"You're a bounty hunter."

"I prefer being called an enforcement officer." Max tried to dilute the ugliness of the words.

"Will you get paid if you take my brother back?" Reagan wanted to know.

"Yes. We collect a portion of the bail."

"Then you're a bounty hunter." She backed away from him, eyes wide and filled with disgust. "Don't try to make it sound better than it is." She bumped into a chair and came to a stop. "You've been using me to find Travis."

"No! If I'd known who you were when we met, I'd have told you."

Her eyes became a clear, cold green. "Instead, you accepted my hospitality, met my children and pretended to care about me." Her eyes roamed across his face. After what seemed an eternity, she turned away and let herself out.

Damn! He'd never wanted to hurt her.

Tomorrow he'd pick up Travis when Reagan was at work and the girls were at school. When he wouldn't have to look into their eyes and see the hurt and anger there.

Tonight he'd work on getting over Reagan.

Dear Reader,

When I was a child, my favorite time of year was summer. My parents would load the family into the car and drive from our home in Montana to visit family in Utah. Even though the trip was long, and I probably drove my parents crazy asking how soon we'd get there, I always looked forward to driving through Yellowstone National Park and the mountains of Wyoming. I loved the way the sun sparkled on snow-capped peaks and then got lost inside dense forests, and I spent countless hours looking out my window, dreaming up stories and imagining what it could be like to live there. To this day, if I close my eyes for a few seconds, I can see the forest lashing past, smell the pine and hear the hum of tires on the road.

A few years ago I loaded my own car and took my children to my childhood vacation spot. Though I hadn't been back in a very long time, I was instantly transported through the years. All the stories I'd dreamed up as a child came back as fully formed as if I'd made them up only yesterday. Before the first day was over, I knew I wouldn't be content until I'd written a book set in those incredible mountains.

The instant I created Serenity and let Reagan walk through town, I knew she belonged there. I trusted that Max would eventually come to appreciate its beauty and the extended-family dynamic that seems unique to small towns everywhere. I hope you'll enjoy their story as much as I enjoyed writing it.

Sherry Lewis

That Woman in Wyoming

Sherry Lewis

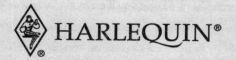

HARLEQUIN®

TORONTO • NEW YORK • LONDON
AMSTERDAM • PARIS • SYDNEY • HAMBURG
STOCKHOLM • ATHENS • TOKYO • MILAN • MADRID
PRAGUE • WARSAW • BUDAPEST • AUCKLAND

ISBN 0-373-70974-9

THAT WOMAN IN WYOMING

Copyright © 2001 by Sherry Lewis.

This edition published by arrangement with Harlequin Books S.A.

® and TM are trademarks of the publisher. Trademarks indicated with
® are registered in the United States Patent and Trademark Office, the
Canadian Trade Marks Office and in other countries.

Visit us at www.eHarlequin.com

Printed in U.S.A.

For Aunt Barbara

CHAPTER ONE

MAX GARDNER COVERED the car's dome light with one hand as his partner, Donovan Reed, slipped inside. A strong gust of cold March wind blew in through the door, bringing the scent of rain with it. Shivering, Max swirled the dregs of hours-old coffee in the bottom of a paper cup while Donovan shut them inside with a nearly inaudible click.

"Is Carmichael in there?" Max asked.

Donovan shook his head and motioned for Max to start the engine. "I couldn't see anything. They've got the windows covered, and there are so many shrubs around the house I couldn't get in close."

Max turned his gaze to the small frame house three doors from where they'd parked. The neighborhood had definitely seen better days. Max had spent more nights than he could count in neighborhoods like this one over the past ten years. Sometimes they got lucky; sometimes not. "So I guess we wait until he shows himself?"

"If he's even there." Donovan held both hands over the defrost vents on the dashboard. "He'd better not have given us the slip this time."

With his black leather vest, shoulder-length hair, thick brown beard and tattoos on both arms, Donovan looked like a biker—the kind of guy most people would instinctively be wary of. Max had worked with him long enough to know that Donovan's scruffy exterior hid a razor-sharp mind and finely honed instincts. He trusted Donovan's judgment.

"Third time's the charm," Max said with a grin. "We've got him this time. I can feel it."

Donovan let out an appreciative sigh as the heat kicked on. "I just hope he comes out before morning. Holly will have my head if we miss our plane."

"A year ago, you'd have thought this was great fun. I think marriage has skewed your priorities."

"Changed 'em," Donovan said with a lopsided smile, "not skewed. And don't try to tell me *you'd* rather cool your heels waiting to collect a bounty than spending a week in Cancún with the most beautiful woman in the world."

Max laughed softly and shut off the engine again. Even for comfort, they couldn't risk calling attention to themselves. "I'd rather cool my heels on a stakeout. A week with *any* woman is too much commitment for me."

"One of these days, some woman's going to help you change your mind," Donovan warned. "I can't wait to see it."

Max took a sip of lukewarm coffee, grimaced and set the cup back in its holder. "You'll keep waiting. It isn't going to happen."

At times he might envy Donovan having a beautiful woman to go home to, but Max couldn't understand how his friend could ask her to live with the uncertainty that came with their jobs. Max was sharply aware of the danger they faced every time they went after a fugitive. It didn't seem right to ask a woman to live with that.

True, some situations were more dangerous than others, but nobody who'd escaped from jail or skipped bail was happy to see them. Some tried to run. Others resisted. The most unlikely people had weapons, and few hesitated to bring them out when bounty hunters came knocking at the door.

To make matters worse, Max and Donovan spent days, sometimes weeks, on the road. The pay was good but sporadic, and they couldn't count on a paycheck until they had it in their hands. Not the ideal career for a family man. Not even close. Max just hoped Donovan and Holly wouldn't eventually regret their decision.

He checked his watch and changed the subject. "It's almost ten o'clock. If our friend at the bar wasn't lying, Carmichael's girlfriend will be leaving for work soon."

Donovan leaned back in the seat and closed his eyes. "If she does, you can charm her. If it looks like she's going to let you into the house, come and get me."

Max glanced at his worn jeans, faded T-shirt and the bulletproof vest beneath his jacket. He ran a hand along the stubble on his chin and laughed. "I'll really charm her, all right."

Donovan opened one eye and grinned. "Use that honest face of yours. It makes women weak in the knees."

"Right. Weak." Max arched his back to work out the kinks—he'd been sitting in the same position for hours. "You're the one with a woman at home. Maybe *you* ought to do the charming."

Donovan gave a lazy shrug and closed his eyes again. "You're the beauty of this partnership. I'm the brawn, remember?"

Max started to answer, but when the front door he'd been watching opened, he nudged Donovan, and nodded toward the shadowy figure stepping onto the porch. "I think we're in luck. Someone's coming out."

Donovan sat upright again, leaned forward and squinted to see through the dark. "It's not Carmichael, unless he's started cross-dressing. Must be the girlfriend. Tall. Blond. Thin. Matches the description I got from the bartender at Lucky's."

Max adjusted his shoulder holster, zipped his jacket and reached for the door handle. "What's her name again?"

"Monique Marshall." This time, Donovan covered the dome light so Max could let himself out into the gathering storm. "She's all yours, partner."

Keeping one eye on the woman and the other on the house, Max set out toward her. She clicked on stiletto heels toward the front gate, wearing a jacket edged with some kind of fur and a skirt that barely grazed the tops of her thighs. She looked half frozen in the sharp March wind.

Max kept his pace slow until she reached the sidewalk, then quickly closed the distance between them. "Excuse me—"

Monique wheeled around to face him, barely managing to keep her balance on the dagger heels. "What in the hell...?" She clutched her purse tightly and glanced over her shoulder for an escape route.

Max held up both hands where she could see them. "Sorry. I didn't mean to frighten you. I'm looking for a friend of mine, and I wonder if you can help."

She pursed a set of crimson lips. "I doubt it."

"His name's Travis Carmichael," Max said, as if she hadn't responded. He kept his smile friendly and his stance nonthreatening, but his gaze drifted between her face, her hands and her oversize purse. He didn't want to be caught off guard if she had a weapon inside.

Monique tossed a lock of platinum hair over one shoulder and hitched her purse high on her shoulder. Her eyes flickered and her lips thinned slightly. "Sorry. Don't know him."

"Are you sure? I was told that you did."

Her eyes stopped flickering and narrowed tightly. "Who told you that?"

"A mutual friend."

Her gaze moved over him rapidly, taking in every detail of his appearance. "You're a cop, aren't you?"

"No."

"Well, you're not a friend. You definitely don't belong in this neighborhood." A lock of hair fell into her eyes. "Travis is in trouble again, isn't he?"

Max figured skipping bail on an armed robbery charge qualified as trouble, but he wasn't going to give her details. "If he is, I'm sure you don't want to be part of it. Why don't you tell me where to find him? I'll make sure you don't get involved." He glanced at the house behind them. "Is he inside?"

"No." Monique chewed one bright red lip and

thought for a moment. "Okay, you're right. I *do* know him. But he hasn't been anywhere near here in over a year. And that's the truth. The only people inside that house are my daughter and her baby-sitter."

Her gaze didn't waver, and Max followed his gut instinct that told him she was telling the truth. "Do you know where I can find him?"

Another gust of wind threatened the slim band of Monique's skirt. She slapped one hand over it to hold it down. "I don't know, and I don't care."

"It's important."

She pushed the hair out of her face impatiently and started toward an aging yellow Volkswagen parked beside the curb. "Look... Travis and I had a thing for a while, but it wasn't serious. I kicked him out last year, and I haven't heard from him since—thank God."

Max followed her into the street. "How about other friends? Do you know anyone else who might have heard from him recently? Like I said, it's important."

Monique glanced at him over her shoulder. "Travis has screwed over everybody *I* know. He's good at that." She spent a second or two wrenching open the dented car door. "If I were you, I'd ask his sister."

"Sister?" Max scowled. Doug Slate hadn't mentioned anything about a sister when he passed the case over to them. "I didn't realize Travis had a sister."

"Believe it or not, even a loser like Travis has family." Monique smiled bitterly. "She's probably the only person who's still speaking to him. He runs through friends pretty fast."

Charming guy. "What can you tell me about her?"

Monique tossed her purse onto the car seat. "I've

never met her, but Travis used to talk about her a lot. I got the feeling they were pretty close.''

Great. Two peas in a pod. ''Any idea where I can find her?''

''He got a couple of letters from her while he was here. Her return address was some little town in Wyoming—something like Peace or Tranquillity.'' Monique scowled thoughtfully and shook her head. ''But those aren't right.'' She slid behind the wheel and put the key into the ignition. ''I remember now. It was Serenity.''

Serenity, Wyoming. Max had never heard of it, but it shouldn't be hard to find. ''What about a name?''

''Ronnie, I think. Yeah…that's it. Ronnie. Travis said he'd take me there to meet her but he never did. He always did talk big, but he wasn't much for keeping promises. Probably still isn't.'' She gave the door a sharp tug. ''Just do me one favor, okay? Don't tell him you talked to me. The last thing I need is Travis Carmichael showing up on my doorstep.''

''You have my word on it.'' If Max had anything to say about it, Travis would be cooling his heels in a jail cell before the weekend was over.

He waited until Monique drove away, then turned back toward the warm car where Donovan waited. ''She hasn't seen him,'' he said when he was back inside. ''But here's an interesting bit of news. Carmichael has a sister living in Serenity, Wyoming.''

Donovan's forehead creased and a scowl tugged at the corners of his mouth. ''Why in the hell didn't Doug tell us about her?''

''Probably because he didn't bother to look.'' Doug Slate might own the bonding company Max and Donovan contracted with, but he was a shining example of incompetence. Max filled Donovan in on the letters and ended with, "Monique got the impression Travis and the sister are close."

"Which means that's the *first* place we should have looked." Donovan shook his head. "I'm telling you, Doug isn't anything like his father. The company's been going to hell in a handbasket since he took over. And you know why? You know what his problem is? He doesn't care."

"Actually, I think it's becoming *our* problem." Max put the Taurus into gear and pulled onto the deserted street. "I'm beginning to wish I'd never promised Harvey I'd stay on for a year after he retired."

"You and me both." Donovan rolled down his window a crack and lit a cigarette. "One of these days Doug's going to get us killed. Personally, I think it's time for you and me to make some decisions. Maybe we should strike out on our own."

Max had the sinking feeling Donovan was right. Breaking with Slate would be easy since they weren't actually Slate's employees. But Max believed in keeping his word, and the idea of cutting loose six months early didn't sit lightly on his shoulders.

"Holly's going to have a fit when I tell her I can't leave tomorrow," Donovan said as he flicked ash out the window.

"You're not going to tell her. There's no reason for you to miss your vacation just because Doug screwed up. Take Holly to Cancún like you planned. I'll track Carmichael down."

Donovan blew out a cloud of smoke and shook his

head. "No way. I don't like the idea of you taking it alone."

Max grinned. "Okay. Then *I'll* take Holly to Cancún and *you* can find Carmichael." He laughed at Donovan's quick scowl. "Quit worrying, would you? I can handle picking up somebody like Travis Carmichael with one hand tied behind my back."

"Assuming nothing goes wrong."

"Nothing will go wrong. Carmichael's an amateur. Sooner or later, he's going to turn up somewhere looking for help, and it's probably going to be at his sister's place. Blood's thicker than water, you know. And if I run into trouble, I'll call Doug. Does that make you feel better?"

"Not much."

Max stopped at the corner and checked for oncoming traffic. "Relax. I'll have Carmichael in custody and be back in San Diego before you get your first sunburn. I guarantee it."

REAGAN MCKENNA HUNCHED to keep the rain from running down her neck as she pulled her mail from the box at the curb. Tucking the envelopes beneath her sweater, she splashed across the wet, winter-brown lawn and ducked inside her house. She paused in the entryway to shake off the moisture, which sent Baby, her silver tabby, skittering out of the way.

Calling out an apology to the cat, Reagan closed the door and kicked off her wet shoes, then started into the living room, sorting the envelopes in her hand as she walked. The bills brought a scowl to her face, and the letter from her stepmother made her smile. The next envelope—one bearing a return address from

Teton Extreme Sports in Jackson and addressed to Jamie McKenna—wiped her smile away.

Reagan paused beside the couch and turned the envelope over in her hand. Jamie had inherited a reckless streak from her father, and the last thing Reagan needed was someone encouraging her to follow it.

"Mom?" A shrill cry followed by two sets of footsteps in the hallway announced her daughters a moment before the two auburn-haired tornadoes burst into the living room. There was only a fifteen-month difference in their ages, and they were so close in size, looks and coloring people often mistook them for twins. But they were as different as summer and winter in personality and temperament.

Fourteen-year-old Danielle's hair bounced on her shoulders as she ran, and jeweled butterflies, clipped into the carefully styled curls, caught the light. She loved clothes, jewelry and makeup almost too much. Jamie was the complete opposite. She wore her hair slicked into a single braid that always seemed about to come undone, chewed her nails and was happy as long as she had jeans, a T-shirt and sneakers.

"I'm so glad you're home," Danielle cried before Reagan could say hello. "You'll never guess what happened today—"

"Let *me* tell her," Jamie interrupted. "Stefani's *my* friend."

"Yeah, but Sean is *my* friend," Danielle countered, "and I was actually there when it happened."

Pushing the envelope into her purse, Reagan sat on the couch and patted the cushions on either side of her. "If Danielle was there, she can finish telling me," she said to Jamie. "I have something else to ask you when she's through."

Jamie sank back into the cushions with a heavy sigh while Danielle launched into the story. Reagan sympathized while Danielle told her about Stefani's lunchtime heartbreak. Baby climbed into Jamie's lap and curled into a contented silver ball.

Reagan tried to keep up as Danielle switched from one urgent story to another, from Stefani's tragedy to a complaint about homework, from that to yet something else. Within minutes, Jamie had stopped pouting and joined in with a few stories of her own.

Curling deeper into the couch, Reagan listened to the rise and fall of their voices. She loved that they still wanted to share their joys and frustrations with her.

She made mental notes of everything she needed to remember—Jamie's basketball game on Thursday and practice Saturday morning. Danielle's piano lesson rescheduled for Wednesday afternoon and a new leotard needed for her jazz class.

She nearly forgot about the envelope from Teton Extreme Sports until Danielle ran off to make a phone call, and Jamie scooped Baby from her lap and stood to leave.

"Wait a second, Jamie. I need to ask you about something."

Jamie perched on the arm of the couch and scratched Baby between the ears. "Yeah? What?"

Reagan pulled the envelope from her purse and held it toward her daughter. "Do you know anything about this?"

Jamie's cinnamon-colored eyes lit up as she took

the envelope, and a wide smile curved her lips. "Oh, cool! It's here." She eagerly retrieved the letter inside.

"You were expecting it?"

Jamie's eyes shuttered. "Kind of."

"Do you mind telling me what it is?"

"Nothing, really. I saw an ad on TV and I called to get some information."

Reagan had seen that look on Paul's face too many times not to recognize it on their daughter's. "Information about what?"

"Nothing much. Just some rock climbing lessons."

Only Jamie and Paul would call that *nothing*. "Without asking me?"

"You weren't home." Jamie returned the letter to its envelope and buried her nose in Baby's neck.

"You should have asked me before you called them."

"I didn't want to forget."

Reagan wanted to believe her, but she had the feeling that Jamie had deliberately tried to sneak it past her. Jamie must have finally noticed the look on Reagan's face because she let Baby jump to the floor and wrapped her arms around her thin knees. "You're mad."

"I'm concerned. You know how I feel about doing things that are dangerous—especially at your age."

"But it's not dangerous. That's the whole point of taking lessons, so it *isn't* dangerous. Besides, they make you use all sorts of safety equipment."

Reagan hated arguing with Jamie, but this was one time when she couldn't back down. "I don't care how much safety equipment they use, you aren't taking classes."

Jamie's eyes narrowed slightly and the fine dusting

of freckles on her nose and cheeks wrinkled. "You're going to say no before I even *ask?* That's not fair." She waved the envelope in the space between them. "I've always wanted to do this, and you won't even consider it."

"Because I don't want you to get hurt."

"I'll be careful, Mom. I promise."

How many times had Paul vowed the same thing? How many times had he been wrong? Reagan had rushed him to doctors' offices and emergency rooms too often in the early years of their marriage to forget. He'd taken his reckless nature onto the streets with him as a police officer, and it had eventually cost his life. Reagan couldn't let Jamie begin the same pattern.

"You can't make a promise like that, sweetheart. Some things are just too risky, and rock climbing happens to be one of them."

Jamie stood abruptly and the letter fluttered to the floor. She scooped it up quickly. "You say that about *everything* I like to do, but you don't even know."

She looked so much like Paul, Reagan's heart lurched. "I don't mind you playing basketball."

Jamie laughed angrily. "Basketball? That's nothing. I only do that because there's nothing else to do around here." She paced, gesturing wildly and almost knocking one of Reagan's favorite figurines from its place on the bookshelf. "Sometimes I think you'd like me better if I was like Danielle. But I don't like sitting in my room listening to CDs all day. I don't like doing makeup and talking about boys and junk. And I *hate* reading."

Reagan caught one of Jamie's flying hands and smiled sadly at the ragged nails and perpetual scratches. "Honey, I know you aren't like Danielle. I don't *want* you to be. I love you exactly as you are."

Jamie tried to pull her hand away. "Yeah. Right."

"Why don't we put our heads together and see if we can find a compromise?"

"Like what?"

"I don't know. Something slightly less risky than climbing up the side of a mountain."

Jamie thought for a second. "Bungee jumping?"

"Let's keep thinking. I don't want you leaping off a building attached to a rubber band, either. How about soccer? Would you like that?"

"*Soccer?*" Jamie jerked her hand away. "You have to be kidding."

Reagan clamped her lips shut on her next suggestion. Softball wouldn't get a better response than soccer had. "Why don't I check at work tomorrow? Maybe the town is offering something you'd like."

Jamie let out a sigh filled with frustration and anger. "*This* town? Forget it, Mom. I might as well just lock myself in my room and stay there. Maybe then you'll be happy." She ran from the room before Reagan could respond, and a few seconds later the bedroom door slammed behind her.

Reagan sank back into the cushions of the couch and aimed the remote at her stereo. Her favorite Colin Raye CD began to play and she tried to relax. Jamie would get over it, she told herself. She was too good-natured to stay upset for long. Meanwhile, she'd keep trying to find a solution they could both live with.

THE NEXT MORNING, Reagan tossed the single-page flyer onto her desk and leaned back in her office chair.

"One tennis lesson a week, swimming Mondays and Thursdays, jazz dance every Wednesday afternoon? These *can't* be the only activities the town offers."

Her friend, Andie Montgomery, looked up from the potted flowers she was positioning along the window ledge of the office they shared. A lock of her straight blond hair had escaped from the barrette at her nape and she had a smudge of dirt on her cheek. She plucked a yellow leaf from a tulip and moved the vase a few inches on the ledge. "I haven't looked at the list for a while, but I'd guess that's all we have. Serenity's never had a very active youth program."

"It's pathetic." Reagan could just imagine Jamie's reaction when she showed her the list. "Why don't we offer more?"

Andie switched a tulip and daffodil and stood back to admire her handiwork. "What would you suggest?"

"I don't know. Something the kids might actually find interesting." Reagan tapped her fingers on her desk. "Jamie will never be satisfied with this."

"She may have to be."

"There's no way," Reagan said as she scoured the list again. "She has a point to make. Who created this list, anyway?"

"That's Wilson Brandt's department." Andie crossed to her desk and pulled out the white bakery bag holding the Danish pastries she brought every morning. "Cheese or apple?"

"Cheese."

"We're lucky to have as many classes as we do," Andie said as she handed Reagan her pastry. "I'm sure Wilson would be happy if we cut the program completely.''

"But that's ridiculous. Serenity might be small, but we still have kids. I can't be the only parent in town who'd like to see this changed.''

"I'm sure you're not. But you know how Wilson is. He's been in charge of Parks and Recreation so long, he pretty much does whatever he wants.''

Reagan rested her chin in her hand. "Why is *he* in charge of the program? He has to be at least eighty. He's probably forgotten what it feels like to be young and full of energy and bored.''

"Because nobody dares to take anything away from him until he's ready to give it up—not even the mayor.''

"Well, somebody needs to do *something*.''

"You're right. Somebody does. Any ideas?''

Reagan looked at her in horror. "Not me, if that's what you're suggesting. I don't have time to take on anything else.'' She gathered their mugs and headed toward the small coffeepot they kept on the filing cabinet. "What about your boys? How do you keep them occupied?''

"It's different for us. We have the ranch, so they have chores and lots of space, and they also have their horses.'' She took the cup Reagan handed her. "I have another advantage, too. Bart's there all the time and he's always finding projects to keep the boys busy.''

"It's not so easy when kids are home alone.'' Reagan rolled her chair back into place at her desk. "But I can't be the *only* single working mother in Serenity.'' She turned the flyer over in her hand, but nothing had magically appeared on the back of the page. "You know Mayor Davidson pretty well, don't you? Why don't you talk to him?''

Andie held up a hand to ward off the suggestion. ''Not a good idea. Davie Davidson and I have butted heads too many times over the years. He still hasn't forgiven me for hitting him over the head when we were twelve.'' Her phone whirred softly and she set aside her pastry to answer. As she listened to the voice on the other end, her gaze shot to the wall clock and she pointed frantically to call Reagan's attention to the time.

It took Reagan about half a heartbeat to realize that she'd forgotten the budget meeting she'd agreed to cover in the mayor's office. Another half a beat to feel her stomach turn over. Bolting to her feet, she grabbed a notepad and a handful of pens and raced toward the door.

''She's on her way,'' Andie said as Reagan sprinted into the hall. ''I'm sure she'll be there any second.''

Reagan chided herself as she raced along the hall and down the stairs. How could she have forgotten the meeting? She'd promised faithfully to take minutes for the mayor's secretary, who was away at a family wedding.

When she hit the ground floor, she slowed to a quick walk. The city office in Serenity might be informal, but she didn't think the mayor and department heads would be impressed if she burst into the meeting at a dead run. In the glassed-in office straight ahead, she could see people milling around as they waited for her.

Her attention was so focused on the opposite end of the hallway, she didn't notice the man coming in through the outside doors until she was almost upon him. Veering sharply, she barely managed to avoid plowing into him and nearly lost her balance.

He caught her arm to steady her. "Whoa. Where's the fire?"

Maybe it was his height that caught her eye. She'd always found tall men attractive. Or it might have been his expensive leather jacket, polished loafers and sharply creased khakis in the heart of cowboy country that made her look twice. Whatever it was, she had trouble looking away.

He pulled off his sunglasses, and she found herself staring at a disconcerting pair of gray eyes. "I'm so sorry," she choked out. "I'm late for a meeting and I wasn't paying attention."

"No harm done. I'm looking for the police department. Am I in the right place?"

His voice was deep and rich, and Reagan felt it all the way to her fingertips. "You are. It's at the end of the hall and down the stairs. You'll see the signs."

The man hooked his sunglasses onto the neckband of his T-shirt and ran his hand along the back of his thick, dark hair, but he didn't take his eyes from hers. "Thanks."

"You're welcome." She was still gazing at him when she heard someone behind her clear his throat and she realized the mayor must be watching. "If you'll excuse me, I'm really late."

The man grinned and started away; Reagan pulled herself together and hotfooted it toward the office. But she couldn't resist sneaking one more peek behind her.

His stride was long and sure, his shoulders strong and square. When he reached the end of the hallway, he glanced back, caught her watching, and tipped his head. Grinning, Reagan pushed through the door into the mayor's office. Running into a handsome stranger in the middle of city hall had definitely put a spin on the morning, but she'd already lost too much time thinking about Jamie. It was time to get her mind back where it belonged.

CHAPTER TWO

BY THAT EVENING, the rain had started again and the temperature had plummeted. Reagan huddled into her warm coat and squinted to see through the windshield wipers as they slapped away the rain. That morning they'd been in shirtsleeves; tonight it felt like winter. They could have snow on the ground by morning or wake to clear skies and sunshine. This was Reagan's third spring in the Rockies, and she was beginning to learn just how unsettled and unpredictable this time of year could be.

Unsettled and unpredictable...like living with teenagers. If Jamie had snapped out of her bad mood, Reagan hadn't been around to see it. She'd worked late, transcribing the minutes from the budget meeting, and come home tired and distracted.

She'd tried joking with Jamie to lighten her mood, but Jamie seemed determined to suffer. Finally, frustrated and confused, Reagan had suggested that they have dinner at the Burger Shack, Serenity's only hamburger stand, rather than reheat leftovers. Danielle had jumped at the chance; Jamie pretended not to care.

Reagan pulled into the parking lot and peered through the driving rain to find an empty spot, but it seemed that everyone in town had decided to eat out tonight. Danielle shifted in her seat to see which of her friends might be inside; Jamie slouched in the back seat, giving Reagan the silent treatment.

It wasn't like Jamie to pout for so long, but Reagan tried not to let it bother her. The girl would get over it eventually.

Reagan gave up trying to find a parking spot close to the building and settled for one at the far edge of the lot near a wide puddle. "Looks like we're going to get wet," she said as she pocketed her keys. "Are you ready to brave it?"

"Let's hurry." Danielle opened her door and bounced outside. Jamie lagged behind, making sure Reagan knew how unhappy she was about being there.

Reagan dodged puddles and hunched her shoulders against the rain as she hurried toward the building. The minute they stepped inside, Danielle spotted two friends in the seating area and ran off to catch up on everything that had happened in the three hours since school let out. Jamie stuffed her hands into her back pockets and scowled up at the menu.

Determined to put an end to their argument, Reagan moved into line beside her. "Do you know what you'd like?"

"Sure. How about rock climbing lessons?"

She was tenacious, Reagan would grant her that. "I don't see that on the menu. You'll have to pick something else."

Jamie sighed heavily and swept her braid off her shoulder with one hand. "I'm not hungry."

"Is that because I won't agree to let you take the lessons? Or don't you feel well?"

Jamie darted an irritated glance at her. "I'm not

sick. I'm just not hungry. If you're going to make me eat, then all I want is a milk shake.''

Reagan fought the urge to insist that Jamie order something else. It wasn't as if the Burger Shack's food was packed with nutrition, and Jamie could make a sandwich or soup if she got hungry enough. ''A milk shake it is, then.''

She motioned Danielle back from her friends and turned toward the counter just as the door opened again and the dark-haired man she'd seen at the city offices that morning stepped inside. He paused at the door to shake off the rain, oblivious to the curious glances coming his way.

He lifted his head and looked into the connecting room where people crammed the tables, his gaze curious, almost predatory, as if he expected to find something or someone.

There was something about him that fascinated Reagan. Something she couldn't understand, much less explain. She tried to convince herself it was just normal curiosity. Judging from the stares of her neighbors, everyone found him interesting. Tourists often passed through on their way to Jackson and the nearby national parks during the summer, but strangers rarely came to Serenity this time of year.

Who was he? And what business did he have with the police?

Dimly, she became aware of Jamie watching her with narrowed eyes. Embarrassed at having been caught, Reagan turned her back on the stranger and concentrated on placing their order. She didn't know if Jamie approved or if she was chalking up one more thing to be angry about.

While she paid for the food, the girls wandered to the sidebar to gather napkins, straws and spoons. Convinced she'd managed to shake off whatever strange emotion had come over her, she picked up the tray and turned around...and found herself looking into the stranger's leather-clad arms folded across his crisp white T-shirt.

She lifted her gaze slowly and met those bemused gray eyes. She caught the hint of a smile as he looked down at her and, *of course,* felt herself blush from the roots of her hair to the tips of her toes.

His lips twitched as he backed away to give her room to maneuver. "Sorry. Didn't mean to block you in."

Reagan tightened her grip on the tray. "You're fine. Don't worry about it." What was *wrong* with her? Yes, he was handsome, but she'd seen good-looking men before and she'd *never* acted like this. She'd always been proud of her common sense. Now she wished she knew where it had gone.

She must have been frozen there, staring, for a long time because the man nodded toward the tray. "Need some help?"

Two familiar giggles worked through her confusion, and the flush burned in her cheeks. The girls were laughing at her. What must everyone else be thinking?

"No. No, I've got it. Thank you." She forced herself to move, mortified by her confusion and by the curious glances of people around her.

She refused to glance back as she walked toward her daughters, even though she could feel his eyes on her until she turned the corner into the small seating area. She didn't start breathing normally again until she'd put a wall between them. And it took another minute for the flush in her cheeks to cool.

Danielle started talking about something that had happened at school, and Reagan tried desperately to concentrate. But she found herself watching for the stranger to come into the dining area. Danielle's words seemed to bounce around and fly off and Reagan couldn't follow what the teenager was saying.

Then through the window, she saw him striding in the rain toward the street, a bag in one hand, a drink in the other. He paused on the curb and waited for traffic, then jogged across the street toward the motel.

"*Mom?* Are you listening?"

Reagan blinked rapidly and snapped her attention back to the girls. "Yes, of course."

"Then can I?"

"Can you what?"

"Sleep over at Ashlee's house on Friday night?"

"I...I don't know. I'll have to think about it, honey."

Jamie picked up her milk shake and grinned at her sister. Danielle shook her head in mock despair. Both girls ducked their heads and giggled.

The only saving grace of the whole, mortifying scene was that Jamie had finally forgotten about her bad mood.

MAX AWOKE THE NEXT MORNING to clear skies beginning to turn gray in the sunrise and mist evaporating from the sides of the mountains. Crocus and daffodils just coming into bloom filled a flower box outside his motel room window, but the rain-damp sidewalks and frosted windows in his car sure made it look cold. The last thing he wanted to do was take his usual morning run.

He'd spent hours searching the Internet the night before trying to trace Carmichael's family. But every lead he got on Carmichael's past turned out to be another dead end. Carmichael must have been on the move for years. Around ten o'clock, Max had gone out for coffee to help him stay awake, but to his disappointment, the Burger Shack had been locked up tight. Ditto for the Chicken Inn and the Hi-Point Diner. Even the town's two gas stations had been dark and deserted. Apparently, if you wanted to eat or drink in Serenity, you had to do it before nine o'clock at night.

He stretched out a few kinks and thought about going back to bed, but he'd always been an early riser. He'd never get back to sleep. And right now, coffee sounded awfully good. Even watery motel room coffee would have been acceptable. But his room didn't have a coffeepot. Talk about being behind the times. If he had to go out, anyway, he might as well run.

He pulled on a pair of sweatpants and a T-shirt, dug running shoes from his duffel bag, and set off along Serenity's narrow Front Street. A sliver of golden light dusted snow-covered peaks in the distance and the scents of pine and loamy soil filled the air. He walked to the corner and stretched again to work out the stiffness from traveling the day before. Halfway across the intersection, he realized the diner was *still* deserted. In fact, every one of the tiny businesses along Serenity's main drag were closed.

If Max hadn't known better, he'd swear he'd dropped into one of those *Twilight Zone* episodes where everyone in town had mysteriously disappeared. Obviously, he wasn't going to get *any* coffee for a while. What a great start to the day.

He started jogging slowly, letting his irritation have its way as he zigzagged through neighborhoods and took in the deserted streets and darkened houses with only an occasional light shining from someone's window. One of these houses belonged to Carmichael's sister, and he found himself wondering which one.

He'd checked in with the chief of police the day before as a courtesy. Not only did Chief Henley not know who Ronnie Carmichael was, he'd insisted that Serenity didn't have a crime rate and *nobody* like the people Max described were living anywhere near. It had taken Max almost an hour to get the chief to agree to keep Max's mission under his hat so that Carmichael wouldn't hear rumors of a search and bolt again before Max could find him.

Max wondered idly as he jogged what kind of woman Carmichael's sister was. How would she react to hearing that Travis was a fugitive, or did she already know? Would she volunteer information, or would she lie to protect her brother?

Max turned down another street, this one pockmarked from a harsh winter, and increased his pace slightly. Here, too, only a few houses had lights on; the rest were still dark. He'd never liked small towns. He was used to heavy traffic by six o'clock in the morning and Starbucks after his morning run. To nightclubs and theaters and stores that stayed open all night. To coffee in his hotel room and food whenever he wanted it.

This town seemed so deserted, the sight of a woman

stepping onto her porch two doors down surprised him. She wore spandex pants that showed off a nice set of legs, a loose-fitting sweatshirt that covered everything else, and a baseball cap. As the sun capped the mountains, she stretched for a second or two, then started across the lawn toward the sidewalk. Max knew she hadn't seen him, so he checked his pace and cleared his throat so she'd know she had company.

Her gaze flew toward him and she stopped with her hand over her heart. "You startled me."

The sun winked off the red curls peeking out from beneath her baseball cap, and Max's complaints vanished like morning mist under a hot sun. He let his gaze linger on her slim legs and follow them to their natural conclusion, then caught himself and met her gaze.

Usually, he didn't let anything interrupt his morning routine, but today he stopped. "Sorry. I tried to make some noise so you'd know I was here."

"No harm done." She closed the gate behind her and took a few steps away from the yard. "So, we meet again."

"It must be fate," he joked.

She laughed softly. "I doubt that. It's kind of hard to miss people in a town this size." She gave him a quick once-over. "Are you new in town, or just passing through?"

"Here on business."

"Really?" She tilted her head and studied him more closely. "What kind of business could you have in Serenity?"

Max gave his standard answer. "I'm in acquisitions."

She looked at him from eyes as green as the sea. The kind of eyes that could probably see a whole lot more than he wanted them to. "Acquisitions as in land?"

He gave a casual shrug and let her think so.

She twitched the brim of her hat and took a couple of steps toward the end of the block. "Any property in particular?"

"I'm not at liberty to discuss it," he said, falling into step beside her. "Sorry."

She darted a glance at him. "That sounds horribly mysterious. You're going to drive people crazy with that answer."

"But not you?"

"I'll wait to hear what the citizens come up with. It should be entertaining."

"I'm sure it will. You'll have to let me know what they're saying." Max took a deep breath of clear mountain air and tried to change the subject. "What time can a guy get a cup of coffee around here?"

She pulled back the sleeve of her sweatshirt and checked her watch. "The diner opens at seven. By the time you get back to town center, coffee will be on."

"Then maybe I'll survive after all." The conversation could have ended there quite naturally, but he wasn't ready to let her go yet. "Were those your daughters with you last night?"

Her expression grew soft and her eyes sparkled. "Yes."

"Twins?"

"No, but people often think so when they first meet them. Danielle is fourteen and Jamie is thirteen."

"Two teenagers must keep you busy."

She increased her pace slightly. "They do."

He matched her gait, huffing slightly from the altitude, reminding himself of his cardinal rule—no women with children. Then again, he was only in town for a few days. There wouldn't be time for things to get complicated. Besides, for all he knew, she had a husband or a boyfriend waiting for her at home.

She paused at the corner, jogging in place while a pickup rolled past. She waved at the old man behind the wheel and moved into the intersection when the way was clear again. "It sounds as if you know about teenagers. Do you have children?"

"Nieces and nephews. No children of my own." He followed her to the other side. "My job keeps me on the road too much to have a family."

"No wife, either?" She didn't look at him, but he knew he wasn't imagining the slight flush on her cheeks.

Her interest pleased him. "No wife. And you?"

She grinned. "I don't have a wife, either."

His laugh echoed in the early morning silence. "Well, that's good. What about a husband?"

She hesitated for a heartbeat before answering. "No."

He liked that. For good measure, he asked, "Significant other?"

"No."

He didn't know why he liked her response so much, but he didn't waste time analyzing his reaction. "Good. Then maybe you won't say no to having breakfast with me when we're through."

Her expression immediately became guarded. "I don't think so."

"I promise you'll be perfectly safe. You can tell me everything there is to know about Serenity." *And maybe point me toward Carmichael's sister.*

She sent him an amused look. "I can tell you about Serenity before we get to the end of the block. Besides, I'm not in the habit of accepting dates with strangers. And I have children to get off to school. *And* I have to be at work in two hours."

He listened intently, trying to keep his mind on what she was saying instead of the shimmer of hair visible from beneath her cap, the bronze glow of her face and arms, the clear green of her eyes. She was a woman who belonged in the sun; shadows didn't do her justice. He had the feeling it would be a long time before he'd watch a sunrise and not remember how she looked bathed in its golden light.

"How about lunch, then? If there's nothing to tell about Serenity, you can tell me everything I need to know about you."

She ground to a halt and put her hands on her hips. "Why would I want to do that?"

"Why wouldn't you?"

"Because I don't know you."

"I can fix that. I'll tell you everything you need to know about me."

She studied him for a moment. "Let's try that first and see how it goes. Start with your name."

"Max Gardner."

She led him around another corner. "Where are you from?"

"Born in Virginia, raised on marine bases all around the world. Currently living in San Diego where I stayed when my dad was reassigned the year I turned eighteen. I'm currently thirty-five years old, the youngest of three boys. My brothers are pillars of society, both are married, and they have seven kids between them. In my mother's eyes, they almost make up for me.'' He paused to catch his breath and grinned. ''Not that I'm a *bad* guy. I'm just not living my mother's dream—no wife, no kids and no house with a white picket fence. So, what do you think? Are you willing to take a chance on sharing a meal with me in a public place?''

She lifted one shoulder slightly. Her lips didn't smile, but her eyes did. ''I suppose it would be safe enough.''

''Terrific. Where should I pick you up?''

''I'll meet you. Be at the Chicken Inn at noon.''

''I know I passed it last night. Not sure I can find it again.''

''You can't miss it. It's the old building made of rock on the corner of Front and Aspen Streets. It used to be a movie theater. They put the lunch specials on the marquee.'' She increased her pace and moved into a patch of clear sunlight. Her hair blazed and seemed to breathe life into the entire valley. She tossed one last thing over her shoulder as she moved away. ''See you then.''

''Wait! At least tell me your name.''

''Reagan.''

''That's it?''

''Reagan McKenna.'' And in a flash of red and gold, she was gone.

Max watched the sway of her hips as she ran, the slim line of her legs. When she disappeared around the next corner, he let out a sigh of pleasure. If Serenity could produce a woman like that, maybe it wasn't such a bad place after all.

AN HOUR LATER, Reagan stood under the hot spray of the shower, wondering what she'd done. It wasn't that she felt disloyal to Paul. She'd loved him dearly and always would, but he'd been gone three years and she knew it was time to move on.

Easy to say. Not so easy to do.

She'd turned down dates with men she knew—perfectly nice men—because she'd been too busy moving, helping the girls adjust and settling into her new life. So why had it been so easy to accept an invitation from a total stranger?

She smiled, thinking about the way Max had looked in his faded sweats, his hair tousled as if he'd done nothing more than run his fingers through it before leaving his motel room, the suggestion of a beard shadowing his cheeks and chin. Seeing him disheveled had put her at ease. If he'd looked the way he had yesterday or last night, she'd probably have been too tongue-tied to talk to him.

She turned off the shower and stepped out into the steamy bathroom. She could hear Danielle and Jamie through the wall separating the two bathrooms arguing mildly about something. How would *they* feel about her accepting Max's invitation to lunch?

She'd rather not make a big deal out of it, but half the town would know about it before she and Max had placed their orders. The girls would never forgive her if they heard about her date from someone else.

She slipped into her faded robe and opened the door just as Danielle skipped past holding a pair of jeans.

Steam billowed into the hallway with her, and the cool air chilled her bare legs and feet.

Jamie careened around the corner, intent upon catching her sister. "You *can't* wear those. I'm going to wear them."

"No you're not." Danielle grabbed Reagan's arm and ducked behind her, using her like a shield. "They're mine and I didn't say you could borrow them."

"They're *mine*," Jamie argued. "I've planned my whole outfit around them." She tried to reach past Reagan to grab the jeans. "*Mom,* make her give me my pants."

Reagan glanced at Jamie in disbelief and held out her hand for the jeans. What was going on with Jamie lately? She never preplanned outfits.

Danielle reluctantly turned over the pants. "Look at the tag, Mom."

For years, Reagan had marked the girls' clothes by snipping a corner from the laundry-care tags in Danielle's things, so it only took a second to see that Danielle was right. She handed the jeans back and looked at Jamie. "Aren't yours in your closet?"

"The ones like that?" Jamie tossed her braid in frustration. "I haven't seen them in a long time. Weeks, maybe."

"I've washed them more recently than that," Reagan told her. "Have you looked under your bed?"

"I've looked *everywhere*. They're gone."

"They have to be somewhere." Reagan slipped her arm around Jamie's shoulder. "Pants don't just get up and walk out the door. And I know they're not waiting to be washed. The laundry's not that backed up." She started toward Jamie's room. "Why don't we look together? Maybe with two sets of eyes we'll find them."

Jamie pulled away from Reagan's arm and stepped in front of the door. "They're not in there, Mom. I swear."

Reagan rarely invaded the privacy of her daughters' bedrooms so the concern on Jamie's face seemed out of place. She hesitated, wondering if there was something wrong. Before she could question Jamie, the telephone rang.

Danielle made a dash into the kitchen, determined not to let Jamie get there before her. Jamie tore after her, insisting that it was her turn to answer.

Reagan stayed behind, looking at the door to Jamie's room and rubbing her forehead. Memories of her brother's behavior when he first started getting into trouble darted through her mind, but she forced them aside. If it hadn't been for that letter from Teton Extreme Sports, she would never have suspected Jamie of hiding something from her. In fact, she could scarcely credit the idea now. But she didn't want to be one of those parents who refused to see the truth, either. She'd have to talk with Jamie later, when they had more time.

Moving her hand to the back of her neck, she tilted her head to work out the knots of tension. Mornings were always a trial and her growing nervousness over her lunch date wasn't making this one easier.

"Mom? It's for you." Jamie had obviously won the battle for the telephone.

Tightening her robe sash, Reagan hurried into the kitchen. "Who is it?" she mouthed to Jamie, who was twirling lazily on a breakfast stool while she held the receiver to her ear.

Jamie covered the mouthpiece with one hand. ''I don't know. Some guy.''

Reagan's spirits plummeted. It had to be Max calling to cancel. Who else could it be? She took the phone and steeled herself for disappointment. It was probably for the best, anyway. But it wasn't Max's deep voice that responded when she answered.

''Sis?''

''Travis?'' She laughed, suddenly giddy with relief and a little dazed. Her brother moved around so often and called so rarely, it was no wonder Jamie hadn't recognized his voice. They hadn't seen him since a few months before Paul died. To Jamie, three years was a lifetime. It felt nearly that long to Reagan. ''Where are you?''

''On my way to see you. I've just got a couple of things I need to do first.'' She could hear traffic in the background, which meant he was calling from a pay or cell phone.

''You're coming *here?*'' She'd written to tell him where they were, but she'd never known whether or not the letters had actually reached him. ''When?''

''I don't know for sure. A day. Maybe two. I've gotta see this guy about some money he owes me first. I just wanted to make sure it's okay if I crash at your place for a few days.''

''You want to stay with us?'' Reagan could scarcely believe it. An internal voice whispered caution, but Reagan ignored it. Paul had never approved of Travis, and his policeman's paranoia had rubbed off on her.

Reagan wasn't blind to Travis's faults, but he *wasn't* as bad as Paul had imagined. On his last visit, he'd been in debt and looking for a loan. The time before that, he'd been hiding from a girlfriend. But those things weren't *bad*. He was just…rebellious.

Travis had changed after their mother died, and their father had been too consumed with grief for months to notice. By the time he'd healed enough to pay attention, the damage had already been done. Reagan had tried to give Travis what he needed, but she'd been young and grief-stricken, and she hadn't done enough. Travis had run away during his junior year of high school and he'd never gone back home.

"Are you in some kind of trouble?" she asked, determined to get that possibility out of the way.

"No. Nothing like that. I'm just… Well, I'm sorta between jobs, that's all."

She was glad that he turned to her when he got in over his head, but she kept hoping he'd find what he was searching for or that she could find a way to help him. "How long do you need to stay?"

"Just long enough to get back on my feet. Is it okay?"

"Of course. You're always welcome here. You know that." She waved to Jamie and Danielle as they ran outside to catch the bus, then reached for the coffeepot and poured a cup. "Have you talked to Dad lately?"

Travis's sudden silence gave her the answer.

"He's worried about you, Trav. You really should call him."

"Why? He'll just think I want money."

"That's because you only call when you want

something. If you'd call him more often, he wouldn't think that.''

"Yeah, but I don't. I don't like telephones. And I really don't like lectures. If *you're* gonna lecture me, I'll find somewhere else to go.''

"No lectures,'' Reagan promised.

"Good. And don't tell Dad about this. I don't want him to call while I'm there.''

"I won't tell him.'' That promise was a little harder to make. "But he will call if you're here longer than a week. I can just about guarantee it.''

"Maybe so, but he doesn't need to know I'm there. In fact,'' Travis continued, "it might be best if you didn't tell anybody that I'm coming. I just want to lie low for a while.''

Reagan didn't bother telling him that everyone in Serenity would know before he'd been here a day. He'd figure it out soon enough. "I'll have to tell the girls.''

"You can tell *them*. I'm okay with that. But nobody else, okay?''

He sounded almost desperate, and her internal warning bells sounded again. "Why, Travis? *Are* you in trouble?''

"I said I wasn't.'' He paused for a moment, and when he went on, his voice had lost its edge. "It's just that I'm not in the mood to meet people right now. I need to get my head together.''

Reagan had been waiting for him to take that step for so long, she wasn't going to jeopardize it now. "Then I won't tell anyone. You have my word.''

CHAPTER THREE

REAGAN TRIED TO PUT her concerns about Jamie and Travis out of her mind as she pulled into the parking lot in front of the Chicken Inn. Suddenly nervous about meeting Max again, she took a minute to check her reflection in the rearview mirror. She'd taken more care than usual with her outfit, hair and makeup, but her long broomstick skirt and matching forest-green sweater suddenly felt shabby, and her makeup seemed overdone.

What would they talk about? It had been so long since she'd had a date, she wasn't sure she knew how to make small talk. Not that Max seemed like the type to be interested in idle chatter. He seemed direct. To the point. Strictly business.

No, she thought with a smile, not *strictly*. The look in his eyes that morning hadn't been exactly businesslike.

She'd have to be careful not to jabber endlessly about the girls. They were the biggest part of her life, her greatest joy, but she didn't want him to think she couldn't talk about anything else.

She couldn't ask about his job. He'd already made it clear that he couldn't discuss it—and though that made her curious, she didn't want him to think she was nosy. But they could discuss sports. Most men liked sports, didn't they? And she liked basketball, if not football, golf and baseball. They both liked to jog. Surely that would be good for five or ten minutes.

What if he didn't like her? Did it matter? What if he tried to kiss her?

Oh, who was she kidding? He'd asked her to lunch, that's all. She was making *far* more of this than she ought to. But even with the stern warnings to herself, her fingers trembled when she readjusted the mirror and opened the car door.

She took a steadying breath and climbed out into the early spring warmth, resisting the urge to check her appearance one last time in the side mirror. When she turned toward the restaurant, she breathed a sigh of relief that she hadn't looked.

Max was waiting for her in front of the building, looking about nine feet tall and five feet wide at the shoulders. His chest tapered to a trim waist and hips, and he wore jeans that could have been created specially to fit his body. He looked lean, mean and dangerous—if only to her peace of mind.

She moistened her lips nervously and started toward him. "Am I late?"

"No, I was early." He touched her arm gently and guided her toward the door.

It was the merest brush of his fingers against her elbow, but she was acutely aware of him—and of the curious glances from customers inside. It was just Reagan's luck that the restaurant was unusually crowded. There'd *definitely* be talk around town this afternoon.

Stares quickly turned to feigned disinterest as Misty Walsh, whose father owned the restaurant, led them toward a table in the far corner, which was about as secluded as you could get at the Chicken Inn. One or two people smiled or said hello, but everyone else pretended they didn't have the slightest interest in Reagan or her date.

Reagan was used to the restaurant, but she suddenly saw it through Max's eyes. Dark wood paneling, mismatched tables in rows with most of the tablecloths off-kilter, metal-backed chairs so old the seat padding was bunched and hard. He probably thought they were terrible hicks.

"You might have a bit of a wait," Misty said as Reagan took a seat. "The other waitress didn't show up for her shift, so I'm the only one here."

"The more time for conversation, the better," Max said, but he looked to Reagan to make sure. "How soon do you need to be back?"

"I'll be fine. I arranged for a long lunch."

Max took off his jacket and placed it on an empty chair as Misty walked away. "Everyone's staring at us," he said as he sat across from her.

"Yes. I'm sorry."

"Don't apologize for looking spectacular." His eyes darkened slightly and darted across her face, dipped down to her breasts and back up again. "I'm not complaining."

She blushed—of course. "Thank you. But that's not why they're staring. They're wondering who you are."

"Should I introduce myself?"

She laughed and shook her head. "No. Leave them guessing."

"All right." He settled comfortably in his seat.

"So, we're here. Are you ready to tell me everything about yourself?"

"Do I have to? Can't I just be mysterious?"

"Sure, if you want to. But I don't know how you can be mysterious for long in a town like this. I'm sure someone would be glad to tell me."

"They would if they could," Reagan said with a teasing grin, "but I'm a pretty private person. Nobody knows very much about me."

"You've managed to keep secrets in this town? I'm impressed. But it only makes me more interested."

"What do you want to know?"

"Whatever you want to tell me. I know your name, where you live, and that you have two daughters. I know you're not married or otherwise attached, and I *think* you must work for the city. How am I doing so far?"

"It's kind of frightening to realize how much someone can learn without much effort. Yes, I work for the city. I'm the one you call if you have something to complain about."

"Divorced?"

"Widowed. My husband died three years ago."

Max's eyes revealed little, she realized, but there were occasional flashes of emotion like the empathy she saw now. "Was it unexpected?"

"He was a police officer for the city of Cincinnati. He was killed in the line of duty."

"I'm sorry."

"Thank you, but that was a long time ago, and I try not to think about the shooting."

"Then we won't." He watched her for a few seconds. "You can relax, Reagan. I won't bite, I promise."

Her cheeks flamed. She hated being so easy to read. "It's just that I haven't been out much since Paul died, and hardly at all since I moved here."

"Why not? It can't be for lack of opportunity."

"I've been busy."

"Too busy for an occasional lunch date?" Max lifted his water glass and shook his head. "Pity."

"*You* seem completely relaxed," she countered. "You must get out a lot."

"Not as often as you might think. I'm on the road too much."

Reagan spread her napkin on her lap to keep her hands busy. "You're on the road now."

"You're right. I am. But believe it or not, I don't do this sort of thing very often."

"Not." His easy tone was beginning to put her at ease. It had been a long time since she'd flirted with anyone, but every word out of his mouth seemed to invite teasing in return. "I bet you do this all the time."

"Only when the woman makes the first move."

"That can't be true. *I* didn't make the first move—"

He grinned mischievously and his eyes looked almost blue. "No? What do you call what happened this morning? There I was, innocently jogging along the street, and you waylaid me."

"I hadn't realized I was so obvious," she countered. "All right, I'll confess. I'd been lying in wait for hours on the chance that you might be an early-morning jogger, and if you were, that you'd come down my street.''

His smile faded. ''Are you trying to say you *didn't* make the first move?''

''I'm afraid not.''

''I'm crushed.''

''Don't be.'' She pulled a menu toward her and made a pretense of studying it, even though she knew it by heart. ''I'm not the kind of person who ever makes a move, so it's nothing personal.''

''Well, then, I'll try not to feel bad.'' He reached for his own menu and his expression changed subtly. ''You lived in Cincinnati before you moved here?''

''We did.''

''What on earth made you decide to move to Serenity?''

''I needed a place to start over after Paul died. When we lost him, our world fell apart. For the girls' sakes I didn't let myself wallow in self-pity for long. They needed me to pull through and make the world right for them again.''

''That couldn't have been easy.''

''It wasn't.'' She didn't think it would ever be possible to explain just how hard it had been, but she liked the way he didn't gush sympathy like so many people had.

''We stayed in our house in Cincinnati for about eight months,'' she said, ''but the memories were so strong that the girls and I were having trouble moving on. Our grief counselor suggested that we leave and start over somewhere new, but I resisted the idea for months.''

Max watched her carefully and listened to every

word as if nothing else were more important. And she found herself saying things she hadn't shared with anyone but a few close friends.

"Police work was Paul's whole life, but I hated the risks he took. I hated that he knowingly put his life on the line every time he walked out the door, and I let him know it. All the disagreements we'd had about his career were in that house, and the guilt was horrible. I finally realized the counselor was right. I had to leave."

"But why Wyoming? Did you have family here? Friends?"

She liked the way Max didn't tell her she should have felt something else. Too many people had tried to shave the edges off her hurt and anger with well-meaning platitudes about how brave Paul had been. But he'd also been careless, and the clichés hadn't helped.

"We didn't know a soul," she said. "That was part of its appeal. I'd thought about moving to Texas to be near my dad and his wife, but Dad and Paul were so close, I was afraid that being around Dad would stir up all the things I wanted to put behind me. One day I found a story about Serenity in a magazine. It appealed to me, and here we are."

Max shook his head slowly. "That took courage. Have you ever regretted your decision?"

"No. I love it here, and I'm getting to know people. I wouldn't want to live anywhere else."

"What about your daughters? Do they like Serenity as much as you do?"

"Danielle does. Jamie thinks it's boring."

Max laughed softly. "This might earn me a black

mark, but I agree with her. Don't get me wrong... It's a perfectly nice town and the people I've met so far have been friendly, but there's not a whole lot to do.''

"That's why I like it.''

His eyes widened slightly. "You like boring?"

"I like *safe*.''

He crooked one shoulder. "A lot of people do, but I'm not sure anyplace is completely safe.''

"Not completely, but some are safer than others.'' She broke off when Misty returned to refill their glasses and waited to speak until the girl quit hovering. "Jamie's a lot like her dad was. She's drawn to things that frighten me to death. Her latest scheme is to sign up for rock climbing lessons.''

"And you object.''

"Of course I do. She's only thirteen. I'd like to see her make it to fourteen.''

Max smiled. "Sounds reasonable. So you said no. How did she take that?''

"Not well. She's still trying to convince me.''

Max's smile grew. "Sounds like a woman after my own heart.'' He stretched his hand across the table and almost touched her fingers. "I don't like taking no for an answer, either.''

Reagan pulled her hand away and tried to catch her breath. "Well, now you know my story. Why don't you tell me more about you?''

"There's not much to tell. My dad was a marine, so we moved around a lot. My mom spent her time trying to make all the new places we moved to feel like home.'' His expression softened when he spoke about his mother, and the look on his face touched her. "She was a career mom. Whatever school we were in, she was a member of the PTA. Whatever sport we wanted to play or club we wanted to join, she got us there, fixed snacks and drove the car pool.''

''What about your dad?''

''He worked. Took orders on base and gave them at home.'' Max pulled a package of crackers from the basket on the table. ''He's mellowed a lot since then.''

''So, why aren't you married?'' It was a gutsy question, but she felt so comfortable around him, it slipped out.

''Never found a woman willing to put up with me.'' Max didn't crack a smile, but his eyes glittered with amusement.

''What's so hard to put up with?''

''My job, for one thing. I'm in the field six days out of seven.''

''What else? Maybe you're always waiting for women to make the first move? Are you shy, is that it?''

He grinned and a chuckle rumbled out from his chest. ''Yeah, I'm painfully shy.''

''If you're always as shy as you've been with me, I can certainly understand the problem.''

His laugh grew a little louder. ''Okay, so the problem is that I work too much, and I'm not sure my career and a family would mix. Other than that, I'm a paragon.''

''I'm sure there are women who could live with your job and be quite happy. I learned to adjust to Paul's hours. It was just the risks he took that bothered me. Some women might like to be married to a man who's not home every single night. Look at all the people in the world who travel for a living. They can't all be single.''

''Maybe.'' Max tore open the package of crackers and crumpled the wrapper in his fist. ''Maybe. But long periods of separation are likely to lead to trouble, don't you think?''

''Not necessarily. Depends on the people. Are you sure you're not using the travel as an excuse?''

''You mean not to get married?''

''Yes.''

''It's not just the travel,'' he said after a few seconds. ''There are other things involved, as well.''

''But that's the part you can't talk about?''

''That's right.''

''I guess you're the one who gets to be mysterious.''

He shook his head without looking at her. ''I just go where I'm sent, pick up what I'm told to, and get paid for my efforts.''

''And do you enjoy the work?''

''Usually.''

''But not always?''

''Not when the job is over too quickly.''

Her heart rocketed and her hands began to tremble. There seemed to be a deeper meaning behind so many of the things he said. His eyes darkened and his lips curved slightly as he watched her. Did he know what kind of effect he was having on her? She was so obvious, how could he *not* know?

Before either of them could say more, Misty arrived to take their orders. Reagan glanced at her watch, surprised to realize how much time had passed. It seemed like only a few minutes. She took advantage of the interruption to pull herself together. But if he kept looking at her like *that*, it wouldn't be easy.

MAX COULDN'T FIGURE OUT why the look on Reagan's face touched him so much. Or why he was blabbering on about himself, revealing more to her in the first five minutes than he had to people he'd known for much longer.

With the waitress hovering, he forced his attention to the menu. "I'm starving. What do you recommend?"

Reagan laughed. "Chicken. It's the only thing they serve. Your choices are baked or fried, white meat or dark."

He set the menu aside and smiled ruefully. "Right. Well, then, I guess I'll have chicken—dark and fried."

Reagan ordered baked white.

When the waitress left, Max found himself looking into Reagan's eyes again. He couldn't seem to look away for more than a few seconds at a time. There was something about her—something warm and genuine that held him spellbound. He *should* be trying to find information about Carmichael's sister. He *could* be keeping an eye open in case Carmichael was in town. But he didn't want to think about Carmichael. He didn't want this moment to end for a while. And there was no law that said he *had* to mix business with pleasure.

"Can you honestly say you're happy living in a town where your only choices are chicken and hamburgers? What if you have a craving for something else?"

"I cook it."

"You said this building used to be the theater. Is there another one in town?"

"No."

"What if you want to take in a play or see a movie?"

She shrugged casually. "Plays are out, but there's a movie theater about twenty miles from here, and we can rent almost anything we want on video. It doesn't really matter that we have to wait a few months because none of the neighbors will have seen it, either." She leaned back in her chair and ran her fingers up the sides of her glass. "How can you stand the traffic, the noise, the crowds and the chaos of the city?"

"It's not chaos, it's energy, and I love it."

"And the crime?"

"There's crime everywhere—even in small towns."

"Not according to Serenity's city fathers." Reagan sent him a thin smile and waved her hand as if she wanted to clear the air. "Maybe we should agree to disagree on that subject. Shall we try sports?"

"Sure."

"What's your favorite?"

"Football."

She laughed as if his answer was inevitable. "I like basketball. Football's too slow."

"This from the lady who lives life in the slow lane?" He chuckled and gave himself over to the conversation, the mood and the teasing smile on her face. "Football requires strategy, brains—"

"But in basketball the action never stops. It's not like football where you spend twenty minutes waiting between every play." Her grin widened and he knew the initial awkwardness between them had passed. "How about pets? Dogs or cats?"

"Dogs. Definitely."

She shook her head sadly. "We have a cat. Dogs are too rough."

"I don't even want to ask about politics or religion."

"I think that's wise." She tilted her head and studied him with mischievous green eyes. "Music?"

"I like rock. Mostly groups from when I was a teenager."

"And I like country. Do you think we have anything in common?"

At this point, Max didn't care. On impulse, he reached across the table and covered her hand with his. The shock of her touch, the warmth of her skin, the silkiness of her fingers stunned him. He lifted his gaze to meet hers and found himself lost in the deep-green sea. He couldn't breathe, and he couldn't let go.

He cleared his throat and managed to get a few words out. "You know what they say... Opposites attract."

"Yes, I suppose they do."

"You suppose? That doesn't sound very promising."

"What do you want me to say?"

He told himself not to say the words that formed on the tip of his tongue. He didn't want to come on too strong. "Oh, I don't know," he heard himself begin. "Maybe that there's a chance we could go on from here."

"Go on?" Reagan's eyes turned the color of emeralds and she drew her hand away slowly, leaving his empty and cold. "Where exactly would that lead us?"

"We'd have to wait and see."

"How long will you be in town?"

"I'm planning on a week. If I can't find what I'm after in that time, I'll move on."

She took a deep breath and pulled herself back to the ground. "I'm not going to pretend I'm not attracted to you, but I think we'd both be smart to keep this in perspective. I have two teenage children, and I have to live in this town long after you're gone. If you're looking for a noncommittal fling while you're here, you're knocking on the wrong door."

"That's not what I want," he said honestly. "It never even crossed my mind." *Until this moment.*

She held his gaze, refusing to look away. "Then what *do* you want?"

"Lunch. Someone interesting to talk to while I eat it. A friendly face while I'm here in town."

"Nothing more?"

Several different answers came to mind, but he made himself give her the one she wanted. "Nothing more."

THAT EVENING, Reagan hummed softly as she lowered her purse to the kitchen counter. She'd had a terrible time trying to concentrate on work after lunch. Andie had peppered her with so many questions about Max she'd ended up making a dozen mistakes on the letters she'd been typing—and those were just the ones she'd caught. She'd hardly paid attention to the road on the drive home. And as she glanced around the kitchen, she realized she hadn't even thought about what to fix for dinner.

But even that couldn't dampen her mood.

Music filled her mind and soul, the budding spring flowers seemed more colorful and fragrant, and just looking at the leaves starting to grow on the trees had sent a shiver of joy through her. Every nerve ending in her body seemed extrasensitive and she felt more womanly, more feminine, and more attractive than she had in years. Max had awoken something inside her.

She hadn't realized until today how long it had been since she'd thought of herself as anything but a mom, and she liked this new awareness of herself as a woman. She just didn't know what she was going to do about it. Serenity wasn't exactly teeming with eligible bachelors.

Not that she was going to start *looking,* she told herself firmly. None of the men she'd met in Serenity appealed to her—at least not in the way Max did—and she'd already turned down invitations from the few who'd shown more than a passing interest. But maybe it *was* time to rejoin the real world. Time to have a few interests other than bills, housework and the division of teenage property.

She shivered, remembering the look in Max's eyes when he'd touched her hand and cooled off again when she remembered why she'd pulled away. She'd done the right thing. Much as she loved Serenity, she couldn't deny that life here was lived under a microscope.

Giving herself a stern shake, she hurried into her bathroom and pulled her hair up. Danielle had a dance lesson in a few hours, and Reagan needed to find *something* for dinner quickly if they were going to make it on time.

Back in the kitchen, she filled a glass with ice and poured a diet soda, then started to search through the refrigerator and cupboards. She thawed a package of ground beef in the microwave, dropped it into the frying pan and began to break it apart with a fork. But it wasn't easy to put Max's gray-blue eyes out of her mind or forget the feel of his hand as it had covered hers.

The back door banged open and pulled Reagan back to earth as Jamie stormed inside, flinging her backpack onto the table and propping her hands on her hips. Whether she'd had a good day or a bad one, Jamie always made a dramatic entrance.

"Hi, sweetheart," Reagan said over her shoulder. "How was school?"

Jamie dropped heavily into one of the ladder-back chairs at the table and let out a deep, soul-wrenching sigh. "It sucked. Mr. Enemoto gave us twice as much math homework as he usually does, and I have a test in Spanish tomorrow."

Real life settled in with a resounding crash. "I guess you won't be watching much television tonight, will you?"

Jamie raked her fingers through her hair, nearly undoing her braid in the process. "It's not fair. All I ever do is homework."

"That's not true," Reagan said. "You have time for basketball practice and the games."

"Yeah, but it's all stuff I don't like."

Reagan turned down the burner and faced her

daughter. "Where is this going, Jamie? Back to the rock climbing lessons?"

Jamie set her mouth stubbornly and lifted her narrow chin. She looked more like Paul than ever. "I *really* want to take them, Mom."

"And I really don't want you to."

Jamie kicked her feet onto a chair and rested her chin in her hand. "You're not being fair. You let Danielle do everything *she* wants."

"I don't let Danielle do everything she wants. If I did, she'd have a friend over every day after school, she'd sleep at someone else's house every other night, and she'd do her homework with her ear attached to the phone. But if you think there's a difference, it *might* be because Danielle doesn't pick out activities that could kill her."

Reagan immediately regretted her outburst. Paul seemed to fill the silence between them and every argument she'd ever had with him echoed in her mind. For an instant, Reagan wondered if she *was* being unfair to her adventurous daughter. The doubt faded almost immediately.

"When you get older, I might consider it," she said as a compromise, "but that won't be for a few more years."

Jamie would probably have argued, but Danielle burst into the room at that moment. She lowered her backpack onto the floor and glared at Reagan. "I can't *believe* you had a date and didn't tell us."

Reagan groaned silently. Jamie's mouth fell open and for a moment the climbing lessons were forgotten. "You had a date?"

"Well, yes. But—"

"You had a *date?*" Jamie sat up quickly and shared a look with her sister. "With who?"

Danielle supplied the answer. "With that guy we saw at the Burger Shack last night."

"With *that* guy?" Jamie's eyes flew wide. "No *wonder* you were acting so weird."

"I hadn't even met him last night," Reagan said quickly. "I'd just bumped into him at work for a second."

"Well, then how—? When? Where? And *why* didn't you tell us?"

"I intended to," Reagan said, "but the morning got away from me before I could. There was the jeans fiasco and then Uncle Travis called, and you had to leave for school before I got off the phone."

Jamie fell back against her chair and blew her bangs out of her eyes. "That was Uncle Travis on the phone this morning?"

"It was."

"One thing at a time," Danielle interrupted. "I want to know about this date. What's his name?" She unzipped her backpack and pulled out a bottle of blue nail polish. "When did he ask you out? What's he like?"

Still mindful of the time, Reagan opened a can of mushroom soup and added it to the pan. "His name is Max Gardner. We ran into each other this morning while we were jogging. We started talking, one thing led to another, and he asked me to have lunch with him. It was that simple."

"He is *so* good-looking," Danielle said dreamily. "What did you talk about?"

"We talked about the two of you. And about your

dad.'' She watched their reactions carefully before going on. ''We talked about his family, and about him. Just the usual stuff.''

Jamie took the direct approach. ''Are you going out with him again?''

''I don't think so. He's only in town for a little while, so it's not as if anything can come of it.'' Funny how sad it made her feel to say that.

''I didn't ask if you were going to marry him,'' Jamie said with a roll of her eyes. ''You *can* date somebody without marrying him, you know.''

''I know.'' Reagan found a bundle of celery in the refrigerator. Why had she worried that the girls would make too much of her date? They were fine.

Danielle readjusted a sparkling clip in her hair, being careful to keep her wet nails from getting smudged. ''Well, *I* think you should go out with him again.''

''So do I.'' Jamie rested her chin in both hands. ''Unless there's something wrong with him.''

There wasn't anything wrong with him physically. Reagan's hands grew clammy just thinking about him. But there were too many other things wrong.

''Go out with him,'' Danielle urged again. ''All you ever do is drive us around to our stuff. You need to have fun, too.''

Reagan looked from one set of brown eyes to the other, surprised by how much she wanted to take their advice. She supposed it might be all right as long as she and Max knew there was no real future together. If they kept things in perspective, could any real harm come from enjoying a little companionship?

"Okay," she said slowly. "If he asks to see me again, I'll say yes."

Jamie found a piece of gum in her pocket and unwrapped it. "Why do you have to wait for him to ask?"

"Because I—"

Danielle pulled polish remover from her backpack and dabbed at a patch of blue on her finger. "I think you should invite him over for dinner."

Reagan laughed. "For hamburger noodle casserole?" She looked at the clutter on the kitchen counter. "I don't think so. Besides, you have a dance lesson."

"Not tonight, then," Jamie said. "Tomorrow. We could help you make lasagna or something."

"I don't know…"

"Oh, come on, Mom. I'll bet he's already sick of eating at the places around here. Besides, you always tell us we're supposed to repay invitations from people."

"Well, yes, I do. But—"

"So?" Danielle scowled up from a package of nail art stickers she'd found somewhere. "Invite him to dinner."

Reagan couldn't believe she was actually considering it. "I suppose asking him to dinner wouldn't hurt."

Danielle and Jamie exchanged grins, as if they'd accomplished something remarkable. Maybe they had.

Reagan went back to cooking dinner, suddenly excited by the prospect of seeing Max again. The memory of his voice drifted in and out of her imagination as she worked, leaving tingles of anticipation racing up her arms, down her sides, through her stomach.

Too bad he wasn't staying in Serenity. It might be interesting to see where this would lead.

CHAPTER FOUR

"COFFEE?"

Rubbing sleep from his eyes with one hand, Max nodded and turned over his cup in its saucer. "Please."

"Looks like you had a rough night."

He blinked up at the pretty, dark-haired waitress who'd served him breakfast the day before. "Very rough."

She filled his cup, then rested the coffeepot on the edge of the table. "I've heard that the beds at the Wagon Wheel aren't the best. If you're going to be here long, maybe you should think about getting an apartment. Joe Walker has some he rents out by the month."

It wasn't the bed that had kept Max up so late he'd decided to skip his morning jog. It had been after two when he'd shut down his laptop without finding any information on Ronnie Carmichael. He'd been working backward, beginning with what he knew about Travis and moving meticulously through search engines, Internet yellow pages and telephone books until his eyes burned and his shoulders ached from sitting in one position for hours.

He took a welcome sip from his cup and tried again to blink away his exhaustion. "I don't plan to be here that long, but thanks for the suggestion. I'll keep it in mind.''

She nodded but made no move to leave. ''I hear you're looking for property. Have you found what you want yet?''

''Not yet.''

''Is it for condominiums?''

''I'm not at liberty to say.''

''Oh. Okay.'' She lifted the coffeepot, then lowered it again. ''I only ask because my brother and I own some really nice land our grandfather left us up near the ridge. It's not close to town, but it has a nice view. I've always thought it would be a good place for condos. I could show it to you if you're interested.''

Max sipped again and smiled at her over the rim of his cup. His eyes started to focus slowly and he could finally read the name tag pinned to her pink uniform. ''Thanks, Stacy. I'll let you know.'' His mind began to clear, ready to get back to business.

''So what'll it be this morning?'' she asked. ''Another omelette?''

''Sounds good. I'll try Spanish this time. White toast. And orange juice.'' He set his cup aside. ''A friend of mine asked me to look up his sister while I'm here, but all I have is a first name. Do you know someone named Ronnie?''

''Ronnie?'' Stacy shook her head. ''No. Sorry. Nobody by that name around here.''

''Are you sure?''

''Positive. Are you sure you have the name right? I know a Bonnie, but no Ronnie.''

''I *could* be wrong, I guess. Where can I find Bonnie?''

"She works in the bakery at the FoodTown. You can find her there most days."

He dug the small black-and-white picture of Travis from his shirt pocket and held it out to her. "Have you ever seen this guy with her?"

Stacy's eyebrows slanted over suspicious brown eyes. "I thought you were here looking for property."

"I am. I'm also trying to find my friend's sister. She might be with this guy." He nodded toward the picture. "Does he look familiar?"

She studied it carefully before handing it back. "Nope. Never seen him before. And I don't think you'll find him with Bonnie, either. She's lived here for about nine hundred years and she just celebrated her fortieth wedding anniversary last month. She lives next door to my grandma."

"Well, then, she's probably not the right person." Max tucked the picture back into his pocket and took another long sip of coffee. "Thanks, anyway."

Stacy picked up the coffeepot and leaned one hip against the table. "Sorry I couldn't be more help."

"No problem. You did what you could." He opened a packet of sugar and dumped it into his cup. "There is one more question you could answer for me, though. Do you know if anyone has moved to town recently?"

Stacy laughed. "People don't move *to* Serenity. They move out. Except for Reagan McKenna. I think she's our newest addition." Her eyes shrouded and her lips curved into a teasing smile. "And speaking of Reagan, I hear *you* had a date with her yesterday."

"I guess it's true what they say about news in a small town."

Stacy drew herself up and looked down at him with a scowl. "News travels at exactly the same speed here as it does everywhere else. It's just that here we all live close together so it just *seems* faster."

"I stand corrected. So, break it to me gently. What are they saying?"

"We're waiting to see what happens next. We don't know either of you well enough to pass judgment yet. Reagan's pretty independent, and she doesn't talk about herself a lot. That's a luxury you don't get if you've lived here all your life."

"I'll bet you don't." Max settled in with his second cup of coffee to wait for breakfast.

By the time his omelette arrived, he was finally fully awake and very hungry. He didn't glance up from his plate until the bell jangled over the door a few minutes later. When he saw Reagan walk through the door, he paused with the fork halfway to his mouth.

She wore a cream-colored sweater that hugged every curve and a dark green skirt that skimmed the tops of her knees. Her hair brushed her shoulders as it had the first time he'd seen her and framed her face in a blaze.

She moved toward him, smiling as if they'd been friends forever. "I was hoping I'd find you here. I thought maybe I'd see you running again this morning."

Mouth suddenly dry, he set his fork aside and motioned for her to sit. "I didn't get out this morning. Rough night. Would you like to join me?"

Her scent caressed him as she sat—not the sweet,

musky scent of perfume—but something more natural. Earth and wind. Sea and sky. Sunrise.

"I've already eaten," she said, waving to Stacy across the room. "I came to ask you something."

"Really? What?"

"If you're still going to be in town this evening, would you like to come to dinner at my place?" A slow flush crept into her cheeks as she added, "We thought maybe you'd be getting tired of eating out."

He could easily let himself forget about finding Carmichael when he looked into her eyes. "It sounds tempting. You have no idea how long it's been since I had a home-cooked meal."

"But...?"

"But it's pretty hard to spend time with you and not let my imagination take over, and from what you said yesterday, I'm pretty sure you don't want that."

She blushed and unconsciously tugged at the neckline of her sweater. "It will be almost impossible to let your imagination go anywhere with my girls in the room."

"The girls will be there?"

"They've heard that we had lunch together yesterday, of course. They're dying to meet you."

"Well, then, maybe it will be safe."

Reagan laughed softly. "I can just about guarantee that it will be."

Max let his gaze travel across the curve of her cheeks, the soft swell of her lips, then linger on the deep green of her eyes. "That's too bad."

The color in her cheeks deepened, but she didn't look away. "Will you come?"

"I'd love to."

"Good." She blinked and broke the spell. "Is lasagna all right? The girls like to help me make it."

"Perfect. I'll bring the wine."

"Seven o'clock?"

"I'll be there."

She stood quickly and smiled down at him, then turned away and walked out the door. He indulged himself for a moment, watching the sway of her hips, the curve of her bottom inside the skirt, the shape of her legs as they tapered to slim ankles on one end and disappeared beneath the swirl of fabric at the other.

He savored the slow warmth of desire that curled in his belly and tightened everything else. He imagined the luxury of a few leisurely hours spent discovering the sweet secrets hidden beneath those clothes. It would be a far more interesting way to spend his time than searching for Carmichael and his sister.

REAGAN LEANED BACK in her office chair and stared at the list in front of her. "I need help. I've talked to four different program coordinators in four different towns, and none of them has anything on their schedule that Jamie would be interested in." Reagan reached for the can of cola on her desk, realized it had grown warm and left it there.

Andie rolled away from her desk and held out a hand for Reagan's half-empty can. "Maybe she's forgotten about rock climbing. My kids get a dozen ideas a week that peter out to nothing within a few days."

"I wish this one would. She hasn't said anything more about it, but I found a list of climbing equipment in her jeans pocket when I was doing laundry last night." Reagan pulled open her desk drawer and grabbed a handful of change from the small dish she kept there.

She loved this about her friendship with Andie—the way they communicated without words, the way they'd fallen into a comfortable routine that marked the hours they spent at the office. They took their break at the same time every day, when the other employees were hard at work and they could have the break room to themselves. She'd always imagined having a sister might be like this.

Andie paused in the doorway and waited for her. "Did you talk to Jamie about the list?"

Reagan pocketed the change and closed her desk drawer. "No. Maybe I should have, but I'm tired of arguing with her about everything."

Andie stuffed her hands into her blazer pockets as they walked. "I suppose that in the grand scheme of things, what she wants to do isn't *so* bad. At least she's not doing drugs or running around with boys and having unprotected sex."

Reagan stopped in front of the soda machine in the employee lunchroom and began feeding it change from her pocket. "If Paul hadn't been such a dare-devil, I might agree with you. But recklessness was like a drug to him." The anger began to curl through her as it always did when she thought of what Paul had done the night he died. Maybe it would never go away. "He had no *right* to be so reckless with his life. If he'd waited for his partner instead of playing hero, my girls would still have a father."

Andie touched her arm gently. "And you'd still have a husband."

Reagan leaned against the machine. "Isn't it weird?

I never think of that when I think of Paul. I used to.''
She added a few more coins and waited while Andie
made her selection. ''I used to lie awake nights missing him—even though he was rarely there when he
was alive. Sometimes I think I missed the idea of him,
the fantasy I had about marriage, more than I actually
missed him. Now I'm just furious with him for robbing the girls of their father.''

Andie opened her soda and took a seat at one of
the small round tables scattered throughout the room.
''I don't know how I'd react if Bart were to do something careless that took his life. But I do know that
the girls are doing fine. They're doing better than most
kids their age would probably do under the circum-
stances, and you're responsible for that. You've made
some good decisions.''

''I've tried.'' Reagan sank into a chair and slipped
off her shoes. She put her feet up and took a long,
cool drink before she realized Andie was watching
her. ''Why do I get the feeling you haven't finished
yet?''

''Because I haven't. Don't get mad at me.''

''Why would I get mad at you?''

''Because I'm going to tell you that I think you
should reconsider and let Jamie take those lessons.
And before you yell at me, let me tell you why.''

''Why?''

''Because, like I said before, she could be doing
things that are worse. Don't shut her down completely, Reagan.''

''I'm *not* shutting her down completely,'' Reagan
snapped.

''Isn't that what she thinks you're doing?''

"Yes, but—"

"Well, then, it doesn't matter what you're really doing, does it? She's going to believe what she wants to."

Reagan nodded grudgingly. "I guess you're right. Travis and I have totally different pictures of our childhood together, and we're both absolutely convinced that we're right. But I can't let Jamie do whatever she wants just so she won't misunderstand my motives. Letting her climb up the side of a mountain hanging by a thread isn't the solution. She's so young and fearless it frightens me to death. Maybe when she's older, when she's learned a little more about setting limits for herself..."

"And in the meantime you're still looking for something she can do here in Serenity that will make her happy?"

"Exactly." Reagan took a long drink and turned the can thoughtfully in her hand for a few seconds. "Enough of this. I don't want to talk about any of it anymore. I'm tired of focusing on what's wrong."

"Well, then, let's talk about what's right. Have you heard from the Handsome Stranger?"

Reagan grinned. That was definitely the change of pace she needed. "He's coming to dinner tonight."

Andie fell back against her seat and let her mouth fall open. "He's what?"

Reagan laughed. "He's coming to dinner. The girls convinced me to ask him."

"Well, good for them. Did you say tonight?"

Reagan nodded. "Yes, and I'm nervous." And getting worse each time she looked at the clock and realized how quickly the time was passing. "He's the first interesting man I've met since Paul."

Andie scooted her chair closer. "You'll be fine. You have to start somewhere, right?"

"I'd rather start somewhere safer—maybe with a guy from accounting with a pocket protector and tape on his glasses. Max doesn't fall into that category."

"So I've heard. Stacy says he's hot…and very nice, even if he didn't jump at the chance to buy that property she and her brother have been trying to get rid of. So, tell me what you're planning to wear. How are you going to do your hair? What are you making?"

"I don't know. Depends on what my hair *wants* to do by tonight. Lasagna, salad and garlic bread."

"How dressy do you want to get?"

"Not very. The girls will be there, so I think it would be best to stay casual."

Andie nodded and tilted her head thoughtfully. "Wear your rust-colored sweater. It looks incredible on you, and it's not too dressy. And your hair down. Definitely. Long, curly and sexy."

Reagan picked up a lock of hair from her shoulder and looked at it. "It looks like a mop."

"No, it doesn't. You have great hair. And if you pull it back off your face here—" Andie leaned forward and scooped hair away from Reagan's face at the temples "—and borrow some of Danielle's sparkly hair clips, it'll look great."

"I'll try that. Thank you."

Andie waved her hand lazily. "Just bring details to work tomorrow. It'll give me something to look forward to."

"We'll be well chaperoned," Reagan said with a laugh. "There probably won't be details."

"Make something up, then. I'm not fussy."

"You're shameless." Reagan took another look at the clock and saw they'd used up their entire break. "Here's a detail for you," she said as she stood. "I stayed up so late last night cleaning just in case he accepted my invitation, I'll probably fall asleep before dinner's over."

"Lovely image," Andie said with a grin. "You, facedown in a plate of lasagna."

"Good thing it's just a friendly dinner and nothing romantic, then, isn't it?"

Andie turned out the lights and closed the door behind them. "A nice romance would be more exciting for those of us who are watching."

"I'm sure it would," Reagan said. "And that is *exactly* why it's going to remain friendly."

THE HOURS DRAGGED BY as Max waited for seven o'clock to arrive. He spent the morning clicking through endless Internet records and making phone calls. He managed to track Travis's life back through two short jail terms and four moves, but he still couldn't find any information on the sister. He was beginning to think Ronnie Carmichael didn't exist.

By noon, he'd had enough of his stuffy motel room, so he shut down the laptop, grabbed his jacket and headed outside for a break. He had a quick lunch at the diner, then killed some time walking through town.

He'd lived so long among large chain stores and shopping malls, the quaint shops lining Front Street fascinated him. A person could buy almost anything he wanted here as long as he knew where to look. Sela's Flowers did weddings, funerals and proms, and also handled the town's cell phone and pager needs. The local tanning bed was in the back room of the stationery store, and a person could send and receive faxes from the hair salon. Not exactly logical, but it appeared to work.

People he'd never seen before waved at him from their cars or commented on the weather as they passed him on the sidewalk, and before long he found himself waving back as if he knew them all. He slipped into the tiny drugstore to pick up a few things and emerged nearly forty-five minutes later with everything he needed and more information about fly-fishing than he'd ever need to know, thanks to an elderly gentleman who apparently spent his days on a bench just inside the front door.

Max made a few discreet inquiries about Ronnie Carmichael, but no one had ever heard of her. Had Monique given him the wrong name? The wrong town? Or was Carmichael's sister as slippery as her brother?

Still at loose ends, he browsed through the Food-Town and bought salsa and tortilla chips to keep in his room for those hours when he was awake and working but the rest of town was locked up tight.

Throughout the afternoon, his mind kept drifting back to the way Reagan had looked that morning, and ahead to their dinner that evening. He didn't know why he was pursuing this attraction for a widow with two children. It didn't make any sense at all, but logic seemed to desert him whenever she was around. Donovan would tell him logic had no place when it came to matters of the heart. Max disagreed.

With only a couple of hours to go, he browsed through Serenity's wine selection. Forget impressing Reagan with his knowledge of wine; Serenity's selection was so limited he had to make a choice from vintages he'd never heard of.

Carrying all of his purchases, he strolled slowly back to the Wagon Wheel, surprised to realize that he'd actually enjoyed the afternoon. He rounded the corner and stopped at the sight of a dark-colored Toyota with South Dakota plates in the motel parking lot.

It might be purely innocent. But it was definitely worth checking. Travis might have detoured through South Dakota on his way here and picked up a car along the way. Max stood there for a second or two, then switched directions and slipped into the motel's office. He'd met the couple who ran the motel, and both of them seemed talkative. Maybe he could get some information about the new guest and save himself time watching at the window.

The small lobby was empty, but he could see Phyllis Graham in the living room of the family's private quarters. She was a heavy-set woman of about fifty, her short brown hair streaked with gray, her face tired and lined. She sat on one end of the green velvet couch with her feet up, engrossed in a daytime talk show complete with screaming guests.

She glanced up and saw Max at the counter, muted the show and struggled to her feet. "Sorry about that," she said as she hurried through the connecting door. "You caught me taking a little break while I wait for the sheets to come out of the dryer."

Max waved away the apology. As far as he could tell, the woman rarely stopped working. She'd been in the office late the night before, up again early to clean rooms, and he'd seen her chasing grandchildren when he left for lunch. She deserved every second she could find to get off her feet. "I'm sorry to bother you. I just picked up a bottle of wine and thought I'd see if you have an extra ice bucket so I can chill it before dinner."

"Of course." Phyllis sent him a weary smile. "But I'd be glad to put it in our refrigerator if that would be easier."

Max shook his head. "The ice will be fine, thanks."

She disappeared into a storeroom and came back a few seconds later with the gray plastic container. "You must be having a special dinner. Are you seeing Reagan McKenna again?"

Max wasn't used to having his personal life dissected by strangers, but he couldn't see much point in denying it. The neighborhood watch would probably report the second he pulled into Reagan's driveway in a couple of hours. "I am. She and her daughters took pity on me and offered me a chance to get out of restaurants for a night."

"That's nice." Mrs. Graham actually looked as if she might pinch his cheek. "I'm always happy when two nice people find each other."

"We're friends," Max told her. "That's all." He leaned an arm on the counter and nodded casually toward the window. "Looks like you have a new guest."

Phyllis nodded. "He got here while you were out. Mr. Carter."

Max hadn't expected it to be so easy to get the guy's name. Only in a small town where people didn't expect anything bad to happen. Carter. Carmichael. Was there a connection? "I guess I'll probably meet him if he's here long enough."

"You might. He's usually only here a day or two."

"He's a regular customer?"

"Fairly regular. He comes through two or three times a year. He's a salesman."

Probably not Carmichael, then. But Max would still check him out, just in case. "While I have you here, maybe you can answer one more question for me," he said, and gave her his story about looking for his friend's sister.

Phyllis listened intently until he finished. "Ronnie? That's all you have? No last name?"

"It used to be Carmichael. I don't know if she still uses that name, or not."

"Ronnie Carmichael." Phyllis repeated the name a couple more times. "I've never heard of her, and I know most everybody around. Are you sure she's living in Serenity?"

"Not positive. My friend thought this was the name of the place she told him."

Phyllis pulled a stool close to the counter and sat. "Maybe you should check with Joe Walker. He has some apartments over on Spring Street and he sometimes rents by the month. It's possible that he's got someone living over there I haven't met."

"I might do that, thanks." Max picked up his bags again.

"If he's not at the apartments, try the newspaper office. He's the editor."

Max glanced back at her, surprised. "Serenity has its own newspaper?"

"A weekly." Phyllis pulled a thin bundle of newsprint from beneath the counter and pushed it toward him. "We don't have enough news for it to come out more often than that."

The *Serenity Sunrise*. Quaint. Max took a look at the front page. The banner headline read Girls Basketball Team Wins Squeaker, but the story beneath made it almost impossible to keep a straight face. Mavis Butterfield Entertains Family for a Week.

"Thanks." He didn't want to seem rude, so he folded the paper and tucked it under his arm. "I needed something to read."

Phyllis arched an eyebrow, as if she knew he was only humoring her. "If somebody new has moved in, or if they're here to visit, chances are it's probably mentioned in there. I don't always get it read cover to cover so sometimes I miss things, but I have issues for about six months back if you're interested in tracking someone down. It seems odd that your friend didn't tell you his sister's last name."

Max's smile faded as he took in her unwavering gaze. She knew something, but how? And what? He settled his bags back on the counter and nodded slowly. "I'm interested."

"I thought you might be. I'll bring the papers to your room when I clean it in the morning. Will that be soon enough?"

"Perfect."

She grinned and crossed her legs. "You're wondering how I figured you out."

"The question crossed my mind."

"I cleaned your room, Mr. Gardner." She lowered her voice and glanced over her shoulder to make sure no one had come up behind her. "You left some of your papers out of your briefcase when you went to lunch, and I had to go back with fresh towels and clean glasses. I didn't mean to pry, but I knocked some papers to the floor when I was gathering up the used glasses. It happened to be a police report."

"I see."

"Are you with the police?"

"I'm what people usually call a bounty hunter, and I'd appreciate it if you'd keep this between the two of us."

"Of course. But why are you hiding why you're really here?"

"This fugitive I'm looking for has slipped away from me twice already. His sister's supposed to be living here, and I'm counting that he'll show up at her place. He could already be there for all I know. I haven't been able to find her yet, and I don't want her to hear about me before I find her. It might give him a chance to get away again."

Phyllis nodded. "And his sister is this Ronnie you're looking for?"

"So I'm told."

"What's *his* name?"

Max pulled the picture of Travis from his pocket. "Travis Carmichael. I don't suppose there's any chance this is our Mr. Carter?"

Phyllis gave the picture a slow once-over and handed it back. "No such luck. Sorry."

"Has the guy in the picture ever stayed with you before?"

"I've never seen him."

"And you've never heard of Ronnie Carmichael."

"No. But I'll keep my eyes and ears open. Just let me give you a word of advice. If you want to keep your reason for being here secret, don't let Elvin know. He's my husband and I love him, but his mouth does tend to run at times. And stay away from Hattie Brown down at the post office. She might know more than anyone else in town, but she can't resist sharing what she knows, either."

"Thanks for the warning."

Phyllis stood and picked up the stool to put it back in the corner. "People have already been asking me and Elvin what we know about you."

"I'm not surprised."

"If it'll help any, I could make up a story to tell everybody. Something juicy that'll keep them busy for days."

The offer helped Max relax again. "I can't ask you to lie. It's enough to know that you won't tell anyone what you know."

Phyllis scowled playfully. "You're not asking me to lie. I'm volunteering. I could say that you're working for a celebrity who wants to escape Hollywood. I could keep people busy for days dropping hints."

Max laughed and shook his head. "I don't want your neighbors to get angry with you when they find out it's a lie."

She pushed a hand at him. "Oh, I don't think they

will. By the time the truth comes out, they'll know it was all in fun. One thing about people around here, Mr. Gardner, most of 'em know how to take a joke as well as play one.'' She settled the stool in the corner and turned back looking younger and more energetic than she had when he came in. "So, tell me, is there anyone special you'd like to work for?"

Laughing, Max pushed open the glass door. "It's your story, Mrs. Graham. I'll leave that part up to you.''

CHAPTER FIVE

A STIFF WIND BLEW down from the mountains as Max pulled into Reagan's driveway that evening. Branches danced overhead, bits of twigs and dirt skittered across the ground in front of him, and he could smell rain. The storm had come out of nowhere a few minutes earlier, dark clouds that seemed to pause at the threshold of the valley, gathering strength before the assault began.

Max gave the house a quick once-over as he rounded the back of the car. It wasn't new by any means, but the paint was fresh white with green shutters and door, and the yard was neat and trimmed. Empty hanging planters swung along a full-length front porch, just waiting to be filled with flowers, and two white Adirondack chairs flanked a low-slung wooden table.

Too bad he wasn't a white-picket-fence kind of guy.

Reagan answered the door wearing a pair of tight black jeans and a rust-colored sweater that was nearly the same color as her hair. Max tried to keep his composure, but it was damn hard to act as if he had nothing but dinner on his mind.

The scents of simmering garlic and spices floated out to meet him, and the appeal of the whole homey picture worked through his defenses. He couldn't remember the last time he'd had a home-cooked meal that wasn't a special occasion at his parents' house, and he was surprised by how much he looked forward to this one.

He handed Reagan the bottle of wine with a dry smile. "I hope this is all right. Your wine selection here in Serenity is a bit limited."

"Just another downside to living in a small town, I guess." She looked at the label and grinned up at him. "It's one of my favorites. Thank you."

Before she could say anything more, her daughters exploded into the entryway, followed by a puff of gray cat. Reagan's smile turned apologetic and she waved one hand to get the girls' attention. "Ladies... Company's here."

"We know." The shorter of the two girls—the one Max guessed was the tomboy—gave a little skip-hop to stand behind Reagan and looked at him over her shoulder. "I'm Jamie, and that's my sister, Danielle."

"Jamie. Danielle." Max nodded at each in turn. "It's nice to meet you. Thanks for inviting me. Something smells delicious."

Reagan turned toward the small living room off the entryway. "The girls made the lasagna. I'm in charge of the salad and garlic bread."

Max followed, surprised to see how much the room looked like her. It was compact, neat and tidy. Everywhere he turned he saw something interesting and unusual, from a shingled birdhouse on the far wall, through a crystal Mickey Mouse on one of the packed bookshelves, to a gleaming brass toadstool beside the couch. The colors matched her, as well—earth tones with splashes of vibrant green or red or yellow to liven things up.

He turned a quizzical glance on her, which earned a delighted laugh. "I like whimsical things," she explained before he could ask. "They make me happy." She waved a hand toward the couch. "Please, make yourself at home. I need to check on a couple of things."

"I'd be glad to help."

"You know how to cook?"

He grinned. "Not very well, but I do know how to stir, and I can throw together a salad. My mother doesn't believe in idle hands, so if you're in her kitchen, you'd better be doing something."

"Well, then, by all means. Let's see just how well you can do with lettuce and tomatoes."

Reagan's smile was like the rest of her, pure sun, all warmth. Max gave himself a stern reminder about the promise he'd made at lunch the day before and followed her down the short hallway. The kitchen bore the same whimsical touches as the living room. He grinned at a ceramic frog that appeared to be climbing the blinds and turned back just in time to see Reagan stretch to reach a bowl in a high cupboard.

Instinctively, he stepped behind her and reached for the bowl. "Let me get that for you." His hand brushed hers, and his hip grazed the curve of her bottom. Her scent filled the space between them and Max had to battle the sudden urge to slip his arms around her waist and pull her close.

Reagan's hand froze, her body stiffened, and she drew away at the same moment Max did. Her wide eyes shot to his and his breath caught as he looked into their depths. His heart began to hammer as the plastic bowl slid from the cupboard, hit the counter and landed on the floor.

The stunned silence was broken only by the sound of plastic rolling across linoleum and bumping into a wall, and of one of the girls whispering something to the other. Max would have to watch himself around those two. They wouldn't miss a thing.

He pulled himself together and forced a laugh. "Okay, so I *don't* know how to get things out of the cupboard."

Reagan bent to pick up the bowl. "I think it was my fault, not yours." She rinsed the dish under the tap and began to towel it dry. "Would you like a glass of wine while you're waiting?"

Max was fairly sure alcohol wouldn't make it any easier to ignore her. "Thanks, but I think I'll wait." He turned away and studied the figurines, painted flowerpots and other decorations she'd placed around the large kitchen and attached dining room. He paused in front of a fragile teapot. It seemed out of sync with the ceramic frogs and brass toadstool, but it seemed as much a part of Reagan as her other treasures.

"This looks old," he said when he realized she was watching him. "Is it an antique?"

"It might be. I found it at a yard sale and I've never bothered to have it appraised."

"I thought maybe it was a family heirloom."

She shook her head and patted lettuce with a paper towel. "I don't have any of those. My dad has his mother's china and crystal, and all of my mom's things are in storage."

"Your mother isn't around?"

"She passed away when I was fourteen."

First her mother, then her husband. No wonder she surrounded herself with things that made her smile. Max pulled out one of the chairs at the table and made himself comfortable. And he tried to imagine her the age of her daughters.

A powerful protective urge swept through him—the desire to keep Reagan and her daughters safe. But why would he feel that way? What *was* he doing? *No women with kids* had always been his number-one rule. For the first time in his life, he had no desire to live by the rules, and he could understand why Donovan had thrown caution out the window when he met Holly. Max had told Donovan that a week with any woman was too long.

Suddenly, it didn't feel long enough.

SEVERAL HOURS LATER, Reagan walked with Max to the front door. Dinner had turned out beautifully, thanks to the girls. Jamie hadn't brought up the rock climbing lessons even once, and Danielle had even managed to stay off the telephone. They'd taken to Max immediately, of course. Their good-natured bickering with him over music had them all laughing, and resulted in a rotation of music on the stereo ranging from Aerosmith to Alan Jackson, the Backstreet Boys to Will Smith.

Max had been great with the girls, and Reagan found it harder than ever to understand why he didn't have a family of his own. She was sure he'd make a terrific dad.

She glanced at him across the dimly lit hallway, acutely aware of everything about him from the set of his shoulders to the length of his legs, the curve of his brow and the strong line of his jaw. She'd absorbed every detail about him during the evening—the way his hand gripped his wineglass during dinner, the way his laugh seemed to begin deep inside and bubble outward, or how his smile started slowly on one side of his mouth and then, without warning, took over his face.

He stopped and turned to face her. "Are you sick of hearing me tell you how great dinner was yet? I haven't eaten like that in ages."

"You make me wish I could take credit for more than the salad."

"*Someone* taught those girls to cook."

She laughed softly and glanced at the closed doors behind which the girls were supposed to be doing their homework. "I'm just glad you enjoyed it. The girls were thrilled."

He followed her gaze and a fond smile curved his lips. "You have great kids, Reagan. They're a lot of fun to be around."

"Thank you."

He leaned one shoulder against the wall and looked deep into her eyes. "It must be a challenge to raise them alone."

"It is at times, I suppose. Although, Paul was gone a lot when he was alive, so I'm used to dealing with problems by myself. But there are times when I wish I had someone to talk things over with, another point of view. Sometimes the decisions feel pretty heavy." She stole another glance at Jamie's bedroom door. "I'm struggling with one right now, as a matter of fact."

"The climbing lessons you mentioned?"

She nodded, touched and a little surprised that he remembered. "She's so determined, it frightens me. Then I wonder if I'm being too rigid...."

"What do you know about this place that's offering the lessons? What kind of safety standards do they have?"

"I don't know anything," she admitted.

"Maybe you'd feel better if you checked it out."

"Maybe. I *know* I'd feel better if she gave up on the idea."

Max glanced down the hall again. "I don't know her like you do, of course, but she doesn't seem like the type of person to give up on anything."

"That's what frightens me most about her. She's so much like her father."

"Is that a bad thing?"

"In this instance, yes." She felt a pang of guilt over her disloyalty to Paul, but she couldn't leave that answer hanging out there without an explanation. "Paul's determination was a wonderful thing in some ways, but once he made up his mind about something, nobody could talk sense into him. I don't want Jamie to be that way."

"You can't change her nature," Max said with a thin smile. "Whether you say yes or no, she's still going to want the lessons. Maybe you should teach her how to be safe rather than just saying no. Otherwise, she may start finding ways to get around you." He glanced at her quickly and pushed away from the wall. "Forget I said that. I don't know her. I don't know you. And I sure as hell don't know anything about being a parent."

"It's all right," she assured him. "There are times when I'm not sure I know all that much, either. This happens to be one of them."

"I'm sure you'll figure it out." His eyes darkened and he brushed her cheek with the tips of his fingers. "How about we talk about something else?"

His touch made her knees weak, and the look in his eyes made her pulse stutter. "Like what?"

"You're a beautiful woman, Reagan. And you're incredible to be around. I'm not sure I've ever known anyone like you."

She put both hands against the wall behind her, needing the contact with something solid to keep her standing. She tried to disregard the sudden longing that tightened her belly, and struggled to remember all the reasons why she couldn't get involved with him.

He drew his hand away slowly. Torn between relief and disappointment, she took a shallow breath. But no matter what logic told her, she wanted to kiss him. Some rebellious part of her brain told her she'd regret it forever if she didn't. She'd spent her entire life being responsible, but she didn't want to lose this moment to caution.

Without giving herself time for second thoughts, she stood on tiptoe and drew his mouth down toward her own. His lips were as full, soft and warm as she'd imagined. His breath mingled with hers and his arms slid around her waist, pulling her against him. His lips opened slightly and his tongue flicked against her mouth.

She moaned softly, completely enveloped in sensation, and her body came fully, immediately, to life. She'd forgotten how a kiss could feel, the way the touch of a man's lips could demand and give at the same time, draw her soul to the surface and lay it bare. She'd forgotten how safe and comforting a man's embrace could be.

Her heart suddenly seemed louder, more intense, and it took her a beat or two to realize it was the loud bass beat of Jamie's music from down the hall. Reagan pulled away quickly and smoothed her hair away from her face.

Questions filled Max's deep gray eyes and she realized she owed him an explanation. "I'm not usually so forward," she said with a thin laugh. "Especially not with men I've only known for two days. But I guess I've never known anyone like you, either."

"No need to apologize," he said with a lopsided grin. "That was some dessert."

She put a little distance between them to make sure she wouldn't give in to temptation again. "I shouldn't have done that. I'm the one who told you I didn't want a temporary fling."

"It *is* a woman's prerogative to change her mind."

"But I haven't changed my mind. I *can't*. My daughters are in the next room."

"If you're worried that I'll take advantage of you, don't. I'm not that kind of guy."

"I know you're not," she assured him. "If I'd thought for one minute you were, I wouldn't have invited you over."

He leaned a little closer. Her breath caught as she waited, torn between the almost overwhelming desire to kiss him again, and the certainty that she shouldn't. She took in every detail of his face, the tiny scar below one ear, the pattern of his whiskers, the arch of his brows. He studied her face just as eagerly, as if he shared the hunger.

But it didn't matter how much they might want each other. Nothing could possibly come of it. Their eyes locked as he drew closer, and Reagan lost the battle between desire and logic. Why did she insist on thinking in terms of forever? What would one more kiss hurt?

Her lips parted, ready, waiting. Her breath caught as she waited, and every feminine part of her came to life with anticipation. But his lips only grazed her cheek.

"Thanks again for dinner, but I think I'd better leave—for a number of reasons."

He slipped out the door and closed it firmly behind him, leaving her to wonder if he'd been at all disappointed, or whether she'd just been given the brush-off.

"Good job, smart guy," Max muttered as he drove away from Reagan's house. "What in the hell was that all about?"

He was supposed to be here on business. He was supposed to be tracking a fugitive. He was *supposed* to be a confirmed bachelor who wanted no ties, no commitment, no responsibility.

But that kiss had changed everything.

It had reached deep into his soul as no kiss ever had. It had stripped away all his walls and masks and left him raw and exposed. He'd been filled with hunger, not just for another kiss, but for something he'd never wanted before—permanence.

Permanence. White picket fence. Homework. Dinner at home. Hell, a place to *call* home. He'd wanted them all for a few seconds, and that had scared the life out of him.

He mopped his face with one hand as he turned onto Front Street and headed toward the motel. *Okay,* he told himself, *let's get real.* That longing for a home of his own might not even be genuine. It might just be the atmosphere. Serenity had a way of making a guy think he actually wanted to settle down. But things could change when he got back to the real world.

Even if it *was* real, even if he found that he actually wanted to change his life, he *wasn't* going to find happily-ever-after with Reagan McKenna. They were too different, and he couldn't make the kinds of changes that would make her happy. No matter what else happened between them, no matter how much or how little they had in common, Reagan would hate what he did for a living...and he couldn't imagine doing anything else.

THE FOLLOWING EVENING, Reagan juggled her purse, two coats, a sweater, two bottles of diet cola and Jamie's backpack as she climbed the bleachers of the junior high school. They'd left the house early, but already a small crowd had gathered and the lower seats were packed with people. Disappointed, Reagan moved toward the higher rows.

The unsettled weather made it chilly outside, so she'd worn her softest faded jeans and her favorite black sweater. But now that she was inside the stifling gymnasium, she wished she'd worn something cooler.

When she caught sight of one team member's father

taking a picture of several girls together, she battled a sharp pang that Paul hadn't lived to see what a fine athlete Jamie had become. It would have meant so much to Jamie to have him here.

Gritting her teeth, she forced her thoughts back to the present. She'd been battling an increasingly foul mood all day. She hadn't heard from Max and she wondered whether that kiss had frightened him off. It had been three days since Travis had called, and she was beginning to doubt that he'd actually show up. And the phone calls she'd made from work trying to find another activity for Jamie had left her discouraged. But Coach Duvall had included Jamie on the starting lineup for tonight's basketball game, and Reagan was determined to put everything else out of her mind while she cheered for her daughter.

She glanced behind her to ask Danielle where she wanted to sit, and found her a few rows below, surrounded by a gaggle of friends. Danielle pointed at the seats beside her and clasped her hands together to ask if she could stay there. Reagan didn't want to sit alone, but she knew Danielle would have more fun with her friends. Reagan nodded permission and moved on until she found a place large enough for herself and all of their things.

As she unloaded their jackets onto the bench, she heard someone call her name. Glancing around, she found Andie waving from a few rows above. Her husband, Bart, leaned his elbows on the seat behind them and stretched his legs onto the bench in front. Andie and Bart had known each other since they were kids, had gone all through school in the same class and married almost immediately after high school graduation.

Bart was long, lean and handsome, his dark hair shot with strands of gray that made him look distinguished, and an engaging, boyish smile when he chose to use it. Their sons, Justin and Tommy, were almost mirror images of him, and they sat on the other side of their mother in nearly identical postures. Reagan grinned at the image of Andie surrounded by the men in her life and battled another pang of envy which she resolutely pushed aside.

Andie cupped her hands around her mouth and called, "Come and sit with us."

Reagan waved a hand over all the things the girls had given her to watch. "Thanks, but I don't think there's enough room for me and all my stuff. And I want to save room for Danielle, just in case she decides to join me."

Andie said something to Bart, then clambered down toward her. "Then I'll keep you company for a few minutes. Bart won't mind. I've been driving him crazy all night, anyway."

Reagan grinned at her friend. "I don't believe that. Bart adores you."

"That doesn't stop him from getting irritated when I nag him about fixing the front porch or tell him where to park." Andie settled on the bench and rested her hands on her knees. "I hear rumors that Jamie's on the starting lineup tonight."

"That's what she tells me." Reagan made herself comfortable on the bench beside her friend. "I'm thrilled, especially since she actually seems excited about it."

"Then it couldn't have come at a better time."
Andie readjusted the clip that held back her hair.
"Maybe it'll help her forget about rock climbing."

"I hope so, but I'm not holding my breath. She
might be enthusiastic about starting the game tonight,
but that didn't stop her from dropping hints about
those lessons on the way here."

Andie let out a soft sigh. "And I'll bet you ignored
every one."

"It was either that or argue with her." Reagan
smiled ruefully. "I'm not in the mood to argue. Or
maybe I should say I could argue too easily. It's been
a long day, and I don't want to say something I'd
regret."

Andie brushed something from her sleeve. "I guess
that answers my next question. Still no word from
Max?"

Reagan found Jamie taking warm-up shots on the
court, and focused on her. "Not a peep."

"Jerk."

"Don't blame him," Reagan said. "I'm the one
who crossed the line."

"It was one kiss," Andie muttered, "not a marriage
proposal."

Sharply aware of all the people who could hear
them, Reagan motioned for Andie to keep her voice
down. "I've spent three-quarters of the day trying not
to think about him," she said. "I'm *not* going to think
about him tonight."

Andie's back stiffened slightly, and Reagan hoped
she hadn't inadvertently offended her. "Really? You
think you can avoid thinking about him?"

"Of course I can. I've been practicing."

''Well, good for you.'' Andie stood and nodded toward the far door. ''Because I do believe he's here.''

Reagan's heart skipped a beat even before she saw him. He stood just inside the doors, tall and trim and looking too good for words in a pair of faded jeans and a tight-fitting T-shirt under his leather jacket. His gaze drifted around the gymnasium as if he was searching for someone, and she knew immediately that he was looking for her.

Her hands grew clammy and her pulse accelerated. The crowd seemed to fade away and she couldn't see anyone but him. The sounds of bouncing balls and shouting voices dimmed, and the only thing she could hear was the thudding of her heart.

''*He* is *gorgeous!*'' Andie said softly. ''I want to meet him later.''

Her voice jerked Reagan back to the moment. The world came into sharp focus as Max caught sight of them and started across the floor. ''You can meet him now if you want.''

''No way. I'm leaving the two of you alone. Later.'' Andie patted Reagan's shoulder and scrambled back toward her family.

At least half the crowd watched Max's progress across the gym; the other half pretended not to. The slow heat of embarrassment crept into Reagan's face and she wished she could adopt Jamie's lack of concern about what people thought. Danielle had always been more like Reagan—not exactly willing to alter her behavior to make someone else happy, but uneasy in the spotlight.

But Danielle seemed like a different girl tonight. The instant she spied Max moving toward the bleachers, she jumped to her feet and waved her arms. "Max. Over here."

He shifted direction, his smile slightly off-kilter as he talked to Danielle. The girl swept one arm in Reagan's direction and announced far too loudly, "Mom's up there."

Reagan couldn't hear Max's reply, but she knew his quick glance made her face an even deeper shade of red, and she didn't miss all the interested glances in her direction. She lifted her chin and tried to look casual in spite of the thundering of her heart and the sudden dryness of her mouth. And when Max reached her row, she forced away the memory of his mouth on hers and greeted him with a smile.

"This is a surprise. I didn't expect to see you here."

"I hope you don't mind that I came. Jamie mentioned that she had a game half a dozen times last night, and I got the impression she wanted me to come."

"I don't mind," Reagan assured him quickly, "and I'm sure she'll be thrilled."

He sat beside her, close enough to brush her thigh with his and set her nerve endings on fire. "Which team am I cheering for?"

"The one in white uniforms. Jamie's number twenty-three." Reagan slanted a glance at him and grinned. "I should warn you, you may occasionally be called upon to howl."

He pulled back sharply. "Howl?"

"Only when one of the kids does something spectacular. We're the Timberwolves. It goes with the name. But don't worry. I'll make sure you know when."

"What a relief."

The starting whistle kept them from talking for the next few minutes while the teams took the floor and a referee conducted tip-off with the tallest two players on the floor. The Timberwolves controlled the ball easily, and Reagan was soon caught up in the game, amazed as always by Jamie's natural athletic ability.

"She's good," Max said after several minutes of play.

"She is, isn't she?"

"Does she take after you?"

Reagan laughed. "I'm afraid not. I can get one foot in front of the other to jog, but that's about it."

Jamie poked the ball away from an opposing player, and the Timberwolves were on the run again. When they finished the play with a basket, Reagan leapt to her feet and Max followed, nearly as excited as she was. As the frenzy subsided, Reagan realized Danielle was climbing the bleachers toward them.

"Did you see that?" Danielle asked as she squeezed into a narrow space beside Reagan. "Jamie should get credit for the assist on that play."

"It was a great pass," Max agreed. "Is she planning to keep playing as she gets older?"

"I wish I knew," Reagan told him.

Danielle watched her sister execute another crisp pass. "She could probably play in college, couldn't she?"

"If she keeps up like this, I wouldn't be surprised." Max stacked Jamie's backpack on top of the jackets and slid over to make more room.

"She's only in seventh grade," Reagan reminded them, scooting into the empty space. "All I care about is getting her through the next six years in one piece. I can worry about college after that.''

"You never know," Max shouted over the roar of the crowd. "If she thought she had a future in basketball she might give up on the idea of hanging off cliffs.''

"She might. And she might come up with something worse.''

Danielle began removing the glittery butterfly clips from her hair. "Max could be right, Mom. You never know.''

Reagan *did* know—at least, she was reasonably certain. Jamie was too much like Paul. But she didn't want to spoil the mood, so she nodded thoughtfully. "That's true. She just might surprise me.''

The opposing coach called time-out and Danielle stood again, holding out the handful of hair clips to Reagan. "Can you put these in your purse? They're starting to pull my hair and I don't want to wear them anymore.''

Reagan held out her hands so Danielle could transfer the clips to her. "Okay, but I'm not responsible if they get broken.''

"Just put 'em in your purse," Danielle said as she started away.

Reagan smiled ruefully. "Easy for her to say. I've already stuffed two pairs of sunglasses, Jamie's watch and her portable CD player into my purse. There isn't room for anything more.''

"Mom's purses are always a catchall. I think it's a law,'' Max joked. He held up Jamie's backpack. "Think they'll be okay in here?''

"Probably as safe as they'd be in my purse.'' Reagan nodded for him to open it. "She has a little pouch inside where she keeps her money. They won't get lost if we put them inside that."

Max lowered the backpack and held out both hands. "I'll hold the clips. You can look. Jamie might not appreciate me going through her things."

Reagan passed the clips to him and opened the drawstring top. Conscious of the look in Max's eyes as he watched her, she felt a burst of confidence, and before she could stop herself, she made a decision. "If you're not doing anything after the game, we'd love to have you join us at the Burger Shack. Going there is sort of a tradition."

"Are you sure I wouldn't be intruding?"

Reagan glanced toward Danielle's retreating back. "I'm positive. The girls would be disappointed if you didn't come."

"Just the girls?"

Reagan lowered her head so he couldn't see her blushing. "Not just the girls. I'd love for you to come."

"In that case, I wouldn't miss it."

She glanced into his eyes, savoring the tingle of anticipation low in her belly. "Good." Her glance fell on the clips in his hands and she forced herself to pay attention to what she was supposed to be doing. "Jamie's money pouch should be here somewhere," she said as she felt inside the pack. "I just can't find it. I don't know what she has in here."

She tugged open the drawstring top a little farther and looked inside. Several pieces of metal rested on top of a coil of reinforced nylon. Curious, Reagan pulled it out of the pack and took in the C-clamp hooks dangling from the end of a tiny scrap harness…exactly the sort of thing Reagan might expect someone to use if they planned to go rock climbing.

CHAPTER SIX

EVERYONE IN TOWN must have been at the Burger Shack, Max thought when he pulled into the parking lot behind Reagan's car. People stood in groups in the lot and clustered beside the building. Inside, they were crowded around tables, squeezed into booths and spilling into the aisles where chairs had been pulled up to accommodate extras. He'd thought she meant coming to the Burger Shack was a tradition for her and the girls. Apparently, everyone was in on the ritual.

He parked and found Reagan in front of the building with Andie and Bart. After a few minutes of barely controlled chaos while everyone decided on what they wanted, placed orders and figured out who would pay for what, they found a table in the back of the adjoining room. And the bedlam began again with Andie, Bart, Reagan, Max and four teenagers all trying to figure out who'd sit where, and who wanted to join friends.

Danielle and Jamie hurried away carrying their milk shakes, and Max caught Reagan's quick frown.

"What is it?"

She shook her head and pulled her sundae closer. "I think Jamie's trying to avoid me."

"Did you talk to her about what you found?"

"Not yet. I'm going to wait until we get home. I

might be angry, but I'm not going to embarrass her in front of everyone.''

They were in such close quarters, Max and Reagan were practically molded together. Her thigh pressed against his, her shoulder fit beneath his, and when she moved her head, her hair brushed his chin. Not that he minded.

Taking his cue from Reagan, he dropped the subject and concentrated on making small talk. ''I had no idea so many people lived in Serenity,'' he said with a glance around.

Bart had to lean across the table to make himself heard over the music blaring from someone's car stereo. ''They don't. A lot of 'em are like us with ranches and farms a few miles out of town. But since this is the closest town around, we come here to shop.''

''And the kids all go to school here in town,'' Andie added, ''so when something happens at school, the town's pretty crowded.'' She waved to someone at the other end of the room and leaned across the aisle to kiss an elderly woman on the cheek. ''Mabel Huntington,'' she explained to Max when she sat down again. ''She was the librarian when Bart and I went to school. She's retired now.''

''I can't imagine living my whole life surrounded by people I know,'' he said. ''I can't imagine having the same neighbors for any length of time. I don't even know my neighbors' names.''

Andie looked incredulous. ''I can't imagine a life like *that*. Friends are so important—don't you think?''

''I have friends,'' Max said with a laugh. ''They just don't live anywhere near me.'' He resisted the urge to slip his arm around Reagan's shoulders, which would have given both of them more room to move. "I've never been a barbecue-with-the-neighbors kind of guy. Maybe it's because we moved around so much when I was a kid."

Reagan slanted a glance at him. "Don't you ever long to settle down in one place?"

"I'm settled. I just don't spend much time there."

"That's not settled," she contended. "Not really."

Max shrugged, uncomfortable with being the center of attention. He was used to keeping his back to the wall and watching other people. It was a tool of the trade that he'd perfected over the years. "It's as settled as I'll probably get." Turning to Bart, he changed the subject again. "You said you're a rancher?"

"All my life." Bart took a sip from a disposable coffee cup and set the cup aside. "And I hear you're here to find property for someone. Have you seen anything you like?"

"A few things," Max said vaguely, "but I haven't found what I'm looking for yet."

Bart fished a toothpick from a plastic cup near the wall and stuck it between his teeth. "Where have you been looking?"

"I probably shouldn't say," Max hedged. "The people I'm working for want me to keep things under my hat."

"I can understand that, I suppose." Bart leaned back in his seat and linked his hands on his stomach. "Business is business. But I'll be glad to give you a hand if you need one. I've lived here for thirty-eight years. I've fished every creek and wandered every field, and built forts on almost every hill. I probably know every inch of land around here.''

''Thanks. I'll keep that in mind.'' Max looked at Reagan, but she was keeping an eye on Jamie and talking to Andie.

''I guess you can't tell us what you want it for.''

''Sorry.''

Bart shrugged casually. ''You're making folks awfully curious, you know. And rumors are flying around the valley so fast it'd make your head spin.''

Max laughed nervously. ''I had no idea people would be so interested.''

''Well, they are.'' Bart shifted his toothpick from one side of his mouth to the other. ''Don't misunderstand, the folks around here are fine people. They just get excited at the prospect of something new happening. I guess I'm not a whole lot different from anyone else.''

Andie came back into their conversation. ''Different about what?''

''Being curious about why Max is here.''

''We're all curious,'' Andie said as she leaned against Bart. The Montgomerys had that same ease around each other that Donovan had with Holly, and a pang of envy shot through Max.

He wondered what they'd say if he blurted out the truth, then decided he didn't want to know.

Reagan looked away from Jamie and stirred her sundae. Her cheeks were flushed and her eyes hard, but she made an effort to join the discussion. ''Have you driven up to Antelope Ridge? You can get a view of the whole valley from there.''

"Not yet. I've been sticking closer to town doing some research."

"The Ridge is a good place," Bart said. "Sunset Rim's another. I could show you around if you'd like."

Looking into Bart's eyes made Max feel guilty. He wished he didn't have to be so deceptive. Worse, he'd have to be careful or Bart would see right through him. "Thanks. But I'd hate to take you away from your work."

"It wouldn't be a problem. I don't have to answer to anyone."

Andie nudged Bart playfully. "What are you trying to do? Get out of the honey-do list I left for you?"

"Me?" Bart kissed her cheek and drawled, "Now, darlin', you know there's nothing I'd rather do than work my way through one of those lists of yours."

Andie shot him a look of playful irritation, and the conversation shifted again. Max joined in, but he knew he'd been lucky. He'd have to be careful to keep people from getting suspicious. If Carmichael's sister was in Serenity, if she was intelligent at all, one slip could give him away.

REAGAN MANAGED TO HOLD on to her temper until she and the girls were home again. Even then, she slipped into her bedroom and took a few minutes to pull herself together. She'd tried to enjoy the laughter and conversation at the Burger Shack, but she hadn't been able to stop thinking about the equipment she'd found in Jamie's backpack. She was furious with Jamie, but she wanted to handle the confrontation wisely or it might backfire. She could shout, threaten or punish, but she had the feeling that none of those reactions would do any good.

Her hands shook as she scrubbed away her makeup and pulled her hair into a ponytail. Her heart hammered as she changed into her favorite pair of flannel pajamas and pulled on her robe. But she couldn't get rid of the dread in her heart whenever she thought of Jamie hanging off the side of a sheer rock face.

Sighing heavily, she flipped off the bathroom light and turned down the covers on her bed. She could hear the girls talking together as they passed in the hall, the steady beat of Jamie's music clashing with the softer sounds of Danielle's.

Finally, unable to stand it any longer, she pulled open her bedroom door. "Jamie? Can you come in here for a minute?"

Jamie peered at her through the open bathroom door. "In a sec, okay?"

"Now, please." Reagan waited until her daughter stepped inside her bedroom, then shut the door behind her and held up the clamps and harness. "Do you want to tell me what these are?"

Jamie's eyes widened in shock, quickly replaced by anger. "How did you find those? Did you look through my backpack?"

"I wasn't spying on you, if that's what you're asking. Now answer my question."

"It's climbing equipment. I borrowed it from a friend just to see what it looked like." Jamie's gaze dropped as she spoke, then shifted back to Reagan's face. "And I wanted to show it to you so you could see that climbing is safe."

"These few pieces of equipment are supposed to

convince me? Everything I'm holding weighs less than five pounds. This little harness and a few ropes would be the only things keeping you from plummeting to your death.'' She dangled the tiny scrap of insulated foam and nylon in front of Jamie. The leg cuffs swayed gently. "And we're dealing with a bigger issue here, Jamie. Even if these things *did* convince me that you'd be safe, you hid this from me. I told you no lessons, and you borrowed equipment, anyway. I don't like feeling as if I'm being manipulated.''

"I'm not trying to manipulate you. I swear I'm not.'' Jamie dropped onto the corner of Reagan's bed and fiddled with the covers. "I had to think of something. Registration closes next week.''

"You're not taking the class. You know how I feel.''

Jamie scrambled onto her knees and grabbed one of Reagan's hands. "Before you say no again, just listen, okay? *Please?*''

Reagan inclined her head a fraction of an inch.

"Okay. Here's the thing… Danielle thinks—and I do, too—that maybe if you actually saw the school and talked to the instructors, maybe you'd feel better about it. I mean, if you *saw* for yourself that they're careful, and that it's safe, and how the equipment works, you'd realize that nothing is going to happen to me, and maybe you wouldn't worry so much.''

"I doubt that, Jamie. It's a dangerous sport.''

"It's not as dangerous as you think. It's really not. Oh, please, Mom? *Please?*'' Jamie released her suddenly and clasped both hands in front of her. "Please talk to them. At least think about it.''

It was on the tip of Reagan's tongue to say no, but the look in Jamie's eyes kept her silent. The briefest recollection of herself at that age, begging her father for art classes she'd never been allowed to take, flickered through her memory.

"Please?"

Reagan's fear didn't abate one bit, but her love for this adventurous child of hers made her relent. "All right," she said softly. "I'll think about it."

Jamie let out a shriek and threw her arms around Reagan's neck. "Thanks, Mom. You're the best. *Seriously* the best."

"I'll *think* about it," Reagan said again. "If we can find time over the weekend and the weather stays good, we can drive to Jackson and take a look. Just don't get your hopes up too high."

"I won't. I swear." Jamie gave Reagan another tight hug and then released her. "I love you, Mom."

Reagan tightened her arms around her daughter. "I love you, too."

The telephone rang and shattered the mood. Reagan's heart rocketed before she even had time to consciously wonder if it might be Max.

Jamie bounced off the bed and ran to the door. "If it's Max, tell him I said hi."

Reagan nodded and smoothed her hair before she answered. She did her best *not* to sound sultry or anxious or silly when she said hello.

"Sis?"

"Travis?" Thank goodness she'd answered in her normal voice. "Where are you? I thought you'd be here by now."

"I got sidetracked for a couple of days."

"Then, you're still coming?"

"That depends." Travis paused and she heard the distinctive click of a lighter followed by the deep, sucking breath that meant he'd lit a cigarette. "Has anybody been there looking for me?"

"Looking for you? Why would someone be looking for you?"

"No reason. I just told a couple of business associates that I might be coming there, and I wondered if they'd called or stopped by."

"You gave out my telephone number and address?" Reagan stared in disbelief at the wall across from her. Paul had been almost paranoid about giving out personal information, and Reagan had become even more cautious now that she and the girls were alone. "You have no right to give my address or telephone number to anyone." Especially the kinds of people he'd been hanging out with the last time she saw him. "I have kids here."

"I know. But, hey, if these guys haven't showed up yet, they probably won't. Does that make you feel better?"

"Not much. What are you up to, Travis?"

"Nothing, I swear."

She could hear something in his voice that made her doubtful. "You can tell me the truth. No matter what it is."

"That *is* the truth. I'm not up to anything. Hell, sis, you're starting to sound like Dad."

"Maybe that's because we both care about you."

He laughed harshly. "Yeah, right. I know *you* do."

"Dad does, too."

"Uh-huh. You know what, sis? I don't want to talk

about Dad.'' A strained silence stretched between them for a few seconds. ''Is it still okay for me to stay with you or what?''

''Of course it's okay. Just promise you won't give out my address and phone number to anyone else.''

''Fine.''

''And I need some idea when you'll get here.''

''I'm almost finished with what I'm doing, so I'll probably be there tomorrow or the next day.''

''Is that a promise?''

''Yeah. Sure. Thanks, sis.'' He disconnected before she could respond, even to tell him that she loved him. And left her listening to the dial tone buzzing in her ear.

Reagan replaced the receiver with a heavy sigh. It had been a hectic few days. She wasn't sure she could handle much more.

THE FOLLOWING MORNING, Reagan pulled into the parking lot of the diner promptly at eight o'clock. Another nearly sleepless night had left her edgy. Her dad had called that morning to chat, and it had been all she could to keep Travis's phone calls a secret. Thankfully, he hadn't asked whether she'd heard from her brother. If he had, she'd have had to choose between a lie and a broken promise. Her life had been steady— almost boring—just a few days ago. Now everything had been tossed upside down.

The only thing she did know for sure was that she wanted to see Max before he started working. She'd been distracted and jumpy last night after they found the climbing equipment, and she owed him an apology.

Or maybe she just wanted to see him, and was making up an excuse to do it.

Laughing softly at herself, she took a quick inventory in the rearview mirror, then climbed out into the cool morning. A perfect, pale blue sky dotted with a few harmless clouds and a hint of warmth beneath the morning chill promised a beautiful day.

She took several deep breaths and stood for a moment in the protective circle of mountains, soaking up the peace. Her life might feel out of control at the moment, but she had to believe that everything would be all right in the end.

Inside the diner, she found Max in his usual booth, nursing a cup of coffee. He wore a tight-fitting pair of faded jeans, a sage-colored shirt open at the neck, and his polished loafers.

Every cell in her body came to life when she saw him, and her worries faded. Max didn't magically make trouble disappear, but for some reason she felt better able to cope when she was with him.

He smiled when he saw her and shifted papers on the table to make room for her. He watched her so closely as she walked toward him that her skin tingled and she felt attractive, even in her jeans and T-shirt.

"This is a nice surprise," he said as she sat. "Don't you have to work today?"

"I work thirty hours a week. I have Fridays off and start late on Monday mornings." She took a look at the newspapers he'd shoved out of her way. "You're reading old copies of the *Sunrise?*"

"Mrs. Graham gave them to me."

"Why?"

He shrugged and smiled. "I guess she thought I'd be interested. Can I buy you breakfast?"

"I ate at home with the girls, but I will have a cup of coffee."

He motioned for Stacy to bring her a cup and leaned back in his seat, letting his eyes travel slowly across her face. "If you have the day off, what are you doing out so early?"

"The girls still have to go to school. And I wanted to apologize for last night. I wasn't exactly the best of company after we found that stuff in Jamie's backpack."

"You were fine. Did you talk to her about it?"

"Yes." Reagan smiled up at Stacy as she filled her cup. "She says that she planned to show it to me and that she'd only borrowed it to convince me she'd be safe if I'd agree to let her take the lessons."

"Do you think she was telling the truth?"

"I do. The poor girl inherited my face. It's almost impossible for us to lie without giving ourselves away." She lifted her cup and smiled at him over the rim. "I agreed to think about it."

Max's eyebrows rose in surprise. "That's a change."

"It's a big change," she admitted. "And don't ask me *why* I did it, because I'm not sure I could explain." She smiled and sipped her coffee, turned her gaze toward the window and the early-morning shadows of the trees along Front Street.

"So, what do you do when the girls are in school and you're off work?"

"Clean house, do laundry. When the weather's warm, I work in the yard. I'm not sure which I'm going to tackle today. Nothing sounds especially appealing.''

''Why don't you spend the day with me?''

Her gaze flew back to his and she smiled slowly. ''Reading copies of the *Sunrise?*''

''Not unless you want to. I was hoping maybe you'd be willing to show me around.''

''Around Serenity?''

''Actually, I was thinking of going a bit farther afield. Do you have time to drive out into the country with me?''

The invitation sounded perfect. The mountains always helped clear her mind. ''I'd love to. Do you think we'll be back by the time the girls get home, or should I take a key to them at school?''

''That depends on how much time you want to spend.''

She glanced at her watch. ''We have seven hours before the girls get home. I'm sure we'll be back. Am I taking you to look at property?''

He stirred a packet of sugar into his coffee before he answered. ''Yeah. I've been told about several places I should check.''

''I know you can't say anything about the people you're working for, but can you at least tell me whether you're more interested in looking for property in the mountains or the valley?''

He lowered his cup slowly. ''Just show me both.''

Okay. ''We could start with Sunset Ridge, I suppose. There's a great view of the entire valley from there.''

''Perfect.''

''Is there anywhere else you'd like to go?''

"I'm going to leave it up to you. Show me the best there is. I'd like to see through your eyes what makes this place so special."

The way she was feeling at the moment, he'd have to look into a mirror to find the answer to that. A twinge of melancholy brushed her when she remembered that he'd be leaving soon, but she shoved it aside along with all of her other concerns. She had an entire day with Max to look forward to, and she didn't want anything to spoil it.

Half an hour later, Max paid the bill and led her outside. "Do you want to drive, or would you like me to?"

"You can," she said quickly. She could imagine how distracted she'd be with him sitting beside her. "I'll navigate."

He took her arm as they walked toward the curb, then moved his hand to the small of her back as they started across the street. After he'd closed the car door behind her, she took advantage of the moment to look around and immerse herself in the essence of him that seemed to be everywhere. The faint trace of his aftershave, a pair of sunglasses dangling from the rearview mirror, a folded map peeking out from beneath the visor. The only thing out of place was the crumpled wrapper from a bag of chips between the seats.

While he started the car, she buckled her seat belt and leaned her head against the headrest. It had been a long time since she'd sat in the passenger seat of a vehicle. "Turn left on Front Street," she told him, "and follow it out of town. We won't turn again for about ten miles."

Within minutes, they left Serenity and drove into

the country where the forest grew down to the highway on both sides and huge stands of lodgepole pine, aspen and spruce threw the highway into deep shade.

Reagan loved the scenery out here. She loved the soft carpet of pine needles that covered the ground, the juxtaposition of forest and meadow, the sprinkling of wildflowers in the tall grass and beneath the canopy of trees. She loved the feeling of solitude, the long moments between passing cars when she could almost believe she and Max were the only two people on earth.

After they'd turned onto the dirt road that would take them to the ridge, Max glanced across the car at her. "You're awfully quiet."

Reagan sat up quickly. "Sorry. I got caught up in the scenery and forgot to talk. Am I horrible company?"

"Not at all. I'm just hoping nothing's wrong."

She adjusted her posture a little more. "Nothing. And certainly nothing you've done." She stifled an unexpected yawn and sent him a sheepish smile. "I didn't sleep much last night."

"Because of Jamie?"

"Partly. Partly work." She stopped herself from finishing the list. She'd promised not to tell anyone about Travis, and she'd keep her word. "It's been quite a week so far."

"Am I part of the problem?"

"Of course not." She shifted in her seat so she could see him better. "Getting to know you has been wonderful. You've given me something to look forward to. But, of course, every day brings us closer to when you have to leave. How much longer will you be here?''

''I gave myself a week to find what I'm after.''

Three more days. Reagan looked away and watched the trees through her window as they bounced over a rutted spot in the road, then motioned toward a turnout on the side of the road. ''This might be a good place to stop. You should be able to get a good view of the valley from here.''

Max stopped the car and came around to open her door. She tried to focus on the deep valley below them—a bowl of green nestled into the jagged, snow-covered mountains. Farms dotted the land, and Serenity, nestled squarely in the valley's center, looked even smaller from this distance.

''Well? What do you think?''

''It's an incredible view.''

''Yes, it is, isn't it?'' She sighed softly and brushed her bangs out of her eyes.

''It's quiet.''

Reagan smiled, wondering whether that was a good thing or a bad one in his mind. ''I don't think I ever heard real silence until I came here.''

''Does it ever bother you?''

''Never.'' She trailed her fingers along the winter-hardened branch of a scrub oak. ''Does it bother you so much?''

''No, but then I haven't been here long.''

And he wouldn't be here long enough to change his mind. She shouldn't waste even a second wishing things were different. But one look at his hair being tousled by the breeze made Reagan wish she had the right to work her fingers through it. One glimpse of the sunlight in his eyes made her wish…

His eyes roamed her face, searched her eyes, settled on her mouth. She couldn't move. She didn't want to. She wanted to feel his lips on hers again, to connect with him on a level beyond words.

Responding to her silent invitation, he dipped his head and kissed her. She gave herself fully to his touch. There could be no future for them, but for just a moment she wanted to forget about reality. She wanted nothing more than this feeling. She was drowning in him, and she couldn't remember ever being happier.

When he finally released her, he brushed one last kiss to her forehead and stepped away. "I probably shouldn't have done that."

"It's what we both wanted."

"Yes, but…"

Reagan brushed a wayward lock of hair out of his eyes and scowled. "But what?"

"I don't want to hurt you."

"You can't hurt me unless I *let* myself be hurt. I'm tougher than I look. I've been through too much to be weak."

He looked deep into her eyes, assessing her answer for a moment. "You're really something, you know that?"

She grinned up at him. "Yeah, but the question is, what?"

He laughed, hugged her quickly and followed up with a brief, chaste kiss. "I'm not sure I know the words to describe exactly what you are."

''Jamie and Danielle could describe it for you. They're always telling me how weird I am.''

''You're different,'' Max whispered hoarsely, ''but definitely not weird. I've never known a woman who could make me forget all about work just by looking at me.''

Her heart skipped a beat. ''What *is* this job of yours?'' She held up one hand before he could answer. ''Don't tell me. I shouldn't have asked. It's just that you're so mysterious about it, and being married to a cop probably made me more suspicious than most people. Just tell me you're not doing something illegal.''

''I'm definitely *not* doing anything against the law.'' He slipped one arm around her waist and drew her close.

Reagan relaxed against him, surprised that she felt so at home in his arms. ''I didn't mean to sound distrusting, it's just that with everything that's been happening lately I'm a little touchy.'' She wanted to tell him about Travis, but again she held back. Talking to Max might help, but she couldn't break her promise to her brother.

Max watched Reagan's eyes flicker and change, darken with some emotion he couldn't read. He probably shouldn't have kissed her, but he wasn't made of stone. ''If I could have one wish right now, do you know what it would be?''

''Tell me.''

''That life wasn't so damn complicated.''

''But it is,'' Reagan said. ''And it seems to get worse all the time.'' She sighed wistfully. ''Maybe we should just forget complications and problems and who's going to get hurt, and just enjoy what we have here for as long as it lasts.''

Max would like nothing more, but it wouldn't be fair to her. ''And when it's over?''

''Then we'll be grateful for every minute we had together.''

Max's pulse thrummed steadily. ''Are you sure that's what you want?''

''Positive.''

''And the girls?''

''We'll still have to be mindful,'' Reagan said slowly. ''At least when we're in town. But for today, at least, let's forget about your job, my job, climbing lessons and *everything* else and just enjoy what we have.''

''For one day?''

''Just one.''

Just one. He should say no, but the look in her eyes was too tempting to resist. And, after all, what could one day hurt?

CHAPTER SEVEN

TEXTBOOKS SPILLED ACROSS the kitchen table, music played softly in the background, and Max would have walked on his knees for a chance at whatever smelled so good on the stove.

Danielle sat at the table, one ear glued to the telephone, the cord wrapped around herself while she laughed at something her friend said. Jamie had both feet propped on the chair in front of her as she pretended to study, but her eyes kept wandering around the room, taking in the smile on Reagan's face and the laughter in Max's eyes. Baby squeezed himself between one set of feet, then another, rubbed up against Danielle's chair, and favored Max with a long, unblinking stare before he yawned and moved on.

Max barely resisted the urge to kiss Reagan as he helped himself to a glass of iced tea from the refrigerator. It wouldn't be fair to the girls to act as if something permanent was on the horizon. "What can I do to help?"

She shook her head quickly, concentrating on the recipe card in front of her. "Everything's under control. Just have a seat. I'll be finished in a few minutes."

He carried his tea into the dining area and leaned against the counter to watch the girls, surprised by how soothing he found the controlled chaos that seemed to come with having teenagers—the phone, the music, the constant chatter.

Jamie glanced up from her homework and let her eyes lock on his, and he could see a faint challenge lurking in their depths. He wondered why. Did she think he was responsible in some way for her mother saying no to the climbing lessons she wanted? Or was she unhappy with the way the relationship was going?

He didn't have to wonder for long.

Reagan gave dinner a quick stir and settled a lid on the pan. ''Would one of you keep an eye on this while I find the recipe book I need for dessert? Just stir it every few minutes and take it off the heat if the mushrooms start getting too dark. And when the water in the other pot boils, just add the pasta.''

''I'll be glad to,'' Max said.

The instant Reagan disappeared, Jamie slipped her feet to the floor and turned to face Max squarely. ''Did you and my mom spend the whole day together?''

Max stiffened slightly, nodded and took a long drink of iced tea. ''Most of it.''

''Doing what?''

''She took me out to Sunset Ridge and showed me around.''

Jamie flicked a glance at her sister; Danielle pretended not to see it. ''Does Mom know why you're really here?''

Max nearly dropped his glass. ''Why I'm really here? I don't know what you mean.''

''People talk, you know. Mom might not get out much, but we hear everything at school.''

''Is that right?'' Max did his best to look unconcerned as he set his glass on the counter behind him. Had Phyllis Graham broken her vow to keep his secret? Had the chief of police? They were the only two people who knew the truth. "And what have you heard?"

"The truth." Jamie leaned a little closer, narrowed her eyes and studied him as if she expected to see a lie printed across his cheeks.

"Are you *sure* it's the truth?"

"Pretty sure."

"How about telling me what you've heard and giving me the chance to defend myself?"

Jamie cocked her head to one side. "Why would you need to defend yourself? If I had your job, I probably wouldn't tell everybody, either. You probably *can't* tell, can you?"

"It depends on the situation." How much did Jamie know? What had she told her mother? Nothing yet, he thought with a glance at the empty doorway. Reagan didn't act like a woman who had even a slight suspicion that things might not be what they seemed.

"But you can tell us, can't you?"

"Tell you what?"

"Who you work for." She leaned a little closer. "I promise I won't tell anybody else."

Max blinked in confusion. "Who I—" He cut himself off, suddenly remembering Phyllis Graham's plan to spread the rumor that he worked for a Hollywood celebrity. "I guess you've heard that I'm working for someone famous."

"Well, yeah." Jamie scowled and nodded toward the kitchen. "Don't you think you should check dinner before Mom comes back?"

Max hustled into the kitchen with Jamie only a step or two behind. Thankfully, the mushrooms looked plump and the water was just coming to a boil. He took one pan off the heat and added pasta to the other, hoping the diversion had distracted Jamie.

"So?" she asked, dashing his hopes immediately. "Can you tell us? If we *swear* not to tell anyone else?"

"I'm afraid not."

"Megan Rasmussen thinks you work for Brad Pitt." The challenge in Jamie's eyes faded, and she looked like any excited teenager. "She's not right, is she?"

"She's not right." Max had to remember to thank Phyllis Graham. She'd obviously done her job well.

"Please tell me who it is. I swear I won't tell anyone else."

The look in her eyes made Max wish Phyllis's story had even an ounce of truth in it. "I can't, Jamie. I'm sorry."

She stuck out her lower lip and pretended to pout. "Thanks a lot. I thought the fact that you're dating my mom would give me an 'in.' But it doesn't matter, I guess. I'll just make something up and tell everybody you told me."

"And what will you do when the truth comes out?"

She shrugged. "Then I'll tell 'em I knew all along, but you made me promise not to tell."

"You won't feel bad about lying to your friends?"

"Not really. I don't have that many friends who really like me. The girls think I'm too much of a tomboy cause I don't like all the stuff they do, and guys don't like girls who can do guy stuff better than they can."

"What kind of guy stuff do you like?"

"Most anything. I play basketball at school just because there's nothing else to do." She lowered her voice and glanced around to be sure her mother hadn't returned. "But I know this guy who's taking rock climbing lessons, and I'd *love* to do that." She looked so hopeful, Max wished he could help her.

But he didn't want to get in the middle of that argument. "What other sports can you play at school?"

The light in Jamie's eyes faded. "Soccer. Softball. The usual boring stuff. You know what else I'd love to do? White-water rafting. The place in Jackson that teaches the climbing lessons does rafting, too."

Reagan would be thrilled to hear that. "You like extreme stuff, huh?"

"I love it. Some day I'm going skydiving, and I don't care *what* my mom says. I read this magazine article about a girl who gave that to herself for her high school graduation present. I think that's what I'm going to do. I'll be eighteen by then, and she won't be able to stop me."

Max wondered if he should warn Reagan how determined Jamie was to have her own way or if telling on the girl would make things worse? He had the strong feeling that no matter how tightly Reagan held on, eventually Jamie would break away. It seemed inevitable, and he wanted to be with Reagan when that happened. The last thing he wanted was to turn his back and drive away in just a few more days.

MAX STILL HADN'T DECIDED how to handle Jamie's confession as he walked with Reagan to the door a few hours later. They'd spent the day together, but he couldn't let himself get too involved in her family life. He reminded himself over and over again of the reasons he shouldn't get in too deep, but the memory of her lips beneath his, her scent as she moved beside him and the soft light in her eyes knocked huge holes in his resolve. There was no question he wanted her.

But he still hadn't told her what he did for a living, and there was a big chance that she'd want nothing more to do with him when he did.

Call him chicken, but Max didn't want to take that chance. He had three days left in Serenity, and he wanted to enjoy all seventy-two hours. The idea of watching the affection in Reagan's eyes die didn't qualify as a good time in his book.

At the door, he put his hands on her waist and leaned in for a quick kiss—the only one he'd allow himself. "You're spoiling me. How am I ever going to be content with restaurant food again?"

She inched her arms around his neck, blowing his resolve right out of the water. "I'm sure you'll adjust. Once you're back in the city and living on fine cuisine, you'll probably wonder how you ever survived here."

"I seriously doubt that."

She pressed her lips to his jaw. "What are you thinking about?"

"How soon I have to leave."

"We're not going to think about that tonight, remember?"

"It's pretty hard not to."

"I know. It keeps creeping into my thoughts, too." Her smile faded, but she shook off the frown that threatened to replace it. "We can have this conversation tomorrow," she insisted. "When I look back on this week, I want some good memories. So far, today's been perfect. I don't want to change that now."

Max tugged her gently outside, making sure the porch light was off before he shut the door. Darkness enveloped them, and he allowed himself to pull her close once more. He knew which memories he'd like to take back to San Diego with him, but he wasn't a *complete* jerk.

He slipped both arms around her waist and crushed her against him, amazed by how good she felt in his arms, how right it felt to be with her. He ran his hands along her hips and gently cupped her bottom. "I keep telling myself I shouldn't do this, but it's damn hard to keep my hands to myself when I'm around you."

"You don't have to stop on my account," she murmured. "Although…" She cast a quick glance at the houses across the street. "I wonder what the neighbors would think if they could see me now."

Max had a pretty good idea what they'd think. He pulled her toward the far edge of the porch where a thick lilac bush provided a shield from prying eyes. "Better?"

"Mmm-hmm." She pressed against him, delighting him with her boldness. "*Much* better."

No man could have resisted her. Max gave up trying. He covered her mouth again and kissed her deeply. He put everything he couldn't say into the kiss, the hopes and dreams he couldn't articulate, the yearning he couldn't acknowledge.

His hands took on a life of their own, moving from

her bottom to her waist, trailing up her sides slowly, driving them both to distraction. When he finally let himself move toward her breasts, her breath caught in her throat and her lips parted slightly.

He circled his thumbs across the tender flesh beneath her T-shirt and she tilted back her head in a gesture of surrender, exposing the long curve of her neck to his lips. She was beautiful, desirable, every inch a woman, and he knew she was as ready as he was to consummate what they felt. But his damn conscience wouldn't let him love her and leave her.

Groaning in frustration, Max pulled her closer. He ached for release, but some rational part of his brain still remembered her daughters inside and the neighbors across the street. Everyone in town would know by morning if he spent the night here or took her back to the Wagon Wheel.

She curved one leg slightly and wrapped it gently around his, and he thought he'd explode. Her hands caressed his chest, leaving a trail of fire in their wake. He pressed his lips to her throat and a moan of desire escaped her.

"I want you."

The words came so softly, he thought he'd imagined them.

"Max... Please. Come back inside. Stay with me for a while."

How was he supposed to resist that? Even as he tried to convince himself to say no, he felt himself nodding. His conscience screamed at him to stop, but he didn't listen. She took his hand and pulled him toward the front door, and he knew he'd found heaven. Surely, there had to be some way to work this out. He'd find a way.

Reagan opened the door and started inside, but the beam of headlights swept across them as a rattletrap van pulled into her driveway. She stopped on the threshold and shielded her eyes against the glare. "Who could this be?"

"Maybe they're just turning around in your driveway," Max growled, irritated by the interruption.

"I don't think so."

The van chugged to a stop, and Reagan took a step closer to it.

"Travis? You're actually here?"

Travis?

The fire burning inside Max turned to ice. *Travis?* It couldn't be. He'd heard wrong.

Reagan caught Max's hand in hers and tugged him toward the porch steps. "It's my brother. Come and meet him."

Numb with disbelief, he stumbled after her. This couldn't be happening. Ronnie. Reagan. How could Monique have mixed up those two names? This had to be another Travis. Max wouldn't *let* it be Carmichael.

Through his stunned denial, a sick dread filled his veins. No wonder he hadn't been able to find any trace of Ronnie. No wonder no one in Serenity knew her. He almost wished he'd given up and left town before he found out. This truth hurt too much.

Travis climbed slowly out of the van. His battered army jacket swayed over his stretched-out T-shirt and worn jeans as he closed the distance between them. His dark auburn hair hung into his eyes and stuck out at odd angles, as if he'd been asleep until just a minute ago. "You look kinda busy," he said in a slow drawl. "Maybe I should drive around the block a couple of times, and then come back."

"No. Stay, please." Reagan looked delighted. "I can't believe you're really here."

"Told you I'd be here." Travis held back, looking Max over cautiously.

Reagan took Travis by the arm and pulled him closer. "I know you don't want to meet people while you're here, but you should at least meet my friend, Max. Max Gardner...my brother, Travis Carmichael."

Travis gripped Max's hand and pumped it a couple of times. "Friend? It looked like more than that to me, but what do I know?" He grinned as if he and Max had been friends for years. "I'm just glad to see her happy."

Happy. She wouldn't be happy for long.

Max's stomach churned and his heart felt like stone. He managed to respond, but he wasn't at all sure that he made any sense. The only thing he knew was the creeping sense of failure.

The one thing he wanted most was the one thing he could never have.

BRIGHT SPRING SUNLIGHT flooded the kitchen the next morning as Reagan carried two cups of coffee to the table. Birds chattered in the trees, and a soft breeze set the blind rattling gently against the open window. The weather had turned unseasonably warm overnight, and the sky was a deep azure with only a trace of clouds. A perfect day in keeping with her mood.

Now that Travis was here, she was even more glad

that she'd gone with Max yesterday. She might not get many more chances to spend time alone with him. He'd gone back to the motel almost immediately after Travis had shown up, insisting that she needed time with her brother. She appreciated his thoughtfulness, but it hadn't really been necessary. Travis had crashed on the couch less than half an hour after Max left.

Yawning, she slid one cup in front of Travis and sat down across the table. She savored the coffee and waited for it to pop her eyes open so she could get started on her day.

Travis sat bare-chested and slouched over the table, both hands laced into his hair as huge yawns racked his body. He looked like the little boy she'd grown up with. He glanced at the cup, murmured a thank-you and took a long, careful sip. "There's nothing like screaming girls to wake a guy up fast."

"Or a mom, either." Reagan rubbed her forehead gently. "I should have woken them last night to tell them you were here. They're not used to finding men sleeping on the couch."

Travis eyed her over the top of his cup. "They scared the hell out of me."

"Sorry." Reagan glanced over her shoulder toward the sounds of mild morning argument drifting from the bathroom. "I'm not sure who scared who the most."

"Trust me," Travis said with a slight frown. "They were a lot better off than I was."

Reagan put her hand over his. "I'm so glad you're actually here. Tell me what's been happening with you."

Travis shrugged. "Same old, same old."

Predictable answer, but Reagan was determined to get through to him this visit. Who knew when she'd have another chance? Besides, Travis wouldn't be here if he wasn't ready to make things better.

"The trouble with that answer," she said, "is that I haven't seen you in so long, I don't know what the same old thing is for you. How about giving me some details—like where you've been working, or if you're seeing someone special."

"There's not that much to tell. I'm not a brain surgeon yet, if that's what you're asking."

Reagan searched his face for a smile, but he looked mulish and defensive. "I'm not being critical, Travis. I just want to know what you've been doing."

"Why? So you can call Dad and tell him?"

"No. I promised you I wouldn't do that." Reagan couldn't help wondering what made him so irritable this morning. "I won't tell Dad, even though I think he deserves to know that you're all right."

Travis's lip curled. "Like he cares."

"He *does* care, Travis. I wish you'd give him a chance to prove it." Reagan pushed away from the table. "Why are we arguing? We've been together less than one day."

"Because I didn't come here to talk about Dad, *or* to have you lecture me about what I ought to do." He hooked his arm over the back of his chair. "I haven't even had my coffee and you're already preaching." He took a long, slow drink, challenging her with his eyes. "If I'm in your way here, just tell me. I can leave. It's no skin off my nose."

Reagan bit back the first response that rose to her lips and tried to put herself in Travis's place. "I didn't mean to lecture you. I really am glad that you're here.''

Travis stood quickly and kissed the top of her head. ''You need to relax, sis. You must drive your kids crazy if you fuss over them all the time like you do me. So, what's up for today?''

''First, we need to get Jamie's things moved into Danielle's room so you have a place to stay.'' And she'd need to do laundry so he had clean sheets. ''Then, I guess we'll see how much time is left after that.''

''I'm surprised,'' Travis said. ''I would have thought you'd have every minute of the day planned. I've always wondered if you allow those girls *any* free time, or if you keep them tied up all day.''

Reagan carried her coffee cup back to the sink. ''It's not a bad thing to keep busy when you're a teen. Too much free time only leads to trouble.''

''And you're scared to death your kids'll turn out like me, aren't you?''

''*Should* I be?''

Travis laughed again and rested both arms on the chair's back. ''One of these days, your daughters are going to rebel.''

He was needling her, trying to get a reaction. But why? She swept some imaginary crumbs into the sink and pulled bowls from the cupboard for cereal. ''I doubt that.''

''Mark my word, sis. Last time I saw you, you had their days packed so tight, they barely had time to go to the bathroom. Nobody can stand living like that forever.''

Suddenly tired of the attack, she rounded on him.

"What makes you such an expert on kids all of a sudden? You don't even have any."

"No, but I was one."

"*You* never played on any teams or took any extra classes. You were…"

"Ignored?"

"That's not what I was going to say."

"But it's the truth, isn't it?"

Reagan pulled two boxes of cereal from the cupboard and closed the door with a bang. "I'm not sure how this happened, but I really hate feeling as if I'm under fire."

"Really?" Travis came into the kitchen behind her. A slow grin curved his mouth. "Gee, *I* kind of like it. I can't get enough."

She had to look up to glare into his eyes. "You've made your point, Travis. You can back off any time now."

He surprised her by bending down to kiss the top of her head once more. "Cool. Then we should be able to have a good visit for the rest of the time I'm here, right?" With that, he shuffled from the room on bare feet, leaving her completely confused.

CHAPTER EIGHT

REAGAN BRUSHED A TRICKLE of perspiration from her forehead as she snapped open a fitted sheet and started putting it on the mattress. After taking Jamie to practice and Danielle to dance rehearsal, she'd done two loads of laundry, dusted and vacuumed Jamie's room, and made several trips from Jamie's room into Danielle's with clothes. The girls had been working to make space in Danielle's room for the roll-away bed ever since they got home.

Reagan had no idea where Travis had gone.

She was trying hard not to be irritated with him, but he made it difficult. He'd mysteriously disappeared as soon as the lifting and carrying started.

To make matters worse, Jamie's mood had gone steadily downhill over the past few hours. Reagan was trying to stay upbeat. She didn't want to argue with anyone today.

Jamie was probably upset at having to give up her room, but Reagan couldn't see any other way to accommodate everyone. Danielle's was the bigger bedroom, and the girls would be more comfortable together there than in Jamie's.

Nudging Travis's backpack out of her way, she tugged the fitted sheet into place. Jamie would adjust, she assured herself. Travis wouldn't be here forever.

He'd probably find some reason to move on in a day or two.

"What time are we leaving?"

Reagan whipped around and found Jamie in the doorway, her arms folded across her chest. "You startled me," Reagan said with a laugh. "I didn't hear you come back. What did you say?"

Jamie leaned against the door frame. "I asked how much longer before we can leave."

Reagan opened the top sheet and smoothed it over the mattress. "Were we supposed to go somewhere?"

Jamie's mouth fell open and her posture grew rigid. "Are you serious?"

Reagan stopped working and took a closer look at her daughter's face. "Have I forgotten something? I wouldn't be surprised. It's been a long week."

"You promised you'd take me to Jackson today, *remember?* You promised you'd talk to the people at the climbing school."

"Oh, Jamie, I—" No wonder the girl had been acting so strangely. "I'm so sorry. I forgot."

"But you promised." Jamie's mouth twisted. Hurt and anger flashed in her eyes. "You *promised.*"

"I said I'd try, honey. That's not the same as a promise. I had no idea Travis would actually show up."

"He told you he was coming. We could have had all this stuff done already."

They could have if Reagan had believed him. She resisted the urge to say so to Jamie. She didn't want to prejudice the girls against their uncle. "Maybe so," she said slowly. "But we didn't. And now that he's here, I can't just leave him sleeping on the couch. We'll never be able to use the living room if I do.''

Jamie propped her hands on her hips. ''Does that mean we're not going?''

Reagan sat on the foot of the bed and patted the mattress for Jamie to join her. ''I know you're disappointed, honey, but I don't see how we can go today. It's already afternoon. Even if we left right now, we'd have trouble getting back before the sun goes down, and you know how I hate driving that canyon after dark—especially at this time of year.''

''But if we don't go, you won't be able to see the school before the registration deadline.''

''Are they open tomorrow?''

''On Sunday?'' Jamie shook her head and slumped against the wall. ''Today's the only chance unless we go after school next week, and I *know* you won't do that.''

Reagan felt about an inch tall. ''I'm really sorry, honey. But there's still so much to do today I don't see how we can go.''

''You never planned on taking me, did you.''

''Of course I did. It's just that things have come up that I didn't foresee. Things that I can't control. Sometimes that happens, and when it does we just have to deal with it.''

''I don't *want* to deal with it. It's not fair.''

The past week had taken its toll on Reagan's patience. There'd been too many changes, both good and bad, and her ability to cope was growing shorter by the minute. She stood again and snapped, ''Life isn't always fair. You're old enough to know that.''

"Yeah," Jamie said bitterly. "But why does it always have to be unfair to *me?*"

Reagan shoved the hem of the sheet under the mattress and reached for a blanket. "It's not always unfair to you. I haven't seen my brother in three years. What would you have me do, ignore him?"

"I don't want you to ignore him, but I don't want you to ignore me, either."

Reagan straightened the blanket without looking at her. "I don't ignore you, Jamie."

"It sure feels like it."

The self-pitying tone frayed Reagan's patience a little further. "I couldn't ignore you if I wanted to, Jamie. You make sure of that." She shoved pillows into cases and tossed them onto the bed. "You won't take no for an answer. I can't even count the number of times I've told you I don't want you to take these lessons."

Jamie's cheeks turned bright red. "If that's how you feel, why did you say you'd take me up there?"

"I intended to take you if I could," Reagan said with the tiny bit of patience she could still muster. "And I would have. But Travis's visit has changed everything, and I need you to understand that."

Jamie stared at her, unmoving, for what felt like forever. "Right. Sure."

The look on her face cut Reagan to the quick. She hated losing her temper with the girls. She hated losing control and saying things she regretted the instant they fell out of her mouth. She took a deep, steadying breath and tried to regroup. "Cut me some slack, Jamie. I'm doing my best here."

"Sure."

"I'm not trying to be unfair."

"Whatever." Jamie turned to leave.

"Don't walk away, sweetheart. Let's talk about this. We can figure something out."

"There's nothing to talk about. You've already decided."

"Jamie, please—"

But Jamie didn't look back. She didn't even slow down. A memory flash of Paul walking away after an argument took the starch out of Reagan's knees. The look in Jamie's eyes had been exactly like the one she'd seen so often in her husband's eyes. It hurt just as much now as if ever had.

MAX WATCHED THE NUMBERS on the clock beside his bed click the minutes away as he tried to figure out what to do. He'd really screwed up this time, and he couldn't see a way out. He'd spent the day thinking, trying to come up with a way to tell Reagan the truth about her brother and about himself. But no matter how Max looked at it, no matter which explanation he tried, he knew she'd believe he'd wormed his way into her life to find her brother. She'd hate him, and the thought of that kept him searching for another solution.

It should have been so easy—a no-brainer. He'd been raised to believe that a man's duty came before anything else. Duty to family, to country, to his career. The old man had drilled it into their heads from the time Max and his brothers could first begin to understand. Yet the idea of hurting Reagan made Max want to forget he even *had* a duty.

He wasn't sure what that said about him.

He paced to the window of his room and peered outside at the Saturday evening activity on Front Street. A few couples walked together hand in hand. A few cars drove slowly past the motel parking lot. Young people laughed and shouted at one another, and music floated across the motel courtyard from some distant radio.

A week ago, Max would have turned up his nose at this sight. Now he found himself wanting to be a part of it. He could almost see himself walking with Reagan to the Burger Shack or to another junior high school basketball game. He could almost envision a future here in Serenity.

He wasn't sure what that said about him, either.

In San Diego he spent Saturday nights at the theater or a fancy new restaurant, usually with an elegant date on his arm. Now his imagination kept taking him back to the Chicken Inn, and Reagan's was the only female face he could conjure.

But she would hate his life, and he'd soon grow bored with hers. He shouldn't even think about any kind of future with her. What he *should* be thinking about was how to get Travis Carmichael into custody.

The answer was simple, of course. Put one foot in front of the other all the way up Reagan's front walk, pull out the handcuffs and do his duty. Get Carmichael off the streets before he pulled another robbery or hurt someone.

It couldn't *be* any simpler.

So why did he keep resisting?

Because he couldn't bear the thought of losing Reagan? He'd lose her, anyway, as soon as he left Serenity.

The telephone shrilled, breaking into his thoughts and making him drop the curtain back into place. It had to be Reagan, but he had no idea what he'd say to her. He strode across the room and answered, anyway.

"Hey! What's up? Still chasing that woman in Wyoming?"

Donovan. Max didn't know if he was disappointed or relieved, but the question bothered him. "Not exactly. How was Cancún?"

"Heaven, buddy. Pure heaven."

"Glad to hear it."

"If you ever manage to get yourself a woman, take her there. Didn't see much of the scenery, but the room was real nice."

Max chuckled because Donovan expected him to, but his heart wasn't in it. "Too bad you didn't do more sightseeing. I'll bet Holly was disappointed."

"You'd lose that bet. Every time I suggested leaving the room, *she* came up with an excuse to stay in." Donovan's voice lowered. "And that woman's got some mighty good excuses. The only thing *she's* upset about is that the week's over, and I'll be spending all my time with you after Monday." He paused, and Max could hear the telltale intake of breath that meant he'd lit a cigarette. "What about you? I thought you were going to be back here with Carmichael before I got my first sunburn."

"To hear you talk, I still have plenty of time." Max leaned against the headboard and stared at the ceiling. "Which is good since he just showed up last night."

"Last night?" Donovan laughed. "You've been

stuck there all this time? I'll bet that's been exciting. What have you been doing with yourself?''

''You wouldn't believe me if I told you. When did you get back?''

''A few hours ago. Tried to call you at home. You weren't there.''

''How'd you find me?''

''Slate. He actually managed not to lose the number you left him.''

''Well. Miracles *do* happen.''

''So, when are you heading back? Give me your flight information and I'll meet you at the airport. We can transport Carmichael to the jail together.''

Max propped the phone between his chin and shoulder and kneaded a knot from the back of his neck. ''I'm going to need a little longer on this one.''

''Longer? The bounty on Carmichael isn't even going to cover your expenses as it is.''

''I know, but things here are more complicated than I expected.''

''Complicated how?''

''It's a long story.''

''You got trouble with the sister or something?''

''No. It's just a little complication.''

''You need me to come out there?''

''No,'' Max said quickly. ''No. Thanks. I've got it under control. Let me ask you something about Carmichael. You've seen his rap sheet. Do you think he's dangerous?''

''No. If I was worried about that, I never would have agreed to let you go after him alone. Why?''

''He's staying with his sister, and she's got two

kids. I don't want to do anything that might put them in danger."

"The kids have to go to school, don't they? Or are they too young?"

"They're teenagers."

"Then wait until they're in school. Or work with the local authorities to get the sister and her kids out of there before you go in."

"Right." Donovan made it sound so easy—and it *should* be. "The sister doesn't know he's on the run."

"She'll figure it out soon enough when you apprehend him." Donovan's voice changed. "What's the problem? You've done this kind of job a hundred times."

"I told you, it's complicated."

"Yeah, but you didn't say how."

"It's hard to explain. I'll fill you in later." If Donovan knew how deeply enmeshed he was, he'd be here in the morning and Max would be off the case. That might be the best solution, but Max hated the thought of Reagan finding out about Travis that way.

"You sure you don't need help?"

"I'm sure. It's not dangerous. Now, quit worrying about me and pay some attention to your wife. I don't need her upset with me for keeping you on the phone all night."

Donovan laughed. "I don't need her upset with me, either. Just keep in touch, okay, buddy? And if you need help, call me."

"You got it." Max disconnected, but the conversation left him even more agitated than he'd been earlier. Now that Donovan had returned, he'd have to get the show on the road. If he wasn't back in San Diego in a couple of days, Donovan would come after him. One way or another, he had to get Travis into custody before that happened.

MAX TIMED HIS MORNING JOG so he could meet up with Reagan. With any luck, she'd invite him back to the house. If not, he'd just have to invite himself. He wanted a chance to size Travis up and take stock of the situation before he did anything.

He was all business this morning—grimly determined to do the job he'd come to do. Jogging slowly past beds of budding flowers, he repeated the vow he'd made to the mirror that morning. No matter what happened, he'd stay in control. He'd remain detached until he had Travis in custody. It wouldn't be easy, but Max felt more equal to the challenge this morning than he had last night. He'd faced tougher ones and come out on top.

He just couldn't remember when.

Sunlight splashed onto the sidewalk in front of him, bringing back the memory of that first morning with Reagan, the fire in her hair and the deep sea-green of her eyes. His sudden, fierce, physical reaction to the memory slowed his step and eventually brought him to a stop in the middle of the sidewalk.

Bending slightly, he gripped his knees and struggled to catch his breath. It took a little more effort to get his mind back on the job. By the time he'd finished his route, he realized he'd either missed Reagan or she'd decided not to run. Switch to plan B, he thought as he started toward her house.

It was still early, but things were already hopping by the time he arrived. Music blared from one of the back rooms and laughter floated out toward him through the open windows, along with the scents of coffee and breakfast.

Stay detached, he reminded himself.

The laughter hushed for a second after he rang the bell, and a set of footsteps raced toward the door. The top of Danielle's head appeared in the window, followed by her eyes as she stood on tiptoe to look out, and an unexpected flash of affection for her left Max a little off step.

Grinning broadly, she threw the door open and shouted over her shoulder, "Max is here!" Before he could get inside, she grabbed his hand and tugged him down the hall.

The rest of the family sat together at the kitchen table, Reagan in a gray University of Texas sweatshirt and a pair of green-and-gray plaid flannel pajama bottoms. She'd pulled her hair high on her head so that curls danced whenever she moved, and her face was clean, scrubbed of makeup and other distractions. She was utterly beautiful.

Travis sat across from her, comfortable in a pair of black sweatpants and a faded T-shirt. "Hey, man." Travis stood when Max entered, shoving out his hand as if they were best friends. "We were just talking about you." He pumped Max's hand for a few seconds. "You want some coffee?"

"Sure." Max smiled at Jamie, who huddled beneath a light blanket and looked as if she'd rather be somewhere else. "Thanks."

Reagan hopped up, but Travis waved her back into her seat and went after the coffee himself. "Take my seat,'' he told Max. ''I'll drag in a chair from the other room.''

Max tried not to let Travis's easy acceptance whip up guilt, but it wasn't easy. ''It sounds like you're having a great time,'' he said as he sat beside Danielle. ''I could hear you laughing all the way up the front walk.''

''Travis has been telling stories about when he and Mom were little.'' Danielle's eyes danced with mischief. ''You should make him tell you the one about Mom's first date.''

''He doesn't need to hear that story. Not from any of you.'' Reagan tried to look stern, but the sparkle in her eyes made it clear that she was enjoying herself thoroughly.

Travis came back into the kitchen with a chair, then poured Max an oversize mug of coffee. ''Reagan just challenged me to a kite-flying contest. You want in?''

Max shook his head quickly. He'd be a fool to let himself become more firmly entrenched in the family unit. Obviously, Reagan and the girls were safe. Travis's eyes looked clear and bright, not clouded from drugs. Nobody seemed frightened. ''I don't think so. I really should get some work done.''

''But it's Sunday,'' Danielle pointed out.

Jamie spoke for the first time. ''You can't do *anything* around here on Sunday.''

''The town's locked up tight, huh?'' Max tried to find another out. ''I haven't flown a kite in so many years, I can't even remember the last time I tried. I'd lose for certain.''

Reagan kicked her feet onto her chair and wrapped her arms around her knees. ''That makes two of us. I was about eight last time I flew a kite, and the girls never have.''

''Yeah,'' Danielle chimed in again. ''So you'll be the same as the rest of us.''

Max knew what his answer should be, but he had a hard time resisting the pull of Reagan's eyes. And if he spent time with them, he could make absolutely certain that Reagan and the girls were really safe. *And dig that hole you're standing in a whole lot deeper.*

Max ignored the warning and focused instead on the circle of shining eyes and smiling faces surrounding him. ''What's at stake?''

''Winner is the one who keeps his kite up longest,'' Travis said. ''Loser has to fix dinner for everyone else tomorrow night.''

''Dinner, huh? That's not so bad, I guess.''

''Now that I think about it,'' Reagan said, ''I'm not sure this is such a good idea. If I remember right, Max isn't all that skilled in the kitchen.'' She turned those eyes on him, all sweetness on the surface with a hint of deviltry shining from their depths.

''As I recall,'' he said, straight-faced, ''the incident you're thinking about wasn't entirely my fault. Besides, I don't intend to lose, so it won't be an issue.''

Danielle laughed softly. Jamie kept her head down, refusing to make eye contact with any of them. Obviously, everything wasn't rosy, but Reagan didn't seem overly concerned so Max tried to ignore the girl's bad mood.

''It has to be more than salad,'' Reagan warned. ''Or hot dogs. And barbecued hamburgers don't count, either.''

''Fair enough.''

Travis shook hair out of his eyes. "So what's it going to be? I'm putting my world-famous chili on the line. Reagan's betting some fancy kind of pasta, and it's sloppy joes for Danielle—and Jamie if she decides to join in."

The look on Jamie's face left no doubt how she felt about taking part. She turned to Reagan with an exaggerated sigh. "I've visited with Travis like you told me to. Can I go back to my room now?"

Disappointment flickered in Reagan's eyes, but she nodded. "If you want to leave, I guess that's okay, but I want you to come with us to fly the kites."

Jamie didn't waste a second shooting to her feet and making a dramatic exit with her blanket trailing behind her and the cat chasing it. If the undercurrents hadn't been so strong, it might even have been comical.

Travis waited until she disappeared, then cut the uneasy silence she left behind. "So, what do you say, Max? Are you in?"

Stand up, Max's inner voice shouted. *Make an excuse. Get the hell out of here before you do something stupid.*

Max ignored it. "Sauerbraten," he said abruptly. "I used to help my mom make it. I'm pretty sure I can do it on my own."

"Sauerbraten?" Reagan arched an eyebrow. "Are you serious?"

"You don't believe I can do it?"

"I didn't say that." She stood and grinned down at him. "I'm sure you can do anything you put your mind to."

Not true. He couldn't keep his mind on business

when he was in the same room with her. He couldn't come up with an easy way to tell her the truth. And he couldn't stop thinking about her when he was alone. It might not have been the most intelligent decision he'd ever made, but he couldn't back out now.

Yesterday had been for Reagan, he rationalized. Today was his day. He'd get back to business tomorrow.

WARMED BY THE WEAK spring sunlight, Max walked hand in hand with Reagan across the still-brown grass of the park. Danielle ran ahead holding the kites they'd spent nearly an hour choosing at FoodTown. Still pouting, Jamie lagged behind her sister and scuffed her feet as she walked.

Travis loped along behind the girls and tossed challenges back over his shoulder every few feet. He zeroed in on Max one minute, on Reagan the next. "I don't think I've ever had sauerbraten," he shouted. "Sure am looking forward to trying it." A few seconds later he added, "What else are you planning to serve with that pasta you're making?"

Max had to admit, the guy had a certain amount of charm. No wonder he'd been able to keep the wool pulled over Reagan's eyes for so long. His enthusiasm was infectious, even to someone who knew the truth about him.

"So, what do you think of my brother?" Reagan asked.

Such hope filled her eyes, Max's heart felt as if someone had twisted it. "I don't know him well enough to have an opinion," he said carefully. "I've just met him."

Reagan's step slowed. "You're right, of course. I

guess I'm just hoping you'll tell me he seems settled, mature, wise, sensible and responsible.''

Those probably wouldn't be the words Max used if he offered an opinion. ''It might take me a little longer than a couple of hours to arrive at all those conclusions,'' he said with a weak smile.

She leaned her head on Max's shoulder. ''I just hope I'm right this time. I hope he's changed. He's always been so irresponsible, so angry and bitter, it breaks my heart.''

''What's he angry about?''

''All sorts of things that happened after our mother died. I sort of raised him, and I'm afraid I didn't do such a great job.''

''You *sort of* raised him? Where was your father?''

''Oh, he was there. He was just so torn up by Mom's death he didn't deal well with either of us for the first few years.'' The sunlight played in her hair. The breeze toyed with her light sweatshirt, molding it against her breasts.

Max tried to keep his focus, but Mother Nature was having a field day at his expense.

''It's funny,'' Reagan continued. ''Travis is twenty-six. I was married and already a mother when I was his age, but I still think of him as a kid.''

''What makes you think you're to blame for the way he turned out?''

She lifted those eyes to meet Max's and he couldn't duck the agony he saw in them. ''Travis could be an incredible person if he'd just try a little harder. He *would* be if I'd been able to give him a firmer hand when he needed it.''

''People aren't always the product of their environment,'' Max argued mildly. ''Some people just are the way they are in spite of the best efforts of the people who love them.''

Reagan pulled back with a frown. ''That's ridiculous. People aren't born bad. Travis certainly wasn't.''

''The two of you had the same childhood, lived in the same house, went through the same tough times. Why did you turn out one way and he another? His personality must have something to do with the difference. It can't all be your fault.''

Her frown deepened. The light in her eyes hardened. ''Why are your two brothers married with children, and you're not? Were you born a confirmed bachelor?''

Judging from the number of times he'd found himself pondering a new lifestyle over the past few days, probably not. ''Point taken,'' he said with a dip of his head. ''How old were you when you had to take over?''

''Fourteen.''

''The same age as Danielle?'' Max let out a low whistle. ''That's hardly old enough to suddenly be responsible for another person.''

Reagan's cheeks colored faintly. ''I didn't mean it to sound as if my dad was totally absent. He took care of the big things. He worked, brought in the money and kept a roof over our heads. He just couldn't be there for the little things, and I should have been able to give them to Travis.''

A host of things about her suddenly seemed much clearer. ''That's why you didn't go to pieces when your husband died. You didn't want to flake out on your kids.'' The sudden, deep flush of red in her cheeks told him he shouldn't have said that aloud.

"My dad didn't *flake out*. He was grief-stricken. My mother's death was completely unexpected."

"So was your husband's, wasn't it?"

Reagan shoved a lock of hair out of her face and looked away. "It wasn't the same."

"You were a kid. You'd just lost your mother. You *aren't* responsible for what happened to your brother any more than Danielle's responsible because Jamie wants to take those climbing lessons. You've told me that Jamie was born with her love of adventure. Why can't the same thing be true of Travis?"

"You think he was born with a love of trouble?"

"Some people are addicted to catastrophe. They hate it and love it at the same time. Even when life's going smoothly, they'll create discord because life doesn't feel right unless something's wrong."

"Travis isn't like that."

Her eyes flashed green fire, and Max knew he'd gone as far as he should for now. "Maybe not. You know him better than I do. And I don't want to argue with you. I don't want to risk losing my fair share of that pasta you'll be making tomorrow."

He held his breath, waiting to see if she'd abandon the argument.

She leaned closer and put her lips just inches from his. "I just hope your mother hasn't lost her sauerbraten recipe. You're going to need it."

The only person she held a grudge against, it seemed, was herself. "No chance." Max didn't pull his mouth away or raise his voice. He kept his tone intimate, as if he were seducing her. "I've got a kite here that'll leave yours in the dust."

"Is that right?"

"Yes, it is."

"I think it's time for you to put your sauerbraten where your mouth is."

Max couldn't resist. He dipped slightly and kissed her. "My mouth," he said in a low whisper, "isn't the slightest bit interested in sauerbraten *or* pasta."

"Neither is mine."

The sudden longing to spend the rest of his life looking into her eyes nearly knocked Max off his feet. He wanted to share more moments like this, to jog with her in the mornings, hold her at night, and share all the moments in between. He wanted to sit at her dinner table in the evenings and worry about Jamie and Danielle with her. An image of himself walking one of the girls down the aisle in a wedding gown flashed in front of his eyes, and he wondered what it would be like to be there for them when that day came.

More than anything, he wanted to spend the rest of his life seeing himself reflected through the light in Reagan's eyes instead of the harsh glare of his mirror.

But could he change his life so drastically? There was a long, tough road ahead before he'd even get the chance to find out.

CHAPTER NINE

IF THEY'D DECIDED the contest by the first try, Max would have lost hands down. In spite of the steady breeze, his kite climbed for about two seconds, then took a nosedive and skidded to a stop near a small stand of trees. Luckily, no one else did much better, so when Reagan suggested time to practice before the contest began, everyone agreed enthusiastically.

Max practiced for a few minutes, then realized now was as good a time as any to have a one-on-one with Travis. He waited until Reagan was busy helping Danielle—Jamie was still moping on a small hill a few feet away—then worked his way across the lawn and came to rest a few feet from Travis. He'd caught a tail wind and was busy letting out string as his kite soared into the air. Max's swooped and swirled out of control, nearly tugging the ball of string out of his hands.

"Looks like you found the good air," he called.

Travis grinned at him. "Good air, nothing. You're looking at pure skill."

He looked so much like Danielle when he smiled, Max had to remind himself that he wasn't an innocent young kid. That he'd used a gun to commit a crime. That he was a fugitive on the run from the law, not just the brother of the woman Max was falling in love with.

Max had no idea what he wanted out of this conversation. A confession? A better understanding of what made Travis tick? Maybe just a deeper look into the eyes of his quarry so he could find something to dislike about him and make his job easier. He *did* know that if Donovan could see him now, he'd either split a side laughing or tell Max to turn in his gun and license.

Max moved a few feet closer and watched Travis at work. "You do that like a pro. I have a feeling we won't be eating chili for dinner."

Travis laughed and nodded toward Max's kite. "You're not doing so bad. We're not judging on how high or how steady your flight is, just on how long you can keep it in the air."

Max moved slightly and felt a tug as the wind finally caught his kite and lifted it. "Reagan tells me you travel a lot."

Travis glanced at his sister and shrugged. "Yeah, I guess so. I don't like staying in one place for too long, that's for sure."

"Where will you be heading after this?"

Travis turned his attention back to his kite. "I haven't decided. I'm weighing my options."

"Yeah?" Max kept his tone easy. "What options?"

"Oh, you know. This and that."

"Well, I've lived all over the country. My father was in the military." Max sawed on the string and tried to save his kite from another savage nosedive. "I could probably tell you about almost any place you're interested in."

Travis pulled his eyes away from the sky. "Okay. If I have any questions, I'll know where to go, then." His kite started to dive and claimed his attention for a few seconds. "So, what made you end up here?"

Max answered without losing a beat. "Work."

"You like it here?"

"Yeah. Yeah, I do." Max realized suddenly that his answer felt like a small fib instead of a blatant lie.

"What do you do?"

"Acquisitions."

"Sounds like the big time. What is it?"

"I look for things other people want."

"Yeah?" Travis sent him a sidelong glance, but Max didn't see any suspicion in his expression. "How do you get into something like that?"

"I heard about it through a friend who did the same thing. I signed up, took some training, and here I am."

"What kind of training?"

He'd be asking Max for a job next. Max shrugged indifferently. "Some general stuff, some more specialized. What do you do for a living? I don't think Reagan mentioned that."

"Probably not. I kind of move around there, too." Travis shoved a shaggy lock of hair out of his eyes. "It's easier to get a good job when you have an education. But since I never finished high school, nobody'll give me a break."

"You could go back. Most places have night classes for adults who want to get their high school diplomas."

Travis shook his head. "Not for me. I sucked at school when I was a kid, and I've probably forgotten everything I ever knew. Even if I *did* go back to school, what good would it do? I'm *not* going to spend the rest of my life working at some minimum-wage job.''

''There are technical schools where you could get training for something that would pay better.''

Travis made a face. ''In what? Computers? Auto mechanics? Bor-ing.''

Compared to the ''thrill'' of robbing people at gunpoint? ''A lot of what makes a job feel right is the people you work with,'' Max told him. ''Even the most exciting career in the world can be a pain if you work with the wrong people. And there's nothing like the feeling of doing a job well—don't you think?''

''There's no feeling like having a wallet full of money,'' Travis said with a grin. ''When you're poor, everybody's got something to say about what you should do or how you should act.''

''Money won't change that. There will always be people who have something to say about what you do.''

''Yeah, but when you have money you don't have to listen.''

''You don't ever *have* to listen. I just hope I'm smart enough to listen when the other person's right.''

Travis took another long, appraising glance at him. ''That makes sense, I guess. You're all right, Max. I think Reagan's going to be okay with you.''

Max could have gone all day without hearing that, he thought. Travis's concern for his sister made it harder for Max to keep his feelings compartmentalized. He started reeling in his kite. ''You through practicing? I think it's about time to get this show on the road.''

"Sure." Travis grinned and began winding his string. "If you're ready to get your butt kicked."

Max forced a laugh and wished he'd waited to talk to Travis until after the fun was over. He had the unsettling feeling he'd just made his job a lot harder.

Travis left him and walked over to the hill where Jamie sat. The girl had made no effort to hide her displeasure at being here. But within minutes, Travis had her on her feet and walking down the hill to join them. The guy had a way with people, that was for sure. Max found himself agreeing with Reagan. Travis could do something good with his life if only he'd try.

Max took his cue from Reagan, who acted as if Jamie's sullen attitude had been a figment of someone's imagination. Reagan, Jamie and Danielle jockeyed for position on the lawn, nudging one another as they vied for the best spots. Travis found a place a little removed from the others, and Max wandered up the hill Jamie had abandoned.

When Travis gave the countdown, they raced like kids across the dry grass, whooping and shouting as they tried to get their kites to catch the wind. The spirit of competition took hold of Max, and everything else flew out of his mind as his kite caught a steady breeze and soared straight into the air.

A shout from Travis pulled his attention back to the others, and he watched Travis battle for control as his kite dipped, swooped, and then spiraled back to earth.

Laughing, Max gave his string a little tug and felt a sense of satisfaction as his kite responded. "What else are you planning to serve with that chili?" he shouted.

Travis waved the question away, but he was grinning broadly. "Looks like you have the good air now."

"Good air, nothing," Max called back. "You're looking at pure dumb luck."

THAT NIGHT, Max paced until his feet hurt, stared at the walls until he knew where every single knothole was in the logs and could have drawn the pattern on the ceiling with his eyes closed. He'd stared out the window for hours, watching the changing shapes of the street lamps as the moon climbed the sky.

Finally, at nearly midnight, when it became clear that he wouldn't sleep until he did something, he punched in Donovan's number. It was an hour earlier in San Diego and Donovan rarely went to bed before Letterman was over.

"You've gotta help me, buddy," he said when Donovan's sleepy voice came over the line.

Donovan murmured something to Holly and yawned noisily into the phone. "What is it? Where are you?"

"I'm still in Serenity. And I'm in big trouble."

Donovan was instantly alert. "What did you do, lose him?"

"No. I know exactly where he is."

"You're not hurt, are you?"

"No. No, nothing like that. It's just that I—" Max mopped his face with one hand and let out his breath in a whoosh. "The thing is, I've met a woman here. I think I'm falling in love with her."

Donovan let out a whoop that earned a grumble from Holly. "Sorry," he said, and lowered his voice to a whisper again. "You're kidding, right?"

"Believe me," Max said miserably, "I wish I were."

"What's the problem?"

"The problem?" Max paced toward the luggage stand. "The *problem* is, she's Travis Carmichael's sister."

Stunned silence echoed between them.

"Did you hear me?" Max demanded. "I'm falling in love with Carmichael's sister." He was suddenly, unreasonably angry with Donovan—as if this were his fault. If Donovan hadn't taken Holly to Cancún, they'd have done the damn job together and Max wouldn't have been in this situation.

"I heard you." Donovan groaned softly and the bed creaked as he climbed out. "I'm just trying to figure out whether *you're* drunk or *I'm* dreaming."

"Neither."

A door shut in the background and Donovan's voice came louder. "Are you crazy, then?"

"Probably." Max kicked the luggage rack, but it didn't relieve his frustration. It only made his foot throb.

"How in the hell did this happen?"

"I didn't know who she was when I met her. I didn't find out until Travis showed up, and by then I was already three-quarters gone."

Donovan chuckled. "In less than a week?" That's even faster than I was. Are you sure? I mean, you can't possibly *know* her, much less *love* her."

"I don't need you to throw my own words back in my face," Max snarled. "I need help. Nothing like this has ever happened to me before. And the worst part of it is, I can't make myself tell her who I really am.''

"She doesn't know?"

"If she did, it wouldn't be a problem." Max resisted the urge to give the luggage rack another boot. "This is crazy, Donovan. I don't know what to do."

Donovan lit a cigarette and exhaled noisily. "There's nothing like falling in love to make a man do strange things."

"I'm not sure I like this feeling. I like having control over the way I feel and the things I do."

"Love ain't about control, Max. The minute you start caring more about another person than yourself, control flies right out the window."

"You're not helping. I've been here six days and Travis is walking about as free as he's ever been. The more I get to know him, the more I doubt whether I *can* bring him in. And the thought of disappointing Reagan makes me feel about an inch high. I can't bear to think about how much she'll hate me when this is all over." Max peeled open a package of crackers and munched one. "That's where you come in."

"Where I...?"

"I've changed my mind. I need you to fly out here and take him into custody."

"You're a day late, buddy. Slate already has me working another case. I'm heading up to Palo Alto in the morning, and to Denver after that."

"Perfect. This is just a short hop on a commuter flight from Denver."

"No can do, Max. Slate's lost two men already because of the changes he's making. He's got half a dozen jobs lined up and he's counting on you being back tomorrow or Tuesday to take a few of 'em. You either need to get Carmichael into custody and bring him back here, or let Slate send someone else after him.''

''I can't do that. You know what loose cannons some of those guys are.''

''Then bring him in yourself. You want the bottom line? I'll give it to you. You can squirm around all you want to, but if you want to keep seeing her when this is all over, she's *going* to find out what you do for a living. It's inevitable.''

''I know you're right,'' Max said quietly. ''And I also know that it would be better to tell her myself than to have her find out some other way. I just keep hoping I can avoid her finding out at all—even though I know that's not possible.''

''Sure it is. Just make an anonymous phone call to the police department there, let one of them pick him up, chalk this up to experience and hightail it out of there. Even if she does find out who you are, you'll never see her again.''

''That's the trouble,'' Max finally admitted. ''I don't want to leave. I don't want this to be over.'' He laughed shortly. ''And I *don't* believe I'm saying that.''

''That makes two of us. So, then, I guess you have a problem, don't you?''

''I thought that's what I said when I called you.''

''You'll have to forgive me. My brain's a little slow tonight. You're going to have to tell her, buddy. There's no way around it.''

''She'll never forgive me.''

''If that's true, maybe she's not the right woman

for you. You, my friend, need someone *very* understanding.''

Max let out a weak laugh. ''I know. Thanks for reminding me.'' He rubbed the back of his neck. ''Tell me something. How does Holly deal with the risks of your job?''

''One day at a time. Is that an issue for you?''

''It will be if I can get past the rest of this mess. Her husband was a cop who was killed in the line of duty. She's not real big on taking risks, and she's got her kids wrapped up in a protective net to keep them safe. I'm not sure she'll be able to get around what I do.''

''I don't know what to tell you on that one. Either she'll be able to, or she won't. If she can't, you'll have to decide which you want more—the woman you love or your career.''

''That's not a choice I want to make.''

''I'm sure it's not. But if I were you, I'd quit worrying about what might happen and take care of your most pressing problem first. Now, hang up and let me get back to my wife, would ya? I'm freezing.''

Max disconnected a minute later and paced once more to the window of his room. Donovan was right, of course. There was no honorable way out that didn't include Reagan finding out the truth. But telling her would probably be the hardest thing he'd ever done.

REAGAN WAS BATTLING exhaustion as Travis switched channels on the TV. The girls had gone to bed, Max had gone back to the Wagon Wheel, and she could almost hear her bed calling to her from the other room. But Travis had headed into the living room and she so desperately wanted to reach him during his visit, she forced herself to stay awake.

She sat in one corner of the couch and leaned back against the arm. Travis sat on the other end, one leg cocked over the other, the television remote dangling from his hand. He kept one eye on the television as she made herself more comfortable.

"I had a good time today," she said, battling a yawn. "I hope you did, too."

"Yeah. It was great."

"The girls are excited to have you here, you know. And I'm glad they're getting a chance to know you. I'd love to see more of you in the future than we have in the past few years."

Travis flicked a glance in her direction. "Yeah? Well, maybe. It's hard to make promises. I never know what's going to happen."

Reagan tried not to let his answer disappoint her. "Maybe some day," she said, then changed the subject. "What did you think of Max?"

"He seems okay." Travis took his eyes away from the TV long enough to really look at her. "*You* like him, don't you?"

"Very much."

"Well, then, it doesn't really matter what I think, does it?"

"It matters."

"You mean, if I don't like him, you'll dump him?"

Reagan smiled and shook her head. "Not necessarily. But it's not that serious, anyway. He's leaving town in a couple of days." She ignored the twist in her heart and tried to keep her smile in place. "But your opinion has always been important to me."

Travis laughed and turned back to the television. "No, it hasn't. I didn't like Paul, and you *married* him."

"Only because the reasons you gave me for not liking him didn't make sense to me at the time." She'd never understood Travis's dislike of the police, but she'd chalked it up to a general disapproval of authority figures. He hadn't liked his teachers or the school principal, either.

"Do they make sense now?"

"A little. You were right about one thing. I wasn't happy being a cop's wife. But not for the reasons you thought. He wasn't egotistical or pushy. He didn't throw his weight around and act like a jerk. He was never mean to me or the girls, and he didn't try to dictate what I did or how I did it." All dire predictions Travis had made before her wedding. "The thing I hated was the risk he took every time he went to work."

"Dad liked him, didn't he?"

"Dad and Paul got along okay." She deliberately downplayed the closeness they'd shared, sensing that it would only reinforce some of Travis's feelings about their father.

"They were exactly alike." Travis paused to listen to the beginning of a news story about a robbery in Cheyenne, then pulled himself back to their conversation. "Paul didn't like me, either."

Reagan started to deny it, then stopped herself. She'd never get through to Travis if she wasn't honest with him. "It wasn't that Paul didn't like *you*," she said carefully. "He just didn't like some of the things you did. He thought you should settle down, find a job and stay with it. He believed you'd be happier if you did.''

''That's the kind of life he wanted, not me. I doubt I'll ever settle down.''

Paul hadn't wanted that kind of life, either, Reagan thought before she could stop herself. He'd married her and then spent the rest of his life avoiding the commitment that came with having a family. He'd chosen a job that hadn't allowed him to be there for his daughters...or his wife. Reagan thought of Max making excuses for his single lifestyle, of Travis, of Paul, and wondered if any man really wanted to marry and make a life with a family, or if she'd just managed to surround herself with the ones who didn't.

Some of the glow from the day faded. She steered the conversation onto something more comfortable. ''You and the girls seemed to be getting along great while we were at the park.''

Travis grinned. ''They're pretty cool for teenage girls. Especially Jamie. Don't get me wrong, I like Danielle, too. But Jamie's more like me, if you know what I mean.''

Reagan wasn't sure she *wanted* to know. ''She's a lot like her dad, too.''

''Yeah.'' Travis nodded, broke off to listen to another news story accompanied by video of police cars and flashing lights, and finally went on. The fact that he had matured enough to pay attention to world events gave Reagan hope. ''So, why won't you let her take the climbing lessons she wants?''

The question surprised her, though she didn't know why it should. Reagan wouldn't worry—as long as Jamie was looking for sympathy and not an ally.

"There are several reasons," she said when she realized Travis was waiting for an answer. "Was she complaining?"

"A little. She thinks you're trying to smother her or turn her into another Danielle."

Had every word she'd said to Jamie flown in one ear and out the other? "I'm not trying to do either," she snapped, then softened it with a weak smile. "I'm sorry. It's not your fault. I shouldn't take out my frustrations on you."

"It's okay. I'm used to it." Travis turned the TV off and shifted to face her. "But really, sis. Why won't you let her take the lessons? What's it going to hurt?"

"I've explained that to Jamie a dozen times. She knows my reasons."

"Why don't you lighten up on her a little?"

"You really don't understand," Reagan began.

"Really?" His mouth twisted. "*I* don't understand what it feels like to have a parent who doesn't approve of you?"

Reagan jerked back as if he'd slapped her. How could he equate trying to keep Jamie safe with what had happened between him and their father? "It's not the same thing at all."

"It's exactly the same thing, sis. Jamie is what she is—and she's great. But she doesn't think you like her much."

"That's not true at all. I love her. She knows that."

"Oh. Okay. Right." The twist of his mouth tightened with bitterness and his voice took on a sharp edge. "Just like I know how much Dad loves me?"

"Dad *does* love you, Travis."

"Uh-huh." He stood abruptly and tossed the remote onto the couch. "Well, you know what's best, I'm sure. I sure as hell don't."

Stunned speechless, Reagan watched him leave the room and fell back against the couch. She'd been in such a good mood only a few minutes ago.

Now she felt as if she'd been run over and left in the middle of the road. She didn't even want to think about what could be next.

"YOU LOOK TIRED this morning," Andie said as Reagan hung her coat on the hook near the door. "Big weekend?"

"Too big." Reagan shoved a lock of hair over her shoulder, wishing she'd had time to do something with it instead of leaving it loose. "My brother is staying with us for a while, and we spent yesterday on the go every minute."

"With or without Max?"

"With, at least most of the time." Reagan fought a yawn and headed for the coffeepot. "Getting ready this morning was a disaster. Travis is staying in Jamie's room, but she didn't take out everything she needed for school. He was dead to the world and didn't even hear her knock on the door, so she kept running in and out of my bedroom while I was getting ready." She sighed, poured a hefty dose of caffeine into her mug and filled another for Andie. "I didn't even have time to make coffee."

Andie tucked a pencil behind her ear and dragged a stack of paper closer. "Nothing like having a man around to upset the routine."

Reagan took a welcome sip and sighed with contentment. "It's not *a* man, it's two of them. And I'm not complaining—not really. I love having Travis around."

"And Max?"

"And Max." Reagan lifted her cup to hide her sudden grin.

"How are things with him?"

"Fine."

"Fine?" Andie scowled playfully. "I don't want to hear *fine*. I want details."

"I'm not sharing details," Reagan said, crossing to her desk.

"I don't mean *that* kind of detail," Andie teased. "I just wonder if things are getting serious."

"I've only known him a week. That's hardly long enough to think serious."

Andie waved aside Reagan's argument and handed her a raspberry Danish. "If it's right, it doesn't have to take forever. I'd just love to see you happy and settled with someone who loves you."

Reagan laughed softly and took another sip before picking up the stack of mail waiting for her in a basket beside her desk. "Well, don't get your hopes up too high. Max isn't here to stay, so nothing permanent is going to come of it."

"You never know. He might decide he loves it here too much to leave."

"I doubt that. He told me he'd be in town for a week, and that was a week ago. Besides, he's a certified, die-hard city boy. He'd never be happy here."

"So, what's to say you can't follow him?"

Reagan plied her letter opener on a thick manila envelope. "For one thing, he hasn't asked." She felt a nervous twinge as she slit open another envelope. "Do you mind if we don't talk about this right now? I'm trying to keep myself in a state of denial, and admitting aloud that it's going to be over soon is making my stomach hurt."

"Okay by me. Besides taking over Danielle's room, how's the visit with your brother going?"

Reagan's stomach knotted again, but she convinced herself it was from hunger this time. "It's going great. I've always wished the family could be closer. Paul was an only child, so Travis is the only uncle the girls have. He seems much more mature than he did last time I saw him, and he seems to like it here. And the best thing is, he's getting along really well with his nieces. Jamie was really upset with me for forgetting about out trip to Jackson until Travis talked to her last night. She actually seemed better this morning."

"What did he tell her?"

"I don't know. Neither of them talked about it and I didn't want to pry." Reagan lowered the mail to her desk and sighed. "I know this is premature, but I'd love it if he decided to find a job and stay around."

"Do you think he will?"

"I don't know. I don't even know what he wants to do with his life. I'm not sure *he* knows. But for the first time in his life, I think he's ready to find out."

Andie dabbed at the corners of her mouth, then dusted her fingers. "If he wants to stay, I could talk to Bart. He'll be looking for help when the weather gets warmer. He might be willing to take Travis on a little early."

Reagan couldn't think of anything more perfect. "What a great idea. Would you talk to him?"

"Sure. No problem. In fact, I'll ask when I call during lunch. Maybe it'll help Travis make up his mind."

Feeling better by the minute, Reagan took another bite of her Danish and picked up another envelope. "I hope it works out. I'm sure that if Travis could find a job he liked, it would be a huge boost to his self-esteem."

"You're such a mother hen," Andie said with a grin. "Don't you ever get tired of making sure everyone around you is tucked safely under your wings?"

Reagan nearly cut her finger with the letter opener. She sat it aside and frowned at her friend. "What do you mean by that?"

"I didn't mean anything bad. It's just that you're always so concerned about everyone else, so determined to make sure everything's all right for everyone around you."

"Is that such a bad thing?"

"No. I just don't want you to be disappointed if Travis doesn't want to work with Bart, or if it doesn't work out for some other reason. I don't want you to feel like it's your fault."

"Well, of course I won't. Really, Andie, you're making it sound as if I smother the people around me."

"I'm not saying that at all. You just try to insulate them—and maybe that's not always such a good thing." Andie linked her hands together on her desk. "When I look back at my life, I realize that the only times I've really grown as a person are the times when I've faced some sort of challenge. You can't expect

Travis to learn anything or get stronger if you protect him all the time.''

"I'm *not* trying to protect him from challenges." Reagan took a deep breath and tried to steady herself. "I just don't want him to make mistakes that he'll have to suffer for."

"But it's the suffering that brings on the growth," Andie insisted.

"That's ridiculous. You're saying I should sit back and do nothing while Travis make mistakes that could ruin his life?"

"I'm saying that maybe it's not your job to decide for him what's a mistake and what isn't. I'm saying that maybe if he makes a few errors in judgment and has to dig himself out, it would be good for him."

Reagan tossed the rest of her Danish into the garbage and picked up the stack of unopened mail. "Would *you* sit back and do nothing while Tommy or Justin did something foolish?"

Andie's cheeks flushed. "Of course not. But I'm their mother, not their sister. And even then, I'd offer my best advice, but I wouldn't throw myself in their path and try to force them to do what *I* think is right for them."

The accusation stung. Reagan shoved her chair under her desk with a bang. "I'm not throwing myself in Travis's path. And I'm tired of arguing with you about it. If you need me, I'll be in the copy room."

"Don't run off mad," Andie called after her.

Reagan stopped at the door and turned back to face her friend. "I'm angry," she said. "And I'm hurt. And if I don't leave, I'm going to say something I'll regret."

Andie looked miserable. "I didn't mean to upset you. You're my best friend. I wouldn't hurt you for the world. But I know that you've been having trouble with Jamie, and now Travis. I just thought—" She broke off at the look on Reagan's face. "Maybe I *didn't* think."

Reagan took a couple of steps back into the office. "I know you didn't hurt me intentionally. In fact, you're not saying anything Travis hasn't already said. But how can I let go? How can I just look the other way? Maybe I am just his sister, but Mom's not around to help him and he won't even speak to Dad. If I could just bring the two of them together again—"

Andie got up and closed the distance between them. "You can't fix the world, Reagan. You'll make yourself sick trying. It's just possible that Travis will have to hit rock bottom before he starts climbing back up again, and if you're always there smoothing the way for him, you're making it possible for him to keep skirting the experiences that might actually make him want to change his life."

"I refuse to believe that," Reagan said stiffly. "I *can't* believe it. Travis just needs some direction, and I'm the only person in the world who believes in him enough to give it to him."

Andie's eyes roamed across her face for a long moment before she sighed in resignation. "You're right. We shouldn't be talking about this. I'm only upsetting you, and that's not what I want to do." She shook herself as if she could get rid of the tension between them that way. "Just forget I said anything, okay?"

"Sure." Reagan shifted the stack of mail in her arms and forced a smile. "It's forgotten."

"I'll call Bart at lunch and ask him about that job."

"Great. Thanks." Reagan turned back toward the copy room, wishing it were as easy as that to put something unpleasant out of her mind. And she wondered—for just a split second—whether there might be some truth in the accusations everyone seemed determined to throw at her.

CHAPTER TEN

BY THE TIME REAGAN got home that evening, she felt only marginally better. The atmosphere between her and Andie had remained strained for most of the day, in spite of their best efforts to smooth things over. She turned her key in the lock, tossed her mail and purse onto the table inside the front door, and stared in disbelief as they hit the floor where the table used to be. Confused, she moved into the living room and ground to a halt just before she ran into the back of the couch.

"Jamie?" she called. "Danielle?" Everything in the living room had been moved as well. The room looked cramped and crowded, and about half its normal size. The girls would never do anything like this without at least calling her. So Travis must be responsible.

Telling herself her irritation was out of place, she took a steadying breath, kicked off her shoes and carried them down the hall toward her bedroom. "Jamie? Danielle? Where is everybody?"

Laughter from outside in the backyard drifted in through one of the partially open windows. She pulled aside the blind and peered outside. The girls lay on the grass looking up at the sky. Travis lounged in a lawn chair she'd put into the garage before winter.

She felt another flash of irritation. Jamie was due

at basketball practice in ten minutes and she obviously hadn't even thought about getting ready. Danielle's jazz dance class started in half an hour, and she was lying on the grass as if she had nothing to do but watch clouds.

Reagan changed quickly into jeans and her favorite light sweater and headed through the kitchen toward the back door. Backpacks lay abandoned on the floor beside the table. The girls hadn't even unzipped them yet.

This wasn't like her daughters. She knew exactly whose influence this was. No matter how much homework he'd been assigned as a kid, Travis had never done it without prompting—*lots* of prompting. And now Jamie and Danielle were following suit.

She stepped out into the backyard and three sets of eyes shot toward her. "It looks like you've all been busy," she said, making an effort to keep her voice light. "What made you decide to rearrange the furniture?"

Travis kicked one foot gently. "I was bored, and it was something to do."

Reagan looked from Jamie to Danielle slowly. "Did you help?"

"A little," Danielle admitted. "Just since we've been home from school."

"What happened to homework?"

"We're going to do it later." Jamie actually sounded proud of their decision.

"When? You know Max is coming to dinner for Travis's chili. And what about practice?"

"I don't want to go to practice." Jamie's expression grew tight and almost haughty. "I don't want to play basketball anymore."

Reagan's temper flashed to the surface. "You *are* going to play. You've made a commitment to the coach and the team, and you're going to keep it."

Jamie's eyes blazed, but she stood, clamped her mouth shut and shuffled toward the house just slow enough to make sure her mother knew how she felt.

Reagan turned to Danielle. "What about dance class? When were you planning to change?"

Danielle's face turned a deep shade of red. "I forgot, too. I'm sorry." She sprinted off toward the house, leaving Reagan alone with Travis.

When Travis stood as if he intended to follow, she motioned him back toward the lawn chair. "Wait a second, okay? I want to talk to you."

He sank back into his chair and eyed her warily. "What now? How did I screw up this time?"

The question diffused Reagan's anger and reminded her of how much Travis needed direction and approval. She perched against the picnic table and crossed one foot over the other. "You didn't screw up, Trav. But in this house, homework always comes first. Next time, I'd appreciate it if you'd remind the girls of that. They can help you when they're through with homework and their other activities."

"Are they *ever* done?"

"Of course they are. They have plenty of spare time." Reagan gripped the edge of the table and gave herself a moment to deal with the flare of irritation left over from her conversation with Andie. "That's not what I wanted to talk to you about."

Travis had leaned forward, arms resting on his

knees, hands linked together. He slanted a glance at her, and he looked so young and vulnerable, her heart softened again. "I've done something else wrong?"

"No. Not at all. I was talking to a friend at work today and she mentioned that her husband is looking for someone to help on their ranch. He's willing to give you the job if you're interested."

Travis shot out of the lawn chair so fast it toppled over. "You told her I was here? I thought I told you not to tell anybody."

"Well, I—" She broke off uncertainly. "I'm sorry, Travis. I know you said you didn't want to meet a lot of people, but—"

"Who else have you told?"

"Nobody. Look, I'm sorry I forgot, but she's a very close friend. She won't say anything if I ask her not to."

"*You* weren't supposed to tell anyone." He took a few jerky steps away and raked his fingers through his hair again. "I trusted you."

His reaction shocked her into silence, but only for a moment. Suspicion began to dawn as she watched him. "Why are you so upset, Travis?"

"Because I *told* you not to say anything about me being here to anybody."

"I know. But why? What are you hiding from? Or should I ask *who?*"

Travis stopped pacing and took a long look at her. A dozen different emotions flickered through his eyes and she could see him trying to decide what to say. "What makes you think I'm hiding?"

"Because of the way you're reacting. Just look at

you. Who cares if you're here? Who's looking for you?''

"Nobody.'' The word snapped out of his mouth. He made a visible effort to pull himself together. "Nobody. I just thought I could trust you, that's all.''

"I wish I could believe you,'' Reagan said. "But you're acting as if it's a matter of life and death.''

"Yeah?'' Travis's eyes narrowed and he gestured angrily. "Well, excuse me. I hate to think how *you'd* act if the shoe was on the other foot. If I made you a promise and then broke it, you'd never let me forget it.'' His voice rose with every word until his voice had become harsh, loud and angry.

"That's ridiculous,'' she shouted back. "If I brought up all the promises you've broken over the years, we'd *never* talk about anything else.''

"Do we ever?'' Travis shoved the lawn chair out of his way. "Thanks a lot, sis. Thanks for the reminder of how things really are. I'd almost forgotten that no matter what I do, I'm always going to be wrong.'' He stormed past her toward the house.

"Dammit, Travis—'' Reagan turned to follow him, but when she saw the girls standing just outside the back door, she broke off guiltily.

She didn't want them to get caught in the middle of an argument, especially since she had no idea what was really bothering Travis. She bit back what she'd been about to say and took a calming breath. "Are you girls ready?''

Danielle nodded without speaking. She could obviously tell this wasn't the time to push.

Jamie watched Travis shove his way into the house before answering. "I guess so,'' she said as the door banged shut behind him. "If you're going to make me go."

"Don't start, Jamie."

"Why don't you believe him?"

"I don't want to talk about it." Reagan straightened the chair Travis had shoved onto its side. "Make sure you have all your things and meet me in the car." She needed a few minutes alone to calm down before she drove anywhere.

MAX GATHERED HIS determination as he followed the front walk toward Reagan's house. Last night Reagan had told him dinner would be a bit late—she had to pick up the girls from practice and dance class—but he'd purposely arrived early so he could have a few minutes alone with Travis. Without Reagan and the girls there, he could take Travis into custody. He didn't even need to step inside. Five minutes, and it could all be over. It was what he should do....

So, what was stopping him?

Every second he postponed the inevitable only ensured that the eventual outcome would be more painful. Every lie he told Reagan only made it more certain that she'd detest him when she learned the truth.

And yet here he was, approaching a possibly armed fugitive without a sidearm of his own. Had he lost his mind? He had half a mind to go back to the car and arm himself, but before he could make that decision, Travis threw open the front door and ran out onto the porch followed by a cloud of smoke.

Gasping, coughing, Travis bent over and grasped his knees while smoke billowed out into the gathering twilight and the scent of burned food filled the air.

Max jumped onto the porch, made sure Travis was breathing, and demanded. "Is anyone else inside?"

Travis shook his head, but when he tried to speak another fit of coughing cut him off.

"Where's the fire?"

Travis gestured with both hands toward the chef's apron he wore and managed to choke out a few words. "Kitchen. Oven."

Max plunged into the house, relieved to find the smoke far less dense than it had first seemed. He found the fire extinguisher he'd noticed hanging inside Reagan's laundry room, pulled the pin and inched toward the kitchen.

Smoke poured from the open door, but Max couldn't see flames. He switched off the oven and opened the patio door and watched the smoke change direction, then made his way to the kitchen window. When he had several windows open, the smoke began to dissipate and he looked up to find Travis watching him.

"Thanks, man." Travis dabbed at his eyes with the corner of his apron. "I was pretty out of it for a minute there."

Max took in the disaster area that had once been Reagan's kitchen, now lost beneath a jumble of empty packages, boxes, bowls and utensils on the counter, food spilled on the floor and something that looked like tomato paste dotting the ceiling.

He suppressed a shudder. "What happened?"

"I forgot to thaw out the hamburger, so I thought I'd do it in the oven."

Max wrinkled his nose against the biting smell of

burned paper and charred meat. "Did you take it out of the wrapper?"

"I couldn't. It was stuck on."

"So you put it into the oven, paper and all?"

"Well, yeah. But only for a few minutes while I had a beer." Travis waved his apron to guide smoke toward the window. "I didn't think this would happen."

Max peered at the oven setting and groaned aloud when he saw that Travis had set it to broil. "Do you know anything about cooking?"

"Apparently not enough."

"How soon will Reagan be back?"

Travis's brows knit as he squinted through the smoke to look at the clock. "Half an hour. Maybe less."

"Then I suggest we get busy. I don't want her coming home to this disaster." He started opening drawers, looking for something he could use to clean the counters. "Why don't you find a garbage bag and start gathering trash?"

Travis nodded weakly. "Sure. Okay."

"Do you know where she keeps her broom and mop?"

"Mop?"

"You know...the thing she uses to clean the floor?"

"I don't know where she keeps it." Travis looked around, his eyes blank.

"We'll find it later. First, let's get rid of some of this mess."

"What about dinner?"

"I think dinner's going to be at the Chicken Inn

tonight.'' Max found a dishcloth and started toward the sink. The guy definitely needed someone to take him in hand and teach him a thing or two.

Now, where had that thought come from? Max shut off the water quickly and gave himself a mental shake. Travis wasn't a kid. He was a grown man, a fugitive from justice, not someone deserving of Max's sympathy.

He stole another glance at the young man who scowled in concentration while he gathered discarded packages and threw them away. He did look young, Max realized. And almost eager to follow Max's directions. Maybe Reagan had a point. Maybe Travis had ended up in this fix because he'd been without proper guidance when he was younger.

Maybe if their father hadn't been so wrapped up in the grief of losing his wife, if he'd been available to instill some values in his son the way Max's father had, Travis wouldn't have drifted into trouble.

Max followed behind Travis, scrubbing the counter as the younger man cleared it, and he tested his reaction over and over again. He'd never been one of those people who believed in blaming a bad childhood for stupid adult choices. Hell, *everyone* could find something in their life to blame for what they didn't like. Max had heard every excuse under the sun, and he'd rolled his eyes in disgust at most of them.

So why was he falling for this one? Was he getting soft? That thought sent a wave of fear through him. He couldn't afford to lose his edge. Not if he wanted to stay successful at his job.

He scrubbed harder, trying to work away the apprehension. He couldn't let this happen to him, not over some two-time punk like Travis Carmichael.

But it wasn't about Travis. It had never been. Max *was* getting soft. He'd turned into a powder puff, and all because of a woman.

TWO HOURS LATER, Max sat at one end of a long table and waited for the waitress to bring their check. Irritation ate at him like a rash, prickling every nerve, making it almost impossible to sit still. Of course, this wasn't *all* Travis's fault. If Max had arrested Travis earlier, he wouldn't have been thawing paper under the broiler.

Reagan was more agitated than Max had ever seen her, but she hadn't reacted to the fire the way Max had expected her to. Any other woman who'd come home to find her kitchen filled with smoke and her house reeking would have come unglued. Reagan had sighed softly and listened to Travis's rambling explanation. He was obviously a master at avoiding responsibility, and Reagan was far too used to letting him get away with it.

Her quiet sadness whenever she looked at Travis only added to Max's frustration. He wanted to shake some sense into her, to make her understand that Travis wasn't likely to start accepting responsibility until she stopped taking it all on herself, but it wasn't his place to say anything.

Now, as the waitress approached the table, Max watched Travis carefully. He wasn't a bit surprised when Travis stood quickly. "Hey," he said to the girls, "come with me. I want to show you something."

Both girls looked to their mother for her okay. They'd been horrified by the sight that greeted them when they got home and had been more subdued all evening than Max had ever seen them. Smart girls. They knew when to push and when to become part of the woodwork.

Though her cheeks flushed slightly, Reagan nodded her permission for them to leave. And Travis made another getaway. He expected someone else to pay for dinner, and someone else would. But, dammit, it wouldn't be Reagan.

Max held up a hand to signal the waitress before Reagan could take the small brown plastic tray. "Dinner's on me tonight."

Reagan smiled but made no move to draw her hand back. "That's sweet of you, but it's not necessary."

"It's not sweet," Max said softly. *Sweet* was about the last thing he felt at the moment. "I just don't see any reason for you to pay for dinner twice."

Her gaze flew to his. "It was Travis's dinner. What makes you think I bought the groceries?"

"Didn't you?"

Her gaze faltered almost imperceptibly.

"I've seen too many guys like Travis in my life, Reagan. I know the score. It's not your fault we had to eat out tonight." Max moved from his seat to the one Jamie had vacated. "Travis should pay the bill, and you know it. But he doesn't seem interested, and I'm sure as hell not going to let *you* pay for it."

"He *can't* pay for it," Reagan murmured. "He doesn't have any money."

"He must have some or he wouldn't have been able to get to Serenity in the first place."

Reagan's eyes flashed. "Are you saying he lied to me?"

"I'm saying it's possible that he hasn't told you the whole truth."

She shook her head emphatically. "Travis might have his problems, but he wouldn't do that."

Her naïveté frustrated and saddened him. Sooner or later, she'd have to face the truth about her brother. And not just the truth Max had to tell her. The whole truth. Every disheartening piece of it.

"He's human," Max said evenly. "Everyone leaves out pieces of the truth from time to time."

She lifted her chin and looked him straight in the eye. "*I* don't."

"Never?" Max laughed in disbelief. "You've *never* left out a little bit of the truth, embellished a little or told an outright lie?"

"Never. At least not since I was little."

"Well, then, I admire you. Most people don't have your control."

"It doesn't take control to be honest," she said, reaching for the dinner check. "Telling the truth is the easiest thing in the world. You don't have to worry about keeping your story straight or remembering to whom you've told what. Lying is always harder...and wrong."

Max pulled the plastic tray away from her. "You've never told a lie to protect someone you cared about?"

"From what?"

"From the truth."

"I've never been in a situation where someone needed to be protected from the truth, and I can't imagine one, either." She stood quickly and held out her hand as if she expected him to hand the bill over to her. "Travis knows how I feel about the truth."

"I'm sure he does. But does he share your opinion?"

Her eyes darkened to a deep emerald green as they darted around the room to see who was listening. Her cheeks flushed and her lips parted slightly. Her breasts rose and fell as she struggled to compose herself. "What's wrong with you tonight? You're acting as if Travis's accident in the kitchen was not only deliberate, but the end of the world."

"It's not that." Max pulled a few rumpled bills from his pocket and tossed them onto the table for the tip. "I know what happened in the kitchen was an accident, but I do think you should be more upset with him for being careless. He was negligent, Reagan. The oven didn't spontaneously combust. And I think he should at least have *offered* to pay for dinner."

Reagan stared at him without speaking, but the frustrations of the past week got the best of him.

"You think I'm making too much out of what happened," he said. "But I think you're making too little. He did something stupid and careless. You're damned lucky you had a house to come home to."

Reagan's eyes narrowed, but not enough to hide the sparks of anger. "It was a *mistake,*" she said through clenched teeth. "Haven't you ever made one?"

Max wished he'd waited until they were outside to start this conversation. "Yes, of course I have. But—"

"Then cut him some slack." She pivoted away and started toward the cashier's station near the front door.

Swearing under his breath, Max followed. Before

he could catch her, she pushed through the heavy glass doors into the night, leaving him to pay the bill. By the time he got away from the chatty hostess and pocketed his change, Reagan, Travis and the girls had disappeared.

Hoping against hope that they were waiting by the cars, Max hurried to the corner and looked at the spot where she'd parked. But the spot next to his car was empty.

He'd blown it.

THE NEXT MORNING, Max sat wearily on the foot of his motel bed and dragged the phone onto his lap. He dialed Reagan's number twice, but hung up both times before the connection went through. He had no idea what he'd say to her.

She'd expect an apology, and maybe he owed her one—if not for what he'd said, then for the way he'd said it. But he'd already let the situation get too far out of hand, and he couldn't keep compounding the problem.

Mopping his face with his hand, he let out a heavy sigh and tapped the receiver gently against his forehead while he thought. Finally, when the dull ache of hard plastic against his skin began to sink through his misery, he punched in the numbers for his phone card and followed it with his parents' number.

Not surprisingly, his mother answered almost immediately. She always kept the phone beside her TV chair in case one of the grandkids called. He could hear the television playing softly in the background and imagined his mother with her glasses perched on the end of her nose, working on one of her counted cross-stitch patterns while she watched.

"Hi, Mom. Am I interrupting your favorite show?"

She laughed delightedly and the background noise disappeared, courtesy the mute button. "You must be a mind reader. I just tried to call you. Did you see our number on your caller ID?"

"I'm not home, Mom." Max closed his eyes and let his mother's voice work away some of his tension. Over the years, her Southern drawl had been blurred by the number of places she'd lived, but the soft natural cadence of the low country remained the same. "I'm still out on a case."

"The same one?"

"The same one. It's taking a little longer than usual."

"I'd say so. Is everything all right?"

The sound of the extension being lifted made Max hold off on his reply. "You there, Dad?"

"I'm here. Sounds like you're in some sort of trouble."

"Not really. I was just telling Mom this case is taking longer than I expected."

"What's the holdup?"

Max smiled and leaned against the headboard. Tom Gardner had never learned to beat around the bush. "It's complicated."

"So...? Spell it out."

"Maybe he doesn't want to talk about it," his mother suggested.

His father snorted a laugh. "Nonsense, Alice. Of course he wants to talk about it. He wouldn't have called otherwise."

Max laughed aloud this time. "You know me too well, Dad. Sometimes even better than I know myself."

"Well?"

"I've gotten myself into a bit of a mess," Max admitted. "I'm not sure how to get myself out of it. No... That's not entirely true. I *know* how to get out of it, I'm just not sure I want to...."

"Maybe you'd better explain that," his mother prodded gently.

"This'll probably make you happy," he said, rubbing his eyes with his fingertips. "It's about a woman."

"You've met someone?" His mother's tone changed abruptly. She sounded elated.

"I have. But—"

"Is it serious?"

"What I want to know," his father interrupted, his voice heavy with disapproval, "is what this woman has to do with the case you're on."

"That's the hard part," Max admitted. "Her brother's the guy I'm after."

"You've gotten involved with a suspect's sister?" his father demanded. "What were you thinking?"

"It wasn't intentional. I didn't know who she was at first."

"You haven't been there that long, Max. How could you possibly be serious about this woman?"

"Don't be so hard on him, Tom," Max's mother scolded. And to Max she added, "*She's* not a criminal, is she?"

"No, Mom. She's a widow with two teenage daughters, and honest as the day is long."

"Well, then?" He could picture his mother leaning up in her chair so she could see his father through the door to his study. "What's wrong with that?"

"What's wrong is that he's compromising his case," his father said. "What's wrong is that he knows better. What's *wrong*—"

His mother interceded again. "Maybe so, but falling in love isn't always logical, is it? Max wouldn't let anything compromise his integrity, and I'd say his happiness is more important than some case."

"You don't understand, Alice—"

"I understand perfectly. I know my son. I know how his mind works and what kind of heart he has."

"The problem," Max put in carefully, "is that she still doesn't know who I am."

"Ooh, Max." Now his mother sounded disappointed. "You haven't told her?"

He felt like dirt. "I can't. I keep telling myself I need to, but then I look into her eyes and I can see how much she'll hate me when I do. I just keep hoping I'll find another way out." He wiped his eyes again. "The thing is, it's not just her. It's her kids, too. They're great. And her brother, too, I guess. I mean, he's done some stupid stuff and I don't question for a minute that he needs to take responsibility for his actions, but—"

"But you're learning that sometimes the world's not black and white?"

"Right is right," Max reminded her. "Isn't that what you always told us kids when we were growing up?"

"I think that's probably more likely what you *heard*," his mother said gently. "If we felt that way, we wouldn't have listened to both sides of every argument between you and your brothers, would we? Sometimes the hardest decisions are between two rights.''

Max sat back against the headboard. ''Okay... But how does that reconcile with what Dad's always preaching about duty?''

''What do I preach?'' his father demanded.

''That duty's almost sacred. *Nothing* should come before a man's duty.''

His father chuckled. ''I'd like to know when you heard me say *that*. If I recall, the only times I said things like that were to your mother. Alone. Usually late at night when you were supposed to be in bed, and always when I was grappling with a problem I couldn't see my way out of. Tell me, son. While you were eavesdropping, did you bother listening to what *she* said?''

''Your voice is louder than hers,'' Max said sheepishly. ''Are you saying you don't feel that way?''

''Duty's important, son. I'm not saying that it isn't. But your mother taught me that other things are important, too.'' His father shifted and the familiar sound of his leather chair creaking transported Max across the miles. ''It's easy to shove other things out the window and let duty be your only concern. Putting them all together is the tough part.''

''Tell me about it.'' Max felt better than he had in days. ''So how did you finally do it?''

''Hard work and a whole lot of soul-searching.''

Max waited for his father to expound, but silence filled the airwaves. ''That's it?'' he demanded after a lengthy pause. "That's the secret to your success? That's all you're going to tell me?"

"That's it, son. You're going to have to figure out just how you want to deal with it for yourself. If either of us told you what to do, your heart and soul wouldn't necessarily be behind the decision. And *you* have to be fully committed, especially on the tough ones."

Max dropped his head to his bent knees and groaned softly. In the background, he could hear his mother talking to his father. The sound of their voices blended into a childhood memory, and the intimacy they shared stirred the longing that had been growing steadily since he first set eyes on Reagan.

When he replaced the receiver a few minutes later, he sat with his head down for a long time while he tried to reconcile the different emotions pulling at him. In the end, his decision was no different from what it had always been.

He had to tell Reagan the truth and take his chances on the outcome.

CHAPTER ELEVEN

REAGAN CAME HOME from work at lunchtime with a splitting headache. Her argument with Max had left her short-tempered and low on patience. Every phone call she'd taken had grated on her nerves. Every new demand placed on her by her supervisor had left her feeling more and more overwhelmed.

Why was she letting Max's opinion bother her so much? He didn't know Travis. He didn't know the first thing about their lives or what had brought them to this point. He'd had a perfect childhood with two parents who were always there and two fine, upstanding brothers who'd probably never spent a minute in detention during school.

He had a hell of a nerve offering an opinion about Travis.

Although...

To be honest, Travis's refusal to discuss his plans was beginning to wear on her. His stubborn silence about what had brought him here was making her edgy. And he *did* seem to have a supply of money from somewhere. Beer and cigarettes were turning up around the house regularly—and *she* certainly wasn't buying them.

Deep inside, she knew she owed Max an apology. She just didn't know how to approach him or what to say. She didn't know how to explain why she got so defensive about Travis, why she excused his behavior time and again and put up with things she wouldn't have tolerated from anyone else.

She let herself inside the house and curled her nose at the lingering smell from last night's disaster. Travis's dishes from breakfast and lunch littered the counter and table and filled the sink. She started toward her bedroom, pausing at the door to Danielle's room. She knocked softly and opened the door—and gasped in shock at the sight that greeted her.

Piles of shoes and clothes covered most of the floor. CD cases, magazines and old school papers filled the blank spots. The bedclothes draped onto the floor and little round nubs of dirty socks dotted its surface.

Gritting her teeth, Reagan picked her way across the floor toward the open drawers of the dresser. A sharp crack underfoot told her she'd stepped on something plastic buried beneath the clothes—clothes she could have sworn neither of the girls had worn this week.

When she stubbed her toe against something solid, hard and painful, she decided enough was enough. She was quickly losing control of her home and her family. She couldn't let things go on the way they had been.

She found Travis lying on the couch, feet up, one arm extended as he lazily flipped through the channels. His hair looked as if he hadn't brushed it all day.

"Turn that off," she said as she entered the room. "We need to talk."

His gaze flicked across her face and returned to the screen. "What about?"

"About you. About your plans."

"I don't have any." He fished a potato chip from a bag on the floor and popped it into his mouth. "I've told you that already."

"Yes, you have. But you need to make some." Reagan grabbed the remote out of his hand and turned off the set, then shoved his feet from the arm of her couch. "Sit up, Travis. The kids see you lying around all day, dropping clothes on the floor, leaving the bed unmade, and they're beginning to follow your example."

"So? Chill out, sis. A little clutter here and there isn't the end of the world."

"This isn't just about clutter," Reagan snapped. "It's about everything."

"It's about you and Max, isn't it?" Travis sat up slowly. "You're upset with him, and you're taking it out on me. That's not fair, you know."

"What's not *fair*," Reagan said, struggling to control her rising temper, "is that you've come here to stay, you claim to have no money to help out with expenses, yet somehow you're managing to bring beer and cigarettes into the house."

"I have a little spending money."

"You're an adult, Travis. Living expenses come first. Or are you expecting me to support you while you spend *your* money on junk?"

He mumbled something she couldn't quite make out.

"You can't sleep half the day and trash my house if you're going to stay here. From now on, I expect you to get up at a reasonable hour and help out around the house."

"I'll help." Travis smiled his little-boy smile. "Just tell me what to do. I'm not a mind reader, you know."

His boyish grin didn't affect her the way it usually did. "Fine. Get rid of all this garbage you've brought into the living room. And then go into the kitchen and clean up what you left in there."

"Fine."

Reagan waited for him to start working, but he only rolled onto his side. "*Now,* Travis. Not after you've finished watching a rerun of some twenty-year-old show."

"Fine." He sat up again, muttering under his breath.

His reaction grated across her raw nerves. "Why can't you make plans? I know you said you were between jobs, but don't you think it's about time you found one?"

"I don't need to find a job, I'm self-employed. I'm just waiting for the right opportunity to come along."

"And it's going to find you on my couch?" Reagan narrowed her eyes and regarded him carefully. "What is it you do, Travis?"

He shrugged lazily. "Whatever suits me at the moment."

"Give me an example."

Travis widened his eyes and tried to look young and injured. "What's with the third degree? If you're upset with Max, why don't you take it out on him?"

"This is the second time you've tried to distract me by bringing Max up," Reagan said. "That kind of thing used to work on me, but it doesn't anymore. Why are you here, Travis? And how will you decide when it's time to leave?"

"I'll just know." He picked up the potato chip sack and nudged an empty soda can with his toe. "If you don't want me here, just say so. I'll find somewhere else to hang. No problem."

Reagan took a deep breath and let it out slowly. "So that's what you're doing here? *Hanging?*"

"Yeah. Sure. I needed a place to...chill."

"To chill? From what? A hard day watching television?"

Travis's expression shuttered. She knew that look. She'd seen it too many times when he was young and hiding something he'd done wrong. She perched on the arm of the couch and stared at him. "From *what,* Travis? If you don't answer my question honestly, I'll not only let you leave, I'll help you pack."

Tension stiffened his shoulders. "There are some people looking for me, that's all. I figured this would be a good place to stay until things cool off again."

"What people, and why are they looking for you?"

"It's nothing," Travis said, but his gaze darted from his feet to the window to her face and she could see the nervousness in his eyes. "It's just some stupid trouble I got into in California, that's all."

"What trouble?"

"The cops say I stole something, and now they're after me."

"The *police?*" Everything inside Reagan went suddenly, bitterly cold. Her fingers grew numb, and she could almost feel the blood drain from her face. No wonder he'd been so adamant about not telling anyone he was here. "What did you steal?"

"Nothing." Travis shot to his feet. "Don't make a federal case out of it."

"*Is* it a federal case?"

"*No.* Hell, Reagan. Chill out, wouldja?" He picked up the empty soda can and started out of the room.

She jumped to her feet and blocked his path. "Don't you dare blame me for being upset, Travis. Don't you *dare* try to make this *my* fault. *What did you steal?*"

"What makes you so sure I stole anything? What if I'm innocent? Have you even considered that? Or are you going to be like everyone else and find me guilty without even listening to me?"

Their voices had risen steadily, and his last words bounced back at her from the walls. She took a steadying breath and lowered her voice. "If you're innocent, why are you hiding?"

Travis's lip curled and his eyes flashed with so much anger, it left her cold. "You're just like Dad, you know that?" He shoved past her into the hallway, throwing the empty can at the wall as he stormed out the door.

STILL TOO AGITATED to think straight, Reagan walked quickly through the center of town. She'd spent the past two hours scrubbing everything in sight and putting her house back in order. She'd hoped hard work would do the same with her thoughts, but the debate over what to do about Travis still tore her apart. The only thought that came to her with any clarity was that she owed Max an apology. He was right about Travis and about her role in his life. And she'd been too blind to see it. Or too stubborn.

A few sprinkles of rain hit the sidewalk in front of her. Another landed on her cheek. The sun disappeared beneath a bank of gray clouds that shrouded the tops of the mountains, and a light wind stirred the trees.

Tugging her sweater closer, she waited for a break in the light traffic, then hurried across the street toward the Wagon Wheel. When she saw Max's car in the parking lot, she closed her eyes for a moment and tried to find the strength she'd need to face him again.

She hurried through the few cars in the lot and knocked on his door just as the rain began in earnest. He seemed surprised to see her, but she couldn't tell whether he was pleased or not. He checked behind her as if he expected to see someone else, and his eyes darkened with curiosity as he turned back to her.

She spoke before he could say anything, hunching her shoulders against a gust of wind. "Can I come in?"

"Of course." He stepped aside and she slipped past him, trying not to appear overly curious as her eyes roamed the room and took in this rare glimpse into his personality. Just like his car, everything was clean and tidy—clothes folded, bed made, a stack of papers on the small, round table near the window. His brush, comb and a bottle of Cool Water aftershave were lined up neatly in front of the bathroom mirror.

The frantic beating of her heart left her almost numb. "I came to apologize for our argument last night."

He leaned one broad shoulder against the wall and smiled ruefully. "I'm not sure you're the one who needs to apologize."

"Well, I am." A gust of wind rattled the window behind her, and she was grateful to be safely inside.

"I shouldn't have left the way I did, but I was angry and I don't think you can accomplish a lot by talking when you're that upset. The temptation to say things you shouldn't is too great."

"Maybe," Max said slowly. "But sometimes waiting until the emotion has passed is equally counterproductive. It takes the passion out of the relationship."

The look in his eyes threatened to weaken her resolve. She couldn't read his expression and it disconcerted her. "I guess there are positives and negatives about both. But that doesn't change the fact that I need to apologize."

He pushed away from the wall and closed the distance between them. Taking her shoulders gently, he turned her back to face him. "And so do I. I shouldn't have said anything about Travis. It really wasn't my place."

"But you were right. That's why I had to come. I just found out why Travis is here."

Something flickered across Max's face. "Do you mind if I ask why?"

"He's in trouble with the law and he's using my house as a hideout."

Did she only imagine the sudden tensing of his shoulders, the tightening of his jaw? "He told you that?"

She nodded without looking at him.

"Did he tell you what kind of trouble he's in?"

"Only that the police think he stole something." She forced herself to meet his gaze, needing to see something in his eyes, dreading censure, praying for understanding. "You were right, Max. I've coddled him too much and now he thinks he can do whatever he wants and I'll always be there to fix it for him.''

Max's eyes darkened and the corners of his mouth pulled into a frown. "Travis made his decisions. He chose to commit that robbery. He chose to run. You aren't to blame for any of it.''

"But I am.'' To her dismay, her lip quivered. "If I'd taught him to accept responsibility a long time ago, maybe he wouldn't have gone this far.''

Max watched her for a moment, then pulled her close and cradled her against his chest. "You aren't responsible for the entire world, Reagan—no matter what you thought when you were a kid. It isn't your job to carry everyone you love on your shoulders.''

The deep rumble of his voice against her ear and cheek moved her to tears. Across the room, the heater kicked on and warm air radiated around them.

It had been so long since anyone held her when things went wrong, so long since anyone allowed her to be weak—even for a moment. She swallowed thickly against the lump that suddenly filled her throat and tried to take a deep breath.

Max pulled back to look at her, then cupped her head with his huge, warm hand and pulled her against him once more. "Reagan. You've had to be tough for a long time, haven't you? It's okay, sweetheart. You can let go now. There's nobody to see but me.'' He brushed a kiss to the top of her head and whispered, "I promise I won't tell anyone.''

She tried to laugh, but it came out sounding like a sob instead. His hands moved across her back, kneading, smoothing, relaxing her. "I'm not tough,'' she said when she could talk again. "I'm frightened to death half the time."

"I have news for you, sweetheart. There's nothing tough about not being afraid. Strength is when you do what has to be done even when you're afraid. And you—" he broke off to kiss her lips lightly "—are the best kind of tough. You're still plenty soft where it counts."

She stood on tiptoe to kiss him back and tried not to think about how much she'd miss him when he was gone. She had enough on her mind without that. "I was feeling so horrible when I came in. How is it that you've already made me feel better?"

"Because you know I'm telling you the truth."

She rested her cheek against his shoulder and breathed in his scent. She wanted to stay like this forever. "Thank you."

His hands slowed, and the circles grew slightly larger. He took a deep breath, and she thought he might say something else. Instead, his lips brushed her hair again and the feeling of comfort gave way to slow-burning desire.

Reagan slowly unclenched her hands. She inched closer, needing to feel him, touch him, to imprint this moment on her memory. The lonely future stretched in front of her, but she wanted desperately to keep it away. She lifted her head to say something—anything—and found his mouth hovering just above hers.

He lowered his lips to hers hesitantly, as if unsure whether to take advantage of this moment or not, but Reagan rose to meet him and trailed her fingers across his chest, circling the hard nubs of his nipples through the thin fabric of his shirt.

He groaned and tightened his arms around her, intensifying his kiss and tracing the outline of her mouth with his tongue. Reagan parted her lips and took him inside, the taste and scent of him mingling, overwhelming her senses. Her breath came in shallow gasps as his embrace loosened and his fingers slowly, slowly inched toward her breasts. And when his fingertips teased her, flicking across the bottom of her breasts, skimming the swell above her bra, and then finally settling in place and oh-so-softly caressing her through the fabric, she knew she needed more.

His tongue continued to explore her mouth. His fingers started a wildfire in her abdomen and sent it swirling outward. Her body seemed to take on a life of its own, pressing up against him as it sought relief from the craving.

Max's lips left hers and traced a path to her neck. She arched against him, moaning aloud when his thigh slid between her legs and he nipped at the soft skin of her neck. She slipped her hands beneath his T-shirt and ran them along his stomach and around to his back.

She felt as if she was floating, completely free of life and its problems. She was ready to offer herself to him, to give and take, to love completely. She needed this. Tomorrow could take care of itself.

His hands shifted again, moving slowly down her sides until he cupped her bottom and pulled her against him. He pressed against her, hot, demanding, and finding an answer in every feminine part of her.

"Yes," she whispered. "Yes, please. Make love to me, Max."

His hands stilled without warning. She opened her

eyes slowly, and his horrified expression brought her back to earth with a resounding crash. He pulled away sharply, looking at his hands as if they'd betrayed him. Shaking his head, he put some distance between them. "We can't do this, Reagan. It's not right."

She felt cold and empty without his arms around her. Needing to touch him again, she took a step toward him. "I don't care what people say anymore," she whispered. "I've moved way beyond that."

"It's not that." He lifted his eyes to look at her and the agony she saw there stunned her. "I can't make love to you. God knows I want to, but I can't. And when you hear why, you'll be glad I didn't." He ran a hand across the back of his neck and turned away as if he couldn't bear to face her.

After Travis's announcement, she didn't need any more surprises, but she forced herself to ask. "Why?"

"I'm not who you think I am." Max darted a glance at her. "I'm not who I told you I was." When she didn't speak, he added, "I've lied to you, Reagan. From the first time we met."

MAX WATCHED HER, waiting for her reaction. A dozen emotions flitted across her face—horror, disbelief, denial, to name a few. She backed a step away and narrowed her eyes. "Who are you, then?"

His stomach churned, but he forced himself to answer. "I told you the truth about my name," he said. "But not about what I do or why I came to Serenity." She looked wounded, and he had to clench his hands to keep from reaching for her. "I'm here because of Travis."

"Because of—" She lifted one trembling hand to her forehead. "What do you have to do with Travis?"

"I came here looking for him," he said gently. "He skipped bail, and I was sent to return him to San Diego so he can stand trial."

"You're a bounty hunter?"

"An enforcement officer," he said, wanting to dilute the ugly sound.

"Will you get paid if you take Travis back?"

"Yes. We collect a portion of the bail."

"Then you're a bounty hunter." She backed away from him, eyes wide and filled with disgust. "Don't try to make it sound better than it is." She ran into a chair and came to a stop. "So, you were using me to find my brother?"

"No. Not that. Never that." Max leaned against the dresser, relieved that she wasn't going to bolt out the door before he had a chance to explain. "If I'd known who you were when we met, I would have told you. But I didn't know, and I make it a policy not to come blasting into town for several reasons—protecting the fugitive's family is one of them. I wouldn't have wanted to start gossip about you and your children by announcing to the world that I was after your brother. We had those two chance meetings the first day, and then I ran into you the next morning. When you asked me what I did, I gave you my standard answer because I had no idea who you were."

"You could have told me after you found out."

"I could have." He dropped his gaze to his fingers. "But by that time, I was already half in love with you. I didn't want you to hate me."

Her eyes turned a clear, cold green. "So you accepted my hospitality, met my children and pretended to care about me because you thought that would somehow keep me from hating you?''

"I didn't pretend to care about you, Reagan. The only thing I've lied about is what brought me here in the first place.''

"You knew about Travis. You knew what he'd done. You knew he was wanted by the police, but you didn't tell me. And you expect me to believe that you *care* about me?''

"I *do* care. And more. I've fallen in love with you. I didn't plan to. I didn't even know what was happening at first. I've never felt like this before—''

"But you didn't tell me.''

"I couldn't.'' He caught himself and mopped his face with his hand. "No, that's not true. I could have told you. I *should* have told you. I thought I could keep an eye on all of you and make sure Travis didn't put you in danger. I started hoping that I could convince him to turn himself in. For a while, I even thought I could arrest him and disappear without ever telling you. But I don't want to disappear. I don't want to lose you.'' He shook his head harshly. "All of this sounded good while I was pacing around here on my own. Now it sounds stupid as hell.''

"Yes,'' she said harshly. "It does.'' There was no softness in her face, no welcome, only anger and distrust.

"After our argument the other night, I decided that I had to tell you the truth. I was just trying to figure out how to do it.''

"You expect me to believe that?''

He rubbed his forehead with his fingers and fought

down a wave of panic. He was losing her, just as he'd known he would. "It's true. But why *should* you believe me? I've proven myself to be anything but trustworthy."

Her eyes flew to his face, wide, round, wondering. For a moment, he thought she might actually believe and forgive. "You still haven't explained why you didn't tell me when I first came here today. Why did you almost make love to me?"

"Almost, Reagan. I didn't make love to you. I'm the one who pulled back, remember? I'm the one who stopped. At least give me credit for that. I *did* tell you, just not soon enough."

She swept her hair over her shoulder and lifted her chin. "So now what?"

"I'm going to have to take Travis into custody. If I don't, someone else will, and considering the charges against him—"

She cut him off. "What are the charges?"

This just kept getting worse and worse. "He didn't tell you?"

"He told me that he's been accused of stealing something."

"He was arrested for armed robbery."

The fire in her eyes died and a deep sadness replaced it. "He used a gun?"

"Yes."

"Are you sure it was him? Maybe the police made a mistake."

"They didn't. He was caught on video by the surveillance cameras. I haven't seen the tape, but according to the information I have, there's no doubt it was him. And it isn't his first offense, either. He's been in and out of jail half a dozen times in the past few years.'' Max chanced a step closer. ''I have to take him back so he can face trial.''

Tears shimmered in her eyes, and Max would have given anything for the right to hold her, to be the one giving comfort, not the one inflicting pain. ''I wish I didn't have to tell you this,'' he said. ''Knowing that I'm hurting you is killing me.''

She didn't move for a long time. Her eyes roamed across his face and he didn't know which of them was hurting more. After what felt like eternity, she turned away and let herself out the door, and Max was left listening to the sound of her receding footsteps.

He argued with himself about going after her. But what good would that do? Anything he could say would just sound lame. He wished she'd yelled at him. That stony silence had nearly ripped his heart in two.

The sooner he arrested Travis, the quicker he could put the whole ugly episode behind him and get on with his life. Maybe he'd even forget about her in time. She'd probably waste no time putting him out of her mind.

He should get it over with right now, but he knew Reagan had a lot of information to process, too many emotions to work through. He couldn't add Travis's arrest to the mix right now. And he couldn't make himself arrest Travis while she and the girls looked on.

He'd pick Travis up tomorrow, he promised himself, when Reagan was at work and the girls were at school. When he wouldn't have to look into their eyes and see the hurt and anger there.

Tonight, he'd work on getting over her.

CHAPTER TWELVE

An hour later Reagan was still shaking with cold and anger. She toweled her hair dry and stepped into her slippers. Her wet shirt and pants lay on the bathroom floor and a pool of water slowly formed beside them. How could she have been so blind? How could she *not* have recognized the coincidence in timing that brought Max to town at the same time Travis warned her people might come looking for him?

It was simple, she realized. She hadn't wanted to see. She'd wanted to believe that Max found her attractive, that she was still woman enough to appeal to a young, handsome, virile man. She'd wanted that so desperately, she'd closed her eyes to everything else.

She pulled the towel away from her hair and studied her reflection in the mirror, not sure whether she was more angry with Max or herself. She should be furious with Max. She should hate him. He'd lied to her, used her and treated her like a fool…hadn't he?

Memories of moments they'd spent together drifted through her mind—the interest when they first met, the sparkle in his eyes when he laughed, the desire that darkened them just before they kissed. The agony she'd seen on his face that afternoon haunted her. Could she really believe that she meant nothing to him?

He'd said he loved her. Even overwhelmed by anger, Reagan knew he wasn't the type to say that if he didn't mean it. And she couldn't lie to herself. She loved him more than she'd ever known it was possible to love.

Gathering her wet clothes, she carried them to the laundry room, then hurried back to her bedroom to change. She couldn't let herself think about Max right now. She had to decide what to do about Travis. No matter how she felt about Max, the fact remained that Travis was in serious trouble. Trouble he'd brought upon himself.

That, at least, was not Max's fault.

What if Travis came back here before Max picked him up? What would she say to him? Did he still have the gun he'd used in the robbery? Had he brought it into her house?

She dressed quickly, tugging on a pair of thick, warm socks with her jeans and snuggling into her favorite sweater. She moved quickly down the hall toward Travis's room, knocked to make sure he hadn't come back, then let herself inside.

Half an hour later, she sat back on her heels and lowered the bedclothes back to the floor. If Travis did have a gun, it wasn't in this room. She sat on the foot of the bed and looked at the pile of clothes he'd left on the floor. The thought of him going to jail made her ache all over, but according to Max it wouldn't be anything new for Travis.

For the first time in her life, she realized Travis had problems she might not be able to solve. Problems that were too big, too serious to be cured by an extra dose of love and a listening ear. Travis needed more help than she could give him, and maybe she'd been doing him another disservice by agreeing not to tell their father about what he was doing. She'd certainly done Charlie Carmichael a disservice. She knew how much he wanted to repair his relationship with Travis, but she was making it almost impossible for him to do it.

She let herself out of Travis's room and closed the door behind her. Travis had gotten enough mileage out of their father's pain, and Reagan was suddenly tired of being in the middle.

In the kitchen, she fixed herself a cup of tea, carried the phone to the table and dialed her father's number. Travis would be furious with her, but this wasn't a game anymore, and he really had no right to be angry after the things he'd done.

"Hi, Dad," she said when he answered. "Are you busy?"

"Never too busy to talk to you. How are you, honey?"

His warm, deep voice filled her with comfort and convinced her she'd made the right decision. "Not so good," she admitted. "We have a problem."

"What's wrong? Is it one of the girls?"

She could almost see her father's thin face, the wrinkles around his eyes, the short-cropped white hair, and she wished he could be here with her instead of so far away. Once-a-week phone calls just weren't enough. "We're all fine. It's about Travis."

"You've heard from him?" There was no denying the concern in her father's voice. "Where is he?"

Reagan wished Travis could recognize how much their father cared. "He's here, with me. At least, he was until this morning."

"How is he, Reagan? Is he doing all right?"

"He's in trouble, Dad. Apparently, he committed an armed robbery in California and then skipped bail. There's a bounty hunter here who's going to take him back."

Her father let out a heavy sigh filled with frustration and sadness. "Did Travis tell you that?"

"Not all of it. He finally told me that the police were accusing him of stealing something. The bounty hunter filled me in on the rest."

"Is he under arrest now?"

"I don't know. He stormed out of here earlier, and he hasn't come back. He doesn't want you to know anything about this. I promised I wouldn't even tell you he was here, but that was before I knew the whole story. Now I think you should know."

"I'm glad you told me." Her father's voice sounded weary.

"You should also know this isn't the first time he's been in trouble with the law. According to Max, he's been in jail several times."

"Max? Is he the bounty hunter?"

"Yes." She couldn't make herself tell him any more.

"I see. Guess I'll have to tell Estelle I'll be gone for a little while."

Reagan smiled at the mention of her stepmother. Marrying Estelle ten years ago was the smartest thing her dad could have done. "Are you coming here?"

"Either there or California, wherever Travis is going to be in the next few days. I'll have to get someone to watch things at the shop before I can leave."

Reagan traced the pattern on her teacup with a fingertip. "What if he doesn't want to see you?"

"Then I guess he'll tell me so. It won't be the first time."

"I know, but— Travis has said some horrible things to you in the past and I hate the thought of you stepping into the line of fire again."

Her father laughed softly. There was silence for a moment. Then she heard, "He's delivered a few zingers, that's for sure, but he's my son. You'd do the same thing if it were Jamie or Danielle. I can't make Travis behave the way I want him to. He's his own person. All I can do is my best. What Travis does after that is up to him."

"You make it sound so easy."

Her father laughed. "I wouldn't say that. But when it gets hard, I just remember your mother. She understood about people better than anyone I've ever known. When Travis was just a baby and throwing a fit at being put on his swing, she told me he'd probably be bucking against the reins his whole life."

Reagan could almost hear Max telling her the same thing. "Even so, I keep thinking that if I'd…"

"You're not still blaming yourself for the way Travis turned out, are you?"

"Not entirely." Reagan looked through the rivulets of rain on the window at the daffodils nodding as the drops hit them. "But you have to admit that Travis changed after Mom died."

"Travis changed, but so did you. So did I. Have you forgotten that?"

"But Travis hasn't changed *back*. He's still so angry it hurts just to be around him."

"And you're still feeling guilty. I think you're half convinced you could have prevented your mother's death if you'd done something different. And I'm pretty sure you've been carrying Paul's death on your shoulders, as well. But if anyone should be shouldering the blame for Travis, it's me. I pulled away from you kids when you needed me most. If I had to do it over again, I'd do everything differently. But that's not possible, so now we have to move on from where we are, regrets or no. You can't hold your breath for the rest of your life to prevent bad things from happening, honey."

"I know that, Dad."

"Do you really? One of the hardest things to learn is that there are some things you can't control."

"I know I can't control everything," she said weakly.

"Ah, but you wish you could, don't you? You've always been just the opposite of Travis. He's irresponsible, but you take too much responsibility. You think you *should* be able to prevent bad things from happening to the people you love, and when you can't, you feel that you've failed."

Her father's voice was so gentle and understanding, tears blurred Reagan's eyes. "Maybe."

"Quit being so hard on yourself, honey. You're a good woman, a wonderful mother, a dynamite daughter, and the best sister Travis could have. We're all lucky to have you. Now, fix yourself a cup of tea—if you haven't already—and relax. And give yourself a break. The ball's in my court now…okay?"

Reagan gulped back a sob and managed a weak "Okay."

"I'll make a few calls and figure out where I can do the most good for your brother. You don't have to worry about it now. I'll call you when I've decided exactly what I'm going to do."

"I can't help but worry," she protested. "But I'll work on trying not to take the blame."

"I can't ask for more than that."

When they disconnected a few minutes later, Reagan actually felt a little better. She puttered around the house and started a batch of laundry, trying not to worry. She was folding towels in the kitchen when the door banged and Danielle tossed her backpack onto the table.

The girl tossed her wet hair and her gaze swept across Reagan's face. "What's wrong, Mom? Are you sick?"

"No. Why?"

"You look terrible."

Reagan added another towel to the stack in front of her. "I got caught in the rain earlier, but I'm fine otherwise. You didn't walk home from school, did you?"

"No. Stefani's mom gave me a ride." Danielle crossed to the refrigerator and pulled out a soda. "Is Jamie still at practice?"

"Yes." Reagan pulled another towel from the laundry basket. "I hope Mrs. Jordan remembers it's her turn to drive. It's awfully wet out there."

Danielle dropped into a chair and took a long drink. "Where's Travis?"

"I'm not sure. Why?"

"Just wondering." She slanted a glance at Reagan

and lowered her can to the table. "I'm kind of glad he's not here. Is that an awful thing to say?"

Reagan's hands stilled on the towel. "No, of course not. Is there any special reason why?"

Danielle tucked a lock of hair behind her ear. "I don't know, Mom. Sometimes he kind of scares me." She pulled her gaze back to Reagan's. "I heard him talking to somebody on the phone the other day when you were at work, and he didn't sound like himself at all."

The knot of apprehension in Reagan's stomach came back—this time fear for her children brought it on. "What did he say?"

"Nothing really, except that he swore a lot. Like, every other word." Danielle rolled her eyes in disgust. "It was more how he sounded than what he said. He sounded...mean."

Reagan sat beside Danielle and ignored the laundry. "What else?"

Danielle's dark eyes roamed her face, checking to make sure she wasn't in trouble. "Well, when I walked in on him, he yelled at me to get out. I know he's your brother, and I know you love him and everything, but I hope he doesn't stay very long."

Reagan slipped an arm around her daughter's shoulders. "I don't think he will, sweetheart." She didn't know how much she should tell the girls. "I have the feeling he'll be leaving very soon."

Danielle's eyes widened. "Really? Why? The way he's been acting, I thought maybe he was going to move in forever."

"I won't let that happen," Reagan assured her. "It wouldn't be good for any of us." Hoping to wipe the worry from Danielle's face, she stood and started toward the kitchen. "What do you say we put a mix into the bread maker? Banana nut sounds good to me."

"Okay." Danielle followed and leaned against the counter to watch while she found the mix and plugged in the machine. "Mom?"

"What, sweetheart?"

"Has Jamie told you what she and Travis talk about all the time?"

Reagan turned slowly and caught Danielle winding a lock of hair around one finger—a sure sign that she was troubled. "I didn't realize they talked so much. Is there a problem?"

"I'm not sure. But they spend a lot of time together when you're at work."

"Do *you* know what they talk about?"

Danielle's gaze faltered. "I'm not sure."

"But you have a guess?"

"I'm not sure," Danielle said again. "I wouldn't want to guess wrong."

Reagan pulled eggs from the refrigerator and cracked one into the bread maker. "I understand why you're reluctant. You don't want to say anything that will get Jamie into trouble, right?"

Danielle nodded. "I don't really *know* what they're talking about, but I'm not sure Travis is giving Jamie the best advice, you know?"

Reagan measured oil and handed Danielle the bottle to put away. "Maybe I can tell you something that will help you decide what to tell me." She waited until Danielle was looking at her again. "I found out this morning that he's in trouble with the law and he's hiding from the police here.''

Danielle's step faltered as she walked back to the counter. ''What kind of trouble?''

''He committed an armed robbery.'' Reagan rested one hip against the counter and kept an eye on her daughter. She didn't want to frighten her. ''But don't worry. I couldn't find a gun in his things, and he'll probably be in jail before the night's over—if he's not already.''

''So, the police know?''

''Max knows.'' Reagan forced a thin smile. ''And that's another thing. I found out today that Max is a bounty hunter. He came here to find Travis and take him back.''

''Back?''

''To California so he can stand trial.''

Danielle's eyes widened and a smile tweaked the corners of her mouth. ''Max is a bounty hunter? Is that cool, or what?''

''I'm not sure what it is,'' Reagan said with a weak smile.

''Well, I think it's cool.'' Danielle flicked absently at one of her fingernails. When Reagan didn't respond right away, she looked up at her with narrowed eyes. ''Are you mad at him?''

''For coming after Travis?'' Reagan had to be honest—both with herself and with Danielle. ''No, not for that. I'm angry that he didn't tell me who he was, and I'm hurt.''

Danielle's eyes clouded. ''Why?''

''Because.'' Reagan pushed away from the counter, disconcerted by the look in her daughter's eyes. Danielle suddenly looked old and wise instead of young and frightened. "I don't really want to talk about it."

"You think he was using you?"

"Maybe." Another wave of memories forced her to be honest. "No, I don't think so."

Danielle let out a relieved laugh. "Well, that's good. I was worried for a minute that there was something wrong with you. I mean, *anybody* can see how much he likes you. It's only obvious."

The sudden rush of relief she felt embarrassed her. "That may be, but I still think it was wrong of him to lie to us."

"He was just doing his job, wasn't he? I mean, if he was after Uncle Travis, how could he tell *you* who he was?" Danielle tore open the bread mix and added it to the rest of the ingredients. "Maybe he wasn't supposed to tell. There were lots of times when Daddy couldn't tell us about stuff because of his job, and that was okay, wasn't it?"

Reagan opened her mouth to explain the differences, but she couldn't think of any that sounded reasonable. "Yes," she said. "That was okay."

"So you're not mad at him?"

"No. I'm not mad at him." But even if she could forgive Max for keeping silent, the sudden awareness of the similarities between his job and Paul's left her cold. She might be able to put the rest behind her, but she knew she could never live with that kind of uncertainty again.

THAT NIGHT, MAX WALKED aimlessly along Front Street and tried to console himself. He told himself over and over again that everything had happened for the best. Things always did. But he was fighting a losing battle.

He'd tried distracting himself with people since Reagan left his room. Dinner at the Chicken Inn had been tasteless and he hadn't let himself get interested in the discussion about whether or not the town needed a traffic light near the post office. It wouldn't matter to him in a day or two, anyway.

He'd stopped by the diner and managed to follow the conversation there for about five minutes before his mind began to wander through town to the little white house with green shutters. Losing himself in a crowd had always worked to keep his mind off things before. Tonight, every face reminded him of what he'd be leaving behind. No matter where he went, he came away feeling worse. But sitting in his lonely motel room wouldn't make things better, either.

Shivering slightly, he came to a stop on a street corner and watched a blanket of light gray clouds drift across the sky to shroud the mountains. He checked his watch in the glow of a streetlight and sighed heavily when he realized how slowly time was passing. He was vaguely aware of a pickup coming to a stop at his side, but he didn't bother to look. He wasn't in the mood for any more pointless conversation.

"You lost?"

He looked toward the truck and found Bart grinning at him from the window. "Not lost," Max said, trying not to look miserable. "Just at loose ends."

"I'm on my way to pick up some fencing from Udy Simmons. If you're not doing anything, I could use a hand. I told him I'd be there before seven, and I'm running late."

"I'd be glad to help," Max said without hesitation. Some good hard work might clear his mind. He climbed into the cab and held his chilled hands over the defrost vents as Bart started driving again.

Bart fished a pack of gum from his pocket and offered it to Max. "How's the search coming?"

Max waved away the offer. "I'm just about through here. In fact, it looks like I'll be leaving town tomorrow."

Bart shot a glance at him. "That soon?"

"I'm afraid so."

"Did you find what you wanted?"

Max nodded slowly. His conversations with Donovan and his father had helped, however the sudden urge to talk to someone who actually knew Reagan was damn strong. But he didn't want to make her hate him more than she already did by talking behind her back.

"Too bad you're leaving." Bart put a piece of gum into his mouth and accelerated at the edge of town. "Andie and I were thinkin' about inviting the two of you to have dinner with us next week."

Max wasn't surprised by the pang of disappointment he felt. He'd learned more about himself in the past eight days than he had in the previous thirty-five years. "I wish I could ask for a rain check," he told Bart, "but I don't think I'll be coming back."

"Oh?" Bart flicked a glance at him from across the truck's cab. "Oh."

"I'm not running out on Reagan, if that's what you think."

"I don't think anything."

If Bart had pushed for an explanation, Max would

have resisted giving him one. His seeming lack of interest made Max *want* to defend himself. How perverse was that? He clamped his mouth shut and turned his gaze out the window.

They rode for several miles before Bart finally broke the silence. ''I like Reagan,'' he said with a sharp glance at Max. ''She's been a great friend to Andie. But I also know that she has her own set of problems to work through. We all do,'' he added with a quick smile.

''Reagan hasn't done anything wrong,'' Max said quietly.

Bart rested his elbow on the window and steered with one hand. ''Look, man, have some heart. If you're leaving and this thing between you and Reagan is over, Andie's going to be dying of curiosity. And when she finds out *I* talked to you, she'll expect me to know something. You don't know Andie very well, but she's persistent. If you have a heart at all, give me *something* I can tell her.''

The look on his face tore an unwitting laugh from Max. ''How much do you need?''

''Not much. Anything that will convince her I tried to pump you for information.''

Max chuckled again and realized with a jolt of surprise that he was at ease with Bart, the same reaction he'd had to Donovan almost immediately. ''Okay. I screwed up. Do you think that's enough?''

''That's good, but it's only going to whet her appetite.''

Max tried to decide how to characterize his mistake. Was it really a lie, or merely an omission of the truth? Did it make a difference? Once again, he had the urge to confide in someone who knew Reagan. Bart knew her better than he did. He might actually be able to help. And if Max truly loved Reagan, shouldn't he do whatever he could to win her back?

"I'll make you a deal," he said, shifting toward Bart. "I'll trade you the whole story—in confidence— for a little advice. I'll let you decide whether telling Andie will help Reagan or hurt her."

Bart flicked his gaze from the road for a fraction of a second, nodded and turned back. "All right."

Max explained as quickly as he could, leaving nothing out. Once he started, the words poured from his mouth and the relief of knowing that someone could eventually help Reagan understand that he'd meant no harm made him feel better than he'd felt in days.

Bart listened without interrupting until he'd finished, then grinned broadly. "I *knew* you weren't looking for property to buy. And Andie told me I was too suspicious...." He pushed air through his teeth and changed hands on the steering wheel. "But that doesn't help you, does it?"

"Not a whole lot."

"You want advice?"

"If you have any."

Bart ran a hand along his chin and thought for a few seconds. "First of all, I'd give her a chance to calm down before you try arguing your case. *Nobody's* rational when they're angry."

"By the time she calms down, I'll be gone."

"There are telephones."

Max laughed softly at himself. "You have a point."

"Second," Bart continued, "you're in luck. Reagan's a pretty sensible woman. Once she can think clearly, she's going to realize that she wouldn't have wanted you to tell everyone in town about Travis.''

"That's good news." *Very* good news.

"I don't know what to tell you about the rest, though. It would have been better if you'd told her the truth when Travis got here.''

"I realize that," Max said miserably. "But I can't go back and undo it.''

Bart nodded as he slowed the truck and turned off the highway. "I still think time is your best bet. Don't try to resolve this before you leave town or you'll push too far, too fast, and you'll lose her for good.''

Max knew he was right, but it wasn't what he wanted to hear. "With my luck, by the time she forgets to be angry with me, she'll have forgotten all about me.''

"I doubt that," Bart said with a scowl. "I hate to break it to you, but there aren't many women—or men, either—who'd forget the guy who came to arrest their brother.''

"That's *not* what I want her to remember about me.''

"Maybe not, but she will." Bart pulled up in front of a brightly lit barn and turned off the engine. "I'm not saying she's always going to hate you for it, I'm just thinking that your best bet is to get real about what's going on here. You and Reagan are going into this thing with a lot of strikes against you. You can't pretend they don't exist. What you have to do is face them and deal with them.''

He was right, Max thought as he opened his door. There were a lot of things working against him and Reagan. The question was, were there too many to get past?

CHAPTER THIRTEEN

WHILE DANIELLE SET the table, Reagan put the finishing touches on the salad and gave Jamie last-minute instructions on serving the chicken. She tried to keep her wits about her, but her nerves were jumping. Danielle hadn't told her what she knew about Jamie's conversations with Travis, and she wouldn't now that Jamie was home. And not knowing about Travis was beginning to wear Reagan down.

Would Max let her know when he had Travis in custody? Or would he leave her in the dark because of the way she'd acted earlier? He could easily arrest Travis and disappear without a word. And she wouldn't blame him if he did.

She picked up the salad and started toward the table when the back door flew open and slammed against the wall. Reagan's heart leapt into her throat and the salad bowl slipped from her fingers. It took less than a second to realize that Travis had come through the door, far longer for her heartbeat to slow and her hands to stop shaking.

She bent to scoop up the ruined salad and caught Danielle's worried glance. Determined not to frighten the girls, she forced a smile. "You startled me," she said to her brother. "I didn't think you'd be back for supper."

He shook droplets of water from his hair and pulled off his rain-wet jacket. "Why not? I know I was angry when I left, but I've been doing a lot of thinking this afternoon and I guess you're right about a few things."

She stood unsteadily and carried the bowl to the garbage disposal. "I'm glad to hear that." She dumped the salad, then turned to the girls. "Would you two give Travis and me a few minutes alone before we eat?"

Travis looked from Reagan to the girls as they scrambled from the table and hurried toward Danielle's room. Shrugging, he crossed to the table, leaving small puddles of water in his wake. "You're still upset."

"I'm more upset than ever," she admitted. She gripped the edge of the counter and faced him squarely. "I know the whole story, Travis. I know you were arrested for armed robbery. I know you skipped bail."

He waved a hand through the air between them. "Oh, come on, sis. Don't be such a prude. It's no big deal."

"It *is* a big deal, Travis. You used a gun to commit a crime."

"I took it with me so they'd take me seriously. I wouldn't have used it."

"I'm certainly glad to hear that, but it was still a foolish and dangerous thing to do. And that doesn't tell me *why* you stole."

"The guy owed me money." Travis snatched a piece of bread from a plate on the table and took a bite. "I did some work for him, and he didn't pay me.

I tried to call him but he blew me off, so I decided to get what belonged to me.''

''I wish I could believe that,'' Reagan said, ''but I've also been told that this isn't the first time you've done something like this.''

''Not exactly like this.'' His expression grew cautious. ''I've never used a gun before.''

She could hardly bear to look at him. ''Why, Travis? *Why?* If you needed money that badly, you could have come to me or called Dad.'' The words echoed in her ears, the same words she'd always said to him, the same ''out'' she'd always given him. But her willingness to help him hadn't done a bit of good.

''You really don't get it, do you?'' Travis's voice rose slightly. ''I don't *want* my big sister taking care of me for the rest of my life, and I'm not asking Dad for anything. I did what I had to do.''

''You didn't *have* to steal,'' Reagan insisted. ''You didn't have to use a gun. You didn't have to run from your responsibility. You took the easy way out, just like you always do.''

He snorted a laugh. ''What do you know about it? Life has been tough for me. I've had one bad break after another. You don't know what it's like.''

Reagan could only stare at him for a second before she rounded the counter to stand in front of him. ''I can't believe you're saying that to me. I lost *my* mother, too. I had to raise my little brother while my dad grieved. I lost my husband, I'm raising two daughters alone, and barely making ends meet. How do you figure that I've had such an easy life compared to yours?''

''Oh, come on, Reagan. You've always been

Daddy's little princess—the one who could do no wrong.''

"And you've always been the one who could do no right?'' She leaned both hands on the table and glared at him. "Quit feeling sorry for yourself, Travis. Life is hard. That's just the way it is. Everyone has disappointments. Everyone loses people they love. Everyone faces tough times. But most people don't lie around feeling sorry for themselves, thinking the world owes them something. They do their best to go on.''

"That's so damn easy for you to say, isn't it? You always have the perfect solution to every problem. When things get rough, just ask Big Sister. She loves telling everybody what they should do.''

His sarcasm cut to the quick. "That's not fair.''

"Why not? It's true.'' Travis glared at her.

She backed a step away, stunned by the anger in his eyes. "Don't you dare blame this on me. For *once,* accept responsibility for what you've done.''

"And do what? Turn myself in?''

"*Yes!* Exactly. Turn yourself in.''

Travis pulled back sharply. "No way. I'm *not* going to jail again.''

Reagan took a steadying breath. She couldn't keep shouting at him or he'd leave—and then anything might happen. She couldn't bear the thought of him running, maybe doing something stupid to avoid being arrested again. "You committed a robbery,'' she said evenly. "It's not as if someone's trying to send you to jail for nothing. And running is only making it worse. They're not going to stop looking for you.''

"They're not going to waste a whole bunch of time and money trying to find me. I'm nobody."

The last word was filled with such agony, Reagan sank into the chair in front of her and blinked away the sudden tears that blurred her vision. "Do you really think you're a nobody?"

The question seemed to catch Travis by surprise. He studied her face for a second or two and some of his tension seemed to fade. "I've always felt that way," he said after a moment. "Always."

"It's not true."

He laughed harshly. "So *you* say."

Reagan took a chance and touched his hand, praying silently that he wouldn't pull away. "It's *not* true," she said firmly. "One of these days I hope you'll believe it. I'd do anything to help you reach that point, but I don't think I'm the right person for that. I think you need to talk to someone else—someone who isn't part of the problem."

His eyes narrowed in suspicion. "Like who?"

"I don't know. A counselor, maybe. I just know that you'll never be free of the past until you stop running from it."

A muscle in Travis's jaw jumped, but he left his hand beneath hers for a long time as he studied her face. "Is that what you really want me to do?"

"Yes." She let out a sigh of relief that he still cared enough to want to please her. "Turn yourself in. Face up to this mistake, and then start working through whatever is bothering you. Max might even know of someone back in California who can help you."

Travis's hand stiffened. "What does Max have to do with this?"

Reagan gulped back a moan at the slip, but Travis would know soon, anyway. And he'd see the lie on her face if she didn't tell him the truth. "He's here to take you back."

"Oh, that's great." Red shot into Travis's face. He jerked away from her, gesturing broadly. "That's just *great!* So you knew about the robbery the whole time? And you just let me walk into the trap?"

"No!" Reagan stood to face him. "I only found out about him this morning."

"Right."

"It's the truth, Travis. I didn't set you up. I wouldn't do that to you." She touched his arm tentatively. "But I know that if you turn yourself in to Max, you'll be safe. I'm not so sure what will happen if someone else comes after you." Travis shook her hand away, but she refused to give up. "Please stop running," she whispered. "I can't stand the thought of something happening to you."

Travis paced from one end of the room to the other. He clenched and unclenched his fists as he walked, and his expression went through a series of changes. Reagan prayed that he wouldn't try to run.

After what felt like forever, he ground to a halt and took a long look at her. "You're really worried about me?"

"You can't even imagine how much."

He nodded slowly, thoughtfully. "Okay."

"You'll do it?" Relief nearly knocked her legs out from under her.

"If it means that much to you."

Tears of relief stung her eyes. She closed the distance between them and put her arms around him. "Thank you, Trav."

He gave in to the hug, and even returned it half heartedly. "Can I do it tomorrow? It'd be great to have one more night here with you and the girls since I don't know when I'll see you again."

Reagan pushed aside the warning whisper in the back of her mind. Travis was willing to compromise, and that's what mattered.

"Max could come for you any minute," she warned. "He might even have been watching for you to come back. But I won't call him until morning, and if he does come I'll ask him to wait until morning to take you in."

Travis nodded, half grinned and started toward the living room. Halfway to the door, he stopped and turned back to her. "You going to marry this guy, or what?"

Reagan shook her head slowly. "No. He's too much like Paul, and I can't live that way again." It was the only answer she could give, and she'd *thought* it a thousand times since that morning. But saying it aloud hurt far more than she'd expected it to.

SUNLIGHT STREAMED into Reagan's bedroom through the window. Birds chirped cheerfully outside. She lay in her bed and watched the sun climb into the clear dawn, amazed at how well she'd slept. Amazed that she'd slept at all after everything that had happened the day before.

She rolled onto her side, still bone-weary. Strong emotion always left her feeling as if she'd been put through a wringer, and even a good night's sleep hadn't eased it. This morning, she had to do one of the hardest things she'd ever done. She couldn't avoid it, but the thought of actually seeing Travis in handcuffs made her slightly nauseous.

She couldn't put off the moment by staying in bed forever, but she couldn't seem to make herself take that first step to get up. Sighing softly, she watched the numbers turn on the digital clock at her bedside, then forced herself to push back the covers and put her feet on the floor.

Stepping into her slippers, she scuffed toward the bathroom. She took her time washing her face and pulling on her robe, still trying to avoid the inevitable until she heard the girls moving around in the main bathroom. Then she lifted her chin and stepped out into the hallway to face the day.

Danielle must have heard her coming because she pulled open the bathroom door and motioned her inside. She sat on the edge of the bathtub, her eyes wide. Jamie concentrated on her reflection as she brushed her hair.

"When is Max coming to take Travis to jail?" Danielle asked.

"I don't think he's coming here. I'm planning to take Travis to the motel after I drop you at school."

Jamie's eyes flashed away from the mirror. "You're not actually going to make us go to school on a day like today, are you?"

"I think it would be best. Don't you?"

"But we don't want to go," Danielle argued. "Can't we go with you?"

"I don't think that would be a very good idea. It's

not a memory I want you to have. Besides, you both need to go to school, don't you?''

"Not really." Jamie separated her hair and began to braid it. "Do you know how hard it'll be to pay attention with all this stuff going on?''

"Nothing will be going on," Reagan said firmly. "Not really. Travis will turn himself in to Max and that will be the end of it.''

"You don't know that for sure.''

"No, but I'm fairly certain.''

Danielle sighed dramatically. "Yeah, but—''

"No buts," Reagan said as she turned back toward the door. "Now, get moving or you'll be late. Danielle, will you knock on Travis's door and tell him to get up while I start breakfast?''

Danielle nodded and let herself out of the bathroom. Jamie started to follow, but Reagan stopped her.

"Are you all right, sweetheart?''

Jamie barely glanced at her. "Yeah. Sure.''

"I'm sorry you and Danielle have to be part of this.''

"Whatever." Jamie reached for the doorknob.

"I know you and Travis have been close, but you do realize that he has to face up to what he's done, don't you?''

"Yeah. Sure." Jamie still didn't look at her. "Can I go now? I'm going to be late.''

Reagan felt as if she'd been slapped, but she kept the hurt inside. Her own emotions were razor-sharp, and Jamie was probably feeling much the same way. "Of course, honey.''

After Jamie left, Reagan found an elastic and pulled

her hair up, then padded into the kitchen to start the coffee.

"Um...Mom?" Danielle's voice pulled her around from the sink. "I think we have a problem."

Now what? Reagan shut off the water. "What kind of problem?"

"Travis isn't in Jamie's room."

"Are you sure? Maybe he's just asleep."

"I opened the door and looked. He's not there."

Reagan held the carafe so tightly, her fingers began to grow numb. "Did you look in the living room? Maybe he's watching TV."

"I don't think so." Danielle took a hesitant step closer. "His stuff is gone, too."

Reagan's hand began to tremble so badly she almost dropped the carafe of water on the floor. She rested it on the counter and tried not to panic. "Are you sure?"

"His backpack's gone, and so are all of his clothes."

The numbness spread up Reagan's arms and a painful knot twisted in her stomach. "What about the van? Is it in the driveway?"

Danielle turned away without answering. Reagan waited, listening to the sound of her running feet as she went to the door. The look on Danielle's face when she came back gave her the answer even before she spoke. "The van's gone, too."

Reagan's stunned disbelief turned into anger. How dare he leave? How *dare* he look her in the eye and lie about turning himself in? She should call Max and let him know what had happened, but she couldn't move for several long seconds.

"What are you going to do?"

"Be ready to leave in ten minutes. I'll drop you at the diner so you can have breakfast while I tell Max that Travis has run away." *Again.* "You can walk to school from the diner, can't you?"

"Sure. It's only a couple of blocks. But, Mom?" Danielle followed her to the door of her bedroom. "You're going to tell on him?"

Reagan pulled her favorite pair of jeans and a comfortable sweater from her dresser. "I have to, sweetheart. What he's done is illegal." She sent her worried daughter a thin smile. "I know it seems harsh, but the things he's done are wrong. I won't be doing him any favors if I shield him from the consequences."

Danielle's brows knit and she tugged on the hem of her pajama tops. "Are you going to tell Grandpa?"

"He knows, sweetie. I thought he deserved to know."

"Travis won't think so. He thinks Grandpa hates him."

Reagan closed the drawer and leaned both arms on the dresser's top. "Grandpa doesn't hate him. The two of them had some trouble when your grandma died, but that was a long time ago and Grandpa has tried really hard to make up for it. Travis just uses it as an excuse for the mistakes he makes." She gathered her underclothes and turned back to the bed. "I guess it's easier to blame somebody else when things go wrong than to take the blame yourself."

"Do you think Travis will be mad at you?"

"Probably." Reagan sat on the foot of her bed and pulled apart her socks. "But I can't worry about that anymore." She smiled at Danielle and nodded toward her bedroom door. "Now, hurry and get ready. I want to let Max know what's happened before Travis gets too far away."

In five minutes she was dressed and ready to leave. Calling for the girls, she strode down the hall and reached for her purse on the side table where she usually left it. But as her hand touched the shoulder strap, she froze and stared at the gaping mouth of the bag. Her wallet lay half out of the purse, as if someone had carelessly tossed it there.

Oh, no, Travis. She pulled the wallet out slowly and stared at it, silently willing this to not be what it looked like. Trembling, she fumbled with the zipper of her money compartment, wrenching it open in frustration when the zipper stuck.

She'd had more than two hundred dollars in grocery money last night. Now she had nothing. Gulping back the bile that rose in her throat, she checked her credit cards. She had only two, along with a debit card that accessed both her checking and savings accounts. To her relief, the credit cards were where they belonged, but the debit card—by far the easiest for Travis to use—was missing. She'd foolishly used a set of numbers for the PIN that her brother would try. She had no illusions left on that score.

MAX CHECKED HIS WATCH for probably the hundredth time that morning, trying to calculate how long he should wait before he picked Travis up. He still didn't want Reagan and the girls to see him make the arrest, but if they *weren't* there Max might never see them again. In spite of Bart's advice, Max didn't know if he could leave without trying once more to earn Reagan's forgiveness.

Opening the curtains in his motel room, he gazed out at the parking lot. The sun was about to crest the mountains and the view made Max's breath catch. Golden sunlight, sparkling snow, deep forest-green, shade and light all came together to make an almost postcard-perfect scene.

This was spring in the Rockies. What would summer be like? How would the mountains look in autumn? And winter? Max suddenly wanted to see it all.

But that was a problem for another day. Like it or not, he couldn't put off going after Travis any longer. As he started to turn away, he caught sight of Reagan's car turning into the parking lot and his heart leapt into his throat. Before he could react, she pulled in front of his room and shot out of the car almost before it stopped moving.

Max bolted outside and caught her as she nearly flew onto the sidewalk. "What's wrong?"

"It's Travis. He's gone."

"Are you sure?"

"His clothes are gone, and so is the van." Her eyes were dark with misery. "I'm sorry, Max. He promised to turn himself in this morning, but he slipped out in the middle of the night. I don't know where he's gone."

Max didn't care. The fact that she was here at all must mean that she forgave him on some level. "Are the girls okay?"

She nodded miserably. "They're fine. But he's disappeared. With all the cash from my wallet and my bank debit card."

"Any idea how long he's been gone?"

"None." Her hands shook as she pushed a lock of hair away from her eyes. "I should have known better than to trust him, but I thought he was finally ready to face up to the things he's done."

Max touched her shoulder gently. "We all want to trust the people we love. It hurts when we find out we can't."

"I don't know whether I'm more hurt or angry. He looked me straight in the eye and lied—and then he stole from me." She blinked back tears and turned partially away.

"What would you like me to do?"

She lifted those sea-green eyes to his again. "I want you to find him."

"Are you sure?"

She nodded. "I'm positive."

Max knew how much it took for her to say that, and he admired her strength more than ever. "Then I'll find him."

"And you'll make sure he doesn't get hurt?"

"I'll do everything in my power to make sure he comes in without a scratch."

She let out a baby-soft sigh. "Thank you."

"Do you have any idea where he's gone?"

She shook her head sadly. "No, but I guess that's one good thing about a small town. There's only one road out of Serenity, only two directions he could have gone."

"Well, that'll make my job easier, then. Are you going to be okay?"

She managed a tremulous smile. "I'm fine. I'll be better when you find my brother. I shouldn't have been so angry with you, Max. It was the shock of finding out that got to me, I guess. If it had been another time or another way, maybe I'd have reacted better.''

"Yes, well. I've learned a few things this week, and one of them is that putting off a tough job only makes it harder to do." He held her gaze and forced the next question. ''Does this mean you've forgiven me?''

"Of course." She started to reach for him but pulled her hand back before she touched him. "I've fallen in love with you, you know that. The girls think the sun rises and sets on you." Her gaze faltered and her voice drifted away.

And Max's heart felt as if it had turned to stone. ''But?''

"But you're leaving Serenity after you find Travis. I'm staying."

"There are phones," he reminded her. "And airplanes, cars, trains... E-mail. We could give it a try and see what might come of it."

She still didn't look at him. "Distance isn't the only problem. I lost my husband because of the career he chose. I can't get involved with another person who takes chances with his life on a daily basis. I can't live with that kind of fear again. And it would be worse this time because now I know it can happen—and not just to someone else."

Max pulled her into his arms and brushed her forehead with a kiss. "I know how frightened you are. But I love you, Reagan. I've never felt like this before. How can you expect me to turn my back and walk away from you?"

"And I love you," she said softly. "I never imagined I could love with my whole heart again, but I do.''

He lowered his lips to hers and poured his heart and soul into the kiss, trying to convince her without words to at least give them a chance. She responded, hesitantly at first, then giving herself over to the moment and clinging to him so tightly, he knew there was at least some part of her that didn't want to let him go.

''I love you,'' he whispered when he could speak again. Needing her desperately, he cradled her against his aching heart. ''There has to be some solution, and I'm determined to find it.''

She pulled away and looked up at him. ''How? It would mean one or the other of us would have to change. Your career isn't just what you do, it's who you are.'' She touched his cheek gently and traced the scowl lines around his mouth with one finger. ''I can't ask you to give that up, but I can't live with it, either.''

''I didn't say there was an *easy* solution. Just that there has to be one.''

''I wish I could be as certain as you are.''

''Just give me a chance. I'll see if I can't convince you.'' He allowed himself one last kiss, then pressed her gently away. ''After I find Travis.''

''You'll be careful?''

''I'll be more careful than I've ever been,'' he vowed. ''I've never had such a good reason to watch my back.''

CHAPTER FOURTEEN

MAX SPENT A FEW MINUTES gathering his things and loading the car. He changed into his steel-toed military-issue boots and padded himself with his bullet-proof vest, just in case. He'd promised Reagan to bring Travis in safely, but he'd be a fool to think Travis would be equally careful with Max's health. From here on out, he had to treat this like any other job, any other search, treat Travis like any other criminal.

He checked his ammunition, slipped his 9 mm into the specially made holster under his seat and his .25 caliber—the pistol Donovan laughingly referred to as his girlie gun—into the glove box. By the time he'd finished, he realized that he wouldn't want Reagan or the girls anywhere near the car, and that realization sharpened the spines on the knot in his stomach.

This was no life for a family. He *knew* that. He'd spent hours in training to learn gun safety, and every year he had to pass the certification test again to keep his various licenses, but he wasn't a gun enthusiast. He had a healthy respect for firearms, but he wouldn't want children in the same house with them.

So how could he even consider a life with Reagan and her daughters?

With effort, he shoved the question to the back of

his mind and forced himself to concentrate. Allowing personal problems to distract him during a chase was the kind of mistake that got people killed.

After locking the car and trunk, he picked up an area map from Phyllis in the motel office and told her he'd be away for a day or two, maybe longer. In spite of his determination to treat this like any other case, he didn't check out of the room. Keeping it meant he'd be coming back, and he suspected that Reagan would need that reassurance as much as he did.

As he stepped outside again, he saw a familiar figure leaning against the trunk of his car. With his thick beard and long hair, leather vest and tattoos, Donovan looked as out of place in this town as Max had felt when he first arrived. Though he hadn't consciously expected Donovan to show up, Max wasn't surprised to see him.

Without breaking stride, he stuffed the map Phyllis had given him into his shirt pocket and crossed the parking lot. "Are you lost?"

"Might be." Donovan crossed one booted foot over the other and looked him over slowly. "Where are you headed?"

"Carmichael gave me the slip again. This time with two-hundred in cash from his sister's wallet and her debit card."

Donovan pushed away from the car and stretched. "Guess we'd better get on the road, then."

Max unlocked the car and looked at Donovan over the car's top. "So, are you going to tell me what made you change your mind about coming?"

"Nope." Donovan slid into his seat and shut the door.

Grinning, Max shook his head and joined his partner in the car. He shut the door and tugged the seat belt across his lap. "I had it covered, you know."

"I know." Donovan rolled down his window a crack and lit a cigarette. He gestured toward the office as Max pulled out of the parking lot. "Nice place."

"I've been comfortable."

"Nice town, too."

"It's not San Diego," Max said with a grin. "Not even close."

"No law that says San Diego's the only place to live, is there?"

Max shook his head and braked for a stop sign. "Nope."

Donovan blew out a cloud of smoke and regarded him thoughtfully. "I didn't think so."

IT HAD BEEN twenty-four hours since Reagan had discovered Travis missing. She was crazy with worry. The girls had gone to school again, under protest and after extracting a promise that Reagan would call them as soon as she heard anything. For the second day in a row, Reagan hadn't been able to face work. She sat at her dining table with her head buried in her hands and listened to the clock ticking and Andie puttering in the kitchen.

Thank God for Andie, who'd also taken the day off in spite of Reagan's protests. And for their supervisor who'd been understanding enough to let her. Reagan had thought she wanted to be alone until she saw her friend's face. Then she realized how much she needed someone with her.

The kettle whistled and spoons clanked against

mugs as Andie made tea. Reagan couldn't seem to make her arms and legs work. Every nerve in her body felt as if it were on fire and her mind raced this way and that, hoping for the best but imagining the worst.

"Here you go." Andie slid a cup in front of her. "This will help."

"Thanks. But unless it's going to knock me senseless, I doubt it will make me feel better. I'm so nervous, I'm not sure anything will help."

"You'll hear something soon."

"I hope so. I'm going out of my mind." Reagan stretched out her hand toward the telephone, tempted to check the dial tone to make sure the line was working but afraid that Max would call that very second and get a busy signal. She'd phoned her dad briefly the night before to tell him Travis had bolted, but she hadn't let herself use the phone since. "Why haven't we heard from Max? It means that something bad's happened, doesn't it?"

"I think this is a case where no news is good news." Andie urged her tea closer. "I'm sure they're both fine. You'd have heard if they weren't."

Reagan clutched Andie's hand. "I'm so glad you're here. I'm not sure I could survive waiting alone."

"You'd do the same thing for me."

"You know I would. Let's just hope I never have to."

Andie smiled gently. "I'll second that."

"I wish I knew how long Travis was gone before we woke up yesterday. Maybe Max won't be able to track him down."

Andie scowled lightly. "Max does this for a living, remember?"

"Apparently, so does Travis." Reagan took a steadying breath, but it didn't help calm her. "How could he *do* something this stupid?"

"There's no telling what goes through people's heads." Andie drizzled honey into her tea and took a sip. "Now, tell me, did you call the bank like I told you to yesterday?"

"Not yet."

"Why not? There's a limit on how much he can get in a single day, you know. If they deactivate your card, you should be able to protect the rest of your money."

"I thought about doing that," Reagan said, linking her hands together, then pulling them apart again. "I'm afraid that if I do, Travis will get desperate. At least if he has access to my money, he might not commit another robbery."

"Yeah," Andie said with a scowl, "but you might not have any money left."

"I'd rather lose every cent than have Travis pull another robbery and end up dead." Reagan lifted her cup, set it aside without tasting it and jerked to her feet. "I can't stand sitting here. It's driving me crazy."

"Waiting is hell," Andie agreed.

"I need to do something."

"You want to mop the floor?"

"No. I'd be done in ten minutes. I need something that takes longer and doesn't require me to think."

"Laundry?"

"Laundry takes *too* long. There's too much waiting time between loads." Reagan paced out of the kitchen, searching for something to occupy her. In the living room, she saw the stack of magazines she'd been meaning to go through for months and let out a shout. "I've found it," she called to Andie. "We can clip coupons. I have enough here to keep us busy for days."

Andie came around the corner and took in the stack of magazines with a raised eyebrow. "Days? It looks like *weeks* to me."

"Good intentions, not enough time." Reagan handed her an armful and picked up an equal stack for herself. In the kitchen, she set her magazines on the table and went to the junk drawer for scissors. "If you find any good recipes, you might as well clip those, too."

Andie nodded and started flipping pages. "So, to change the subject, what ever happened with those climbing lessons Jamie was asking you for?"

Reagan pushed her hair over her shoulder and sighed. "I'm not sure. One minute she was gung-ho about them and hardly speaking to me. The next, it was like she didn't care anymore. I don't know what happened, and I've been afraid to bring it up." She set a coupon she'd clipped to one side and flipped another few pages. "If she's forgotten, I don't want to remind her."

Andie laughed and added a coupon to the stack. "I knew she'd forget in time. Tommy's that way. He gets a bug in his ear one day and nothing is more important. A few days later, he's moved on to something else."

"I hope Jamie doesn't move on to something else. I shudder to think what she might come up with."

"Why are you worried? Her next idea might be

perfectly harmless. Like rattlesnake wrestling, or something.''

Reagan laughed. ''You know her, don't you?'' She sobered again almost instantly. ''I wish it was a phase she'd grow out of. Of course, I always thought Travis would outgrow his rebellious stage, and look at him now.''

Andie rested both arms on the table and looked her in the eye. ''Jamie isn't Travis. She isn't Paul, either. Do her a favor and remember that.''

''I know she's not.''

''Jamie's just pushing to find out what her boundaries are, testing to find out who she is and what she likes. We all do that. Travis knows *exactly* where the boundaries are but he's hell-bent on pushing past them to get back at somebody.''

''At me.''

Andie shrugged and went back to clipping. ''Maybe. Maybe your dad. Maybe even your mom for leaving him. Did Travis ever go to counseling after your mom died?''

''For a while, but it was a horrible counseling center that the county ran for free.'' Reagan hadn't thought of that clinic in years and the memory made her shudder. ''The counselors acted as if they were either bored or irritated with us for interrupting them. We both hated it.''

''And I'll bet Travis never tried counseling again.''

''Not that I know of.'' Reagan held her scissors over the page she was about to cut. ''I'm sure he hasn't. It was hard enough for me to get help after Paul died.'' She scratched her forehead lightly. ''And Daddy never did go. It was only because our Aunt

Helen got tired of watching us all flounder that Travis and I went. She convinced Daddy to sign the paperwork, but that's all he did. She drove us to every appointment."

"Maybe that was one more thing that made Travis think your dad didn't care about him."

"I'm sure it was." Reagan set her scissors aside and leaned back in her seat. "Just talking about it, *I'm* suddenly feeling anger I never knew I had left." She rubbed her forehead again. "Travis needs help, doesn't he?"

"I think so."

"I'm doing the right thing."

"Absolutely."

"This is the only way he's ever going to get help, isn't it?"

"Probably." The telephone rang and startled them both. Andie lunged for it before Reagan could move. "I'll get it. That way I can get rid of whoever it is— unless it's Max or your dad, of course."

Reagan listened anxiously while Andie answered, and when Andie held out the phone to her, mouthing Max's name, her heart nearly jumped out of her chest. Her hand trembled so violently, she could hardly hold the phone. "Max? Where are you?"

"In Thayne."

"That's not even sixty miles away. Have you found him?"

"Not yet."

Reagan's heart plummeted. "Do you have any leads?"

"A couple." Max waited while a truck rumbled past. "We found a clerk at the grocery store who remembers him buying food and supplies this morning.''

"We?"

"My partner showed up yesterday before I left town.''

"There's someone else with you?"

"Don't worry, Reagan. He's a good man. He knows why it's so important to bring Travis in without harm, and he won't do anything I wouldn't do.''

"Okay." She had to trust him. What options did she have?

"We got a feel for the kinds of food and supplies Travis was buying here, so we took a chance and checked with the sporting shops. It's beginning to look like he's headed into the mountains.''

Reagan's gaze shot to the window and the white-capped mountains. They looked cold and distant and isolated, and she wondered how anyone could survive the cold and snow—especially someone pampered like Travis. "He could be anywhere up there," she whispered. "He could get lost and nobody will ever find him.''

"*I'll* find him," Max said firmly. "I've had some mountain training. I'll find his trail, and I'll find him. I promise you that.''

Reagan closed her eyes against the sudden sting of tears. "I'm trying to believe you.''

"I won't come back down until I have Travis with me. I'll call again as soon as I have news. Meanwhile, I want you to take care of yourself and the girls. No staying awake all night. No skipping meals.''

In spite of her aching heart, she laughed and sent a guilty glance toward the bowl of fruit. Other than a few sips of coffee and tea, she hadn't put anything in her stomach all day. "What makes you think I'd do either?"

"Call it a wild guess." He covered the mouthpiece against the noise of passing traffic. "I'd better go before it gets any later. Donovan and I want to use daylight as long as we can." He paused again and lowered his voice. "I love you, Reagan. Try not to worry."

Not worry? she thought as she replaced the receiver a few minutes later. How could she not worry? Travis had no experience in the mountains. Anything might happen to him. And anything could happen to Max as he tried to keep his promise to her. Reagan loved her brother, but she didn't know what to expect from him. It hurt to realize that she couldn't trust him.

She trusted Max not to hurt Travis, but she wasn't at all convinced that the trust could go both ways.

MAX PULLED HIS FOOT out of three inches of clinging mud and tried to find a solid place to take his next step. Two days' tracking Travis through the mountains, including several false trails, and he doubted they were an inch closer than they'd been when they started.

"Oh, this is *fun*." Donovan's sarcasm sounded from behind deep inside a patch of aspen where he'd probably found the same wet mud as Max had. "Tell me again why we're out here?" He appeared between two trees, his boots and the lower few inches of his jeans thoroughly caked in mud. "That tiny bounty on Carmichael isn't worth *this*."

If it hadn't been for Reagan, Max would've agreed.

The snow had been getting steadily deeper and the air more frigid as they climbed. His breath formed soft white clouds in front of his face, his nose and ears ached from the cold, and his fingers were growing numb.

They'd followed Travis's trail into the high mountain area by car until they found the van abandoned in front of the chains draped across the snow-blocked roads. They'd been on foot ever since. And after two long days uphill, the pack on his back felt as if it weighed a ton.

"Don't think about the money," he suggested. "Make it a matter of pride."

"Well, *my* pride doesn't want me walking around in the middle of nowhere looking like the creature from the black lagoon." Donovan found a dry spot to leave his pack and tried to kick off a clump of mud that was hanging from his boot. "Seriously, Max. How much longer are we going to chase this guy?"

"Until we find him." According to people they'd talked with in Thayne, there were a number of summer cabins in the high country, and they suspected that Travis might be making for those.

"Why don't we go back down the mountain," Donovan suggested. "We could get warm and dry, catch the Lakers game on TV, and wait for Carmichael to resurface. Or we could ask the local authorities for help."

"Is that what you'd do if he was Holly's brother?"

Donovan tried scraping the mud off on the trunk of a young tree. "Hell, no. I wouldn't want to risk some hotdog getting excited and taking a shot at him. I'd probably do exactly what you're doing—go after him myself. But I look at it this way. If we were chasing Holly's brother, you'd be complaining. So, I figure it's pretty much my duty to gripe now.''

Max laughed and stopped walking to wait for his friend. ''You're a good friend, Donovan. Thanks.''

''For nothing.'' Donovan checked the bottom of his boot and scowled darkly. ''What's in this dirt, anyway? Superglue?''

A chilled gust of wind whipped past them, tousling Max's hair and stinging his ears. Even after they made camp, there'd be little relief. They'd spent two nights sleeping on the hard ground, cooking over an open fire—if emptying a can of stew into the one cheap pan they'd bought at the supply store could be counted as cooking—washing up with melted snow, and choking down coffee that tasted like tar, and that was the *best* thing about it. He couldn't remember the last time he'd felt so wretched.

Now, watching Donovan, he wondered if he was letting his personal feelings take over too much. ''Let me ask you a question,'' he said as Donovan began digging away chunks of mud with a broken twig. ''How far would you really go if this *was* Holly's brother?''

''The truth?''

''If you don't mind.''

''At least this far. I'd push up to the cabins and either find him or discover he wasn't there, and then I'd decide what to do next.''

''You don't have to come with me, you know. You have the luxury of deciding. I'm skating on such thin ice, I can't go back without him.''

Donovan's twig snapped. He swore and tossed it

aside. "If the ice is that thin, are you sure she's the right woman for you? You haven't even known her two weeks yet, man. And those weren't good weeks, either."

"The relationship was perfect until her brother showed up."

"Perfect? How perfect can it be when one partner doesn't know who the other is or what they do?" Donovan gave up on the mud and closed some of the distance between them. "I'm not being funny, and I'm not just trying to be obnoxious, either. It's a legitimate question."

"I've asked myself the same thing," Max admitted. He found a fallen log and tested his weight on it before sitting. The chill immediately shot through his jeans. "The only answer I have is that everything else was true. How I felt, what I shared about myself, who I *really* am inside—all that was true. And that's the man she fell in love with. At least, I hope it was."

Donovan lit a cigarette and studied the sky. "I hope so. I know I've joked around about you settling down, but I don't want to see you rush into something you'll regret. For some reason I like your sorry butt, and I don't want to see you get hurt."

"That makes two of us."

"So, assuming she did fall in love with the real Max Gardner, what are you going to do about it?"

"That's the million-dollar question. We're going to have to work something out—a compromise."

Donovan scowled at the clouds gathering overhead. "If I understand you right, she doesn't want to leave Serenity and she hates what you do for a living, which means in order to be with her, you'd have to give up your condo, move here and change careers.'' He lowered his gaze and looked Max in the eye. ''Where's the compromise in that?''

Max jerked to his feet and put some distance between them. ''You don't get it, Donovan. You haven't even met her. It's not like that.''

''Okay, explain it to me.''

Max opened his mouth, but nothing would come out. The trouble was, Donovan *had* nailed the problem squarely. Max wasn't sure he liked the sound of it any better than Donovan did. But that was the old Max talking, he convinced himself. The one who'd find any excuse to avoid a commitment.

''Look,'' he said patiently, ''I've spent my entire adult lifetime alone—and I'll be alone forever if I don't learn how to give a little.''

Donovan tossed his cigarette to the ground, crushed it out with the toe of his boot and scooped snow over it for good measure. ''Just don't give up who and what you are, thinking it'll make her happy. It won't.''

''Giving *her* up won't make *me* happy.'' Max shifted his pack on his back and glared at his friend. ''I'm not giving up.''

Donovan moved onto the trail beside him and gave him another long look. ''She means that much to you?''

''She does.''

''Hmm. Imagine that.'' Shaking his head in wonder, Donovan started walking again. Max was left to wonder what exactly his friend was implying. He'd have to confront Donovan later, he realized as the wind gusted again. Right now, they needed to find shelter before this storm hit.

CHAPTER FIFTEEN

REAGAN SPRAYED THE TOP of her television with furniture polish and began to work it into the wood with a rag. In the two days since she'd heard from Max, she'd not only clipped every coupon she could find, but sorted them, reorganized the silverware drawer and vacuumed every inch of carpeting in the house. She'd washed every stitch of dirty laundry, worked through her stack of mending and replaced missing buttons on things she'd almost forgotten they owned. She'd dusted the books on her shelves and every figurine in her house, swept all the corners for cobwebs, and still spent more time than she would have believed possible watching the television for news bulletins.

And there was still no word from Max.

Thankfully, she hadn't used her vacation days so she'd had no problem taking the time off. Her concentration was at an all-time low, and she'd have been more trouble than she was worth at the office. Most important, she didn't want to leave the telephone. She even carried the cordless into the bathroom with her when the need arose.

Her dad had called last night to tell her he'd made it to Denver. He'd missed the commuter flight to Jackson and, with the storm hovering over the mountains, couldn't get another until tomorrow. In spite of Reagan's eagerness to see him, she'd urged him to stay where he was. She didn't want him to rent a car and drive in the storm. She trusted Max to find shelter somewhere; but what would Travis do?

She finished the television and moved on to one of the end tables flanking her couch. The girls would be home from school soon. Having them around didn't completely take her mind off Max and Travis, but they did help distract her a little.

Thinking of the girls made her slow the circular motions of her hands. Danielle had been anxious to talk about anything and everything last night, probably to keep herself from worrying. But Jamie still wasn't herself. Something was bothering her, but she resisted every effort Reagan made to talk about it.

She started polishing again, putting all her frustrations into her arms and hands. Admittedly, she'd been so worried about Travis and so busy falling in love with Max, she hadn't discussed the climbing lessons with Jamie. And she had put off making a final decision longer than she should have. She really did owe Jamie better than she'd been giving lately.

Gathering the polish and rag, she moved to the other table. As she sprayed the wood surface, the kitchen door opened and banged shut again.

"Mom?"

"In the living room," Reagan called back. She smiled at Danielle when she entered the room. "Where's Jamie?"

"I thought she was home already." Danielle dropped onto the couch. "She wasn't at her locker after school so I thought maybe she got sick or something and you came to get her."

"I didn't leave the house. How long did you wait for her?"

"Twenty minutes." Danielle picked up Baby and buried her face in the fur at his neck. "Maybe longer. I looked for her on the way home, but I didn't see her."

"She's probably with one of her friends."

"I don't think so. I saw Nikki and Heather walking home. Jamie wasn't with them."

"What about Angela? Did you see her?"

"Uh-uh." Danielle lowered Baby to the couch. "Do you want me to call her and see if Jamie's there?"

"Sure." Reagan gave the cat an absent scratch. "If Angela doesn't know where she is, I'll call the school. Maybe Jamie had to stay after for one of her classes."

Danielle disappeared into the kitchen and came back a minute later. "She's not at Angela's."

Reagan moved Baby to the floor and picked up her dust rag and can of polish. "I wish she'd called to let me know she was going to be late. She's been acting so different lately."

"Mom?"

The tone of Danielle's voice made Reagan turn around. "What, honey?"

"Angela said she hasn't seen Jamie since before lunch."

A nervous knot formed in Reagan's stomach, but she tried to tell herself she was reacting to everything else, not to Jamie being late. "Is that unusual?"

"Yeah. They have their last two classes together. Jamie wasn't in either one."

"Is Angela sure about that?"

"They sit right next to each other."

"You mean Jamie's been gone for over two hours?"

"Or three."

Reagan's hands began to shake. "Does Angela have any idea where she is?"

"No. You know Jamie. She didn't say anything, but Angela said she was acting weird all day. Kind of nervous and edgy."

Reagan tried desperately to stay calm and process what Danielle was telling her. She thought about how drawn and tired Jamie had looked at breakfast. She should have taken time to talk with her then.

Dread settled in her heart, but she couldn't let herself lapse into self-blame and self-pity. She put an arm around Danielle's shoulders. "Don't worry, sweetheart. Maybe Angela was mistaken about her being out of class, or maybe she had a practice that Angela didn't know about."

"If she'd had practice, Stefani would have, too," Danielle reminded her. "And Stefani didn't."

"I'll call the school," Reagan said firmly, as if by sheer force of will she could make Jamie be there.

She dialed and waited impatiently while the phone rang. After what felt like forever, a woman answered. "Serenity Junior High School. May I help you?"

"I hope so." Reagan fought to remain calm. "I'm looking for my daughter. She hasn't come home from school and I'm wondering if she might be at basketball practice, or if one of her teachers had her stay later than usual."

"I can check for you, but I know there's not a practice. I just saw the coach leaving a few minutes ago."

Reagan clutched the phone so tightly her fingers numbed. "Her name is Jamie McKenna. She's in the seventh grade. If you could check with her teachers, I'd appreciate it."

"Sure. Hang on and I'll see what I can find out."

Reagan forced herself to smile at Danielle, who was leaning across the kitchen counter, her eyes dark with worry. "She's looking."

"Jamie's not there, Mom."

"She *might* be." Reagan heard the sharpness in her voice and tried to soften it. "She might be, Danielle. Let's not panic until we've checked everywhere."

Danielle rested her head on her arms. "What if she's *not* there?"

Reagan couldn't bear the thought. "I'll figure that out if it comes to it," she said uneasily, and turned away to compose herself. She paced as far as the cord would stretch and doubled back again several times before the school secretary returned.

"Mrs. McKenna?"

"Yes. Did you find her?"

"No. I'm sorry. I paged her over the loudspeaker, but I didn't get a response."

"Is there any way you could tell me whether or not she was in her last two classes?"

"I'm afraid not. I don't have that information."

"Can you please check? One of her friends thinks she may have missed her afternoon classes."

"I'm afraid I can't, Mrs. McKenna. I don't have that information and I don't know where to get it. Most of the teachers have already left the building, and the principal has gone for the day. If your daughter missed any classes, you should receive a call from the computerized system sometime tonight.''

"I can't wait that long," Reagan snapped. She tried again to pull herself under control. "I need to know now. Please."

Her panic must have been evident because the secretary's tone changed. "I can't make any promises, of course, but I'll see what I can do. If I can find out anything, I'll call you back."

"Thank you." Reagan barely got the words out around the growing lump in her throat, and struggled to give the secretary her number. This couldn't be happening.

She disconnected and watched almost as if in a dream as her trembling hand replaced the receiver. "Grab some paper and a pen," she said to Danielle. "I need all of her friends' numbers and the names of everyone on her team. Jamie *has* to be somewhere, and I'm going to find out where."

The sudden need to have Max beside her came out of nowhere. But he was putting out another fire for her. She was on her own.

BY THE TIME Max and Donovan reached the first cabin in the small cluster, they didn't wonder any longer whether Travis had come this way. His footprints sank into the knee-deep snow, giving them a clear trail to follow.

Thankfully, the storm had held off so far, but the wind was rising steadily and the temperature was dropping just as quickly. Max hoped Travis had taken shelter here. He wanted to get this over with quickly and get back down the mountain before the storm hit.

Donovan signaled him forward, and Max stayed in the cover of the forest as he followed Travis's trail past the first two cabins. Just before the third cabin, the footprints veered sharply off the path toward a two-story log house set back from the road, almost hidden in a thick stand of spruce, aspen and pine.

A wooden sign hung from a low branch proclaiming it the Robbers' Roost. Obviously, Travis hadn't lost his sense of humor.

Max motioned for Donovan to join him and checked the perimeter of the cabin to make sure Travis hadn't slipped past this one to another. The footprints seemed to stop, and a flash of white fabric billowing from a window near the front door showed up against the lead-colored sky. Max could make out bits of fabric clinging to the broken shards of glass.

"He's in there," he said when Donovan came up behind him.

"Sure looks like it." Donovan pulled his weapon from his holster and checked the barrel. "How do you want to handle it?"

"I'm going in after him. Alone."

Donovan scowled at him. "Don't be a fool."

"I promised Reagan that I'd bring him back in one piece."

"And you will. I'm not going to shoot unless he opens fire first."

"You can come in if he starts shooting. I've got to try to get through to him first. Maybe it's a fool's mission," he said before Donovan could argue, "but with any luck at all, Travis will be my brother-in-law. I've been asking myself for hours what I'd do if he were my own brother, and I know damn well I'd go in alone. I can't do less for Reagan's brother.''

Donovan looked as if he'd like to throttle Max. ''I'll be watching. And listening. Let's hope he's smart enough not to make any mistakes.'' Leaving his pack on a patch of dry ground, Donovan slipped into the trees to find the best vantage point to watch the cabin.

Max settled his pack beside Donovan's and ducked into the trees in the opposite direction. The snow made his approach slow and difficult, but he was in no real hurry. Finally he reached the edge of the clearing and stopped again to check the house, but the only things moving were the curtains in the windows. Either Travis didn't know he was out here, or he was watching and waiting to see what Max would do. At the last minute, he pulled his weapon, praying he wouldn't need it.

He tore across the clearing, ducking to make himself a smaller target. On the porch, he pressed against the wall and gave himself a minute to catch his breath while he listened.

Then, keeping to one side of the door, Max tried the knob but the door was locked. He inched toward the window and peered in, but he couldn't see a damn thing. Knowing that Donovan would be chomping at the bit by now, he took a deep breath and let it out slowly, steeling himself.

His heart hammered in his chest; adrenaline made his nerves jump and heightened all his senses. He'd felt it all before, but today he was acutely aware of the possibility for disaster.

Holding his gun in both hands, he trained it on the ground between his feet and shouted, ''Travis!''

A loud *thunk* from somewhere inside convinced him he'd surprised the kid.

"Come on, Travis. I know you're in there." The muffled sound of scrambling feet on hardwood floors reached him through the broken window. "You know why I'm here. Come out and let's do this the easy way."

"I know why you're here," Travis shouted back. "But I'm not coming out. You're not going to put me in jail."

From the sound of his voice, Max placed him somewhere in the middle of the house. "You're going to have to stand trial. You can't avoid it."

"You think I'm stupid?" Travis's voice came from the back of the house this time.

"If you think you're going out that sliding door, then yes." Max weighed his options and decided to stay where he was. Donovan undoubtedly had the back of the house covered. "I'm not alone, and my partner's not nearly as nice as I am."

"I'm *not* going back."

"You're not getting away."

"You won't hurt me," Travis taunted. "Reagan would never forgive you."

"Reagan has nothing to do with this," Max shouted back. "This is between you and me."

"Yeah? Well, you didn't mind using her to get to me in the first place, did you?"

"I'm not talking about Reagan until you and I are face-to-face."

Travis laughed harshly. "Don't hold your breath for *that* to happen. You know what I like about you, Max? You're as big a screwup as I am."

"Not quite," Max called back. "*I* don't have to spend the rest of my life hiding." He caught a glimpse of Donovan moving through the trees behind the house. "Look, man, for what it's worth, I know you're a decent guy. You've got a real chance to be somebody if you'll just stop running around in this circle you've been on. You've already added breaking and entering to the list. You'll be damned lucky if you don't have to face charges for the money and bank card you stole from Reagan. Don't make it worse. Let me inside, and let's talk this over."

"Right." Travis's mocking laughter echoed. "I've had enough of your brand of friendship."

"All right," Max shouted in frustration. "I made a mistake. A *big* one. I'm trying like hell to make up for it. But you know what, Travis? If Reagan doesn't forgive me, I'll have only myself to blame. Your situation's no different."

"There's a helluva difference," Travis argued. "I'll be in jail. You'll still be free."

"Have you ever been in love, Travis? Ever met a woman you couldn't be happy without? There's not much to look forward to when you're about to lose someone you feel that way about." When Travis didn't answer, he went on. "Look, Travis, give me a break. There's no way you can get out of here, and shooting you might be a bad way to introduce myself to the rest of your family."

A long silence followed. Max kept his eyes peeled in case Travis made a break for it. Donovan would warn him if Travis slipped out a window on the opposite side of the cabin.

"You're that serious about Reagan?" Travis's voice sounded closer.

"I'm that serious."

"You didn't just use her to get to me?"

"I didn't even know she was your sister until the night you showed up. Believe me, you have nothing to do with what I feel for Reagan." He waited for an answer. "Come on," he said after several long minutes. "Let me in. It's getting cold out here." Other than the soft keening of the wind and the sound of Max's heartbeat, nothing broke the stillness for a long time.

"You can come in, I guess," Travis said at last. "But just to talk. Don't try anything."

It was a start, Max told himself as the door creaked open. He just hoped he didn't have to leave Donovan freezing outside for long. He stepped inside and gave Travis a quick once-over. He wore a slim-fitting T-shirt tucked into a pair of tight jeans and he'd taken off his shoes, probably to dry them out. The only place he might be hiding a gun was under his plaid wool jacket.

Travis lifted its hem to show the rest of his waistband. "No weapon. You want to pat me down to make sure I'm not lying?"

Max made his decision quickly. "I believe you. Besides, my partner's right outside. Even if you shoot me, you won't get far."

He took in his surroundings as he talked, making note of the large windows looking out onto the forest, the sliding glass doors leading onto a back deck, the narrow hallway that stretched from the front of the cabin to the back and widened into a kitchen in the middle. He could see two large fireplaces from where he stood, but Travis hadn't built a fire in either one, so it wasn't much warmer inside than out.

"How long were you planning to hole up here?"

Travis shrugged and closed the door. "However long I need to. There's canned food and instant coffee in the kitchen, so I won't starve for a few days."

"And what then? Where were you planning to go from here?"

Travis sent an uneasy glance out the window. "Back down the mountain, I guess." His hands fluttered nervously at his side. "I haven't thought that far ahead."

Max perched on the arm of the leather sofa, still ready for anything but hoping to put Travis at ease. "No offense, Travis, but don't you think that's part of the problem here? You're living from minute to minute, flying by the seat of your pants, and never getting anywhere."

Travis huffed a contemptuous laugh. "Depends on whose definition you're going by. I'm doing fine."

"You're wanted by the law and holed up in a cabin surrounded by bail enforcement officers. The only reason my partner's out there waiting instead of rushing the place is because I asked him to hold back as a personal favor. I hate to break it to you, but I don't think that qualifies as 'fine' in anybody's book."

Travis turned away from him and shoved his fingers through his hair. "Like you care."

"I care. So does Reagan."

Travis eyed him speculatively. "And that's supposed to make a difference to me?"

"If you want it to."

Travis took a couple of long, jerky steps toward the window. "I'll tell you something else that's up to me. I'm not going to jail, no matter what."

"You're willing to chance the alternative?"

"Getting away? Sure. Why not?"

Max shook his head slowly. "If you think that's the alternative, you're making a serious error in judgment. My partner and I aren't in the habit of letting fugitives walk away free. You might be Reagan's brother, but you're a fugitive first, and I have a job to do."

"You can try."

"I'm good at what I do, Travis. Make no mistake about that. And my partner's even better. I'm giving you a chance to walk in to the police department on your own. If you don't want to take it, we'll just go to plan B. For someone who claims to hate jail so much, you sure keep trying to get there. Wouldn't it make more sense to go straight?"

"And what would that get me?"

"Maybe nothing. Maybe a little self-pride. Who knows? Have you ever tried it?"

"Self-pride." Travis snorted in derision. "What good would that do?"

"What good does it do to live without it? Can you honestly say you're happy living on the run?"

"Happier than I'd be in jail."

"Jail doesn't have to be more than a temporary setback," Max said. "But if you keep going the way you have been, you could be looking at a lifetime spent in prison."

"No way." Travis shoved the blinds covering the window out of his way and glared outside. "Never."

"Then change the way you're doing things." Max

forced himself to stay put so he wouldn't spook
Travis. "It's up to you. You choose what your future
brings. You can come down the mountain with me
voluntarily, or you can fight it and take another few
strikes into court with you—assuming my partner lets
you make it that far."

"Maybe I won't go to court at all."

Max took a beat or two to think about how to respond. Instinct told him that he could rush Travis and
take him down before the kid could react, but his
promise to Reagan kept echoing through his mind.
"Why are you so determined to make life miserable
for yourself? What are you getting out of it?"

"I'm not getting anything out of it. My life stinks."

"You're getting *something*," Max insisted, "or you
wouldn't keep doing the same thing over and over."

"What the hell do you know about it?" Travis demanded. "Why do you care?"

"I care because Reagan cares," Max said honestly.
"And because your nieces care. And because I got to
know you a little, and I think that underneath it all,
you're actually a decent guy." He stood slowly so
Donovan could see him through the window and realize that he was still all right. "I could be all wrong
about this, but I think you're trying to find reassurance
from your family. The more screwed up your life gets,
the more Reagan tries to fix it for you. But she's already reached the breaking point and you're going to
end up with nothing but a screwed-up life and a nice
cozy prison cell to spend your old age in."

Travis's shoulders hunched slightly, the only sign
that he heard a word.

"No matter what you're looking for," Max continued, ''nobody else but you will be sitting in that jail cell—not your dad, not Reagan, not any of your friends who were with you when you started in this direction…just you. Think about it. Whether you're looking for something or trying to get back at somebody, is it really worth the price you're going to pay?''

Travis's expression hardened, but he still didn't speak. Max was running out of things to say.

He caught a glimpse of Donovan moving closer through the trees. ''It's your ball, Travis. And it's time to decide how you're going to play it this time. But I'd suggest you do it quickly. I don't think my partner's going to wait outside in the cold much longer.''

BY EIGHT O'CLOCK that evening, Reagan was so worried about Jamie, she couldn't think clearly. She clutched the steering wheel of her car as she drove slowly through the streets of Serenity, staring into the inky shadows and praying frantically for help. Her thoughts twisted and curled, alternating between hope that Jamie would show up unharmed and the desperate fear that she wouldn't.

She'd entertained one brief moment of hope that afternoon when she'd concluded that Jamie had probably run off to take the climbing lessons. With her heart in her throat, she'd called Teton Extreme Sports, expecting to be told that Jamie had signed up for the lessons.

But the hope had been short-lived. Jamie's name wasn't on the class list. In desperation, Reagan had called the police. The officer had been sympathetic but not overly concerned. His own children had pushed the envelope by staying out later than they should when they were teenagers and they'd always come back safe and sound. Reagan wished she could be as certain. Her options of places to look were rapidly dwindling.

As she rolled slowly past the diner, she wiped her burning eyes and realized she really was a hazard on the road. She pulled into the parking lot and shut off the motor. She dialed home on her cell phone to check in with Andie and Danielle, then pocketed her keys and crossed the parking lot.

A dozen pairs of eyes looked up as she entered, and the expressions on their faces told her that word had spread about Jamie's disappearance. Reagan wanted no part of their pity. They already assumed the worst, but she wouldn't allow herself to believe it, even for a moment.

Stacy came out from behind the counter and slipped an arm around Reagan's waist. "Have you heard anything yet?"

"Not yet, but I'm sure it's just a matter of time." She stepped away from Stacy and nodded toward a booth with a clear view of the street. "Do you mind if I sit there?"

"It's all yours. Do you want coffee?"

"Please. Lots of it." While Stacy hurried away, Reagan sank into the seat and rested her elbows on the table and her chin in her hands.

Stacy returned carrying a coffeepot and a stack of napkins. "She's going to be fine," she said as she filled Reagan's cup. "You'll find her." She put the pot on the counter behind her and took a seat across from Reagan. "You know how kids that age are—always up to something."

"I know." Reagan picked up her cup and held it, but her hands shook so badly she spilled some of the scalding liquid on her fingers.

Stacy took the cup from her and settled it in the saucer. "Listen, Reagan, I know you like to be independent. You've kept mostly to yourself since you came here, but don't make the mistake of doing it now. This is the time when you need friends and neighbors."

Reagan met Stacy's warm gaze and let out a shaky breath. "I just don't understand how she could disappear so completely. Nobody seems to know anything."

"Somebody does," Stacy assured her. "You just haven't found that person yet."

"I've talked to everyone she knows. I've driven up and down every street in town a dozen times or more. I've called every one of her friends and even kids she doesn't like. I've talked to the school, to her teachers—" her voice cracked and the lump that had been sitting in her throat all evening swelled "—and she's *nowhere*."

"I know. I know." Stacy leaned across the table and put a hand over hers. "You look all done in. You can't keep going like this."

"I can't stop! I can't go home and take a nap and forget that my daughter is missing."

"Look," Stacy said. "I get off work in half an hour. I'll be glad to help you look. And I know a lot of other people feel the same way. They're just waiting for you to ask."

Reagan sat back. She'd never considered asking for help. If Andie hadn't insisted on calling Bart, Reagan would have searched alone until the police thought enough time had passed to get involved.

But why *hadn't* she thought of asking? Why hadn't she looked outside herself for help? Why did she always think she needed to solve every problem, handle every crisis on her own?

"I can put out some calls if you want," Stacy was saying. "We could get a whole crew of people here in minutes."

Reagan fought back a wave of grateful tears. "I— I'd like that."

"We'll all put our heads together and come up with something. We'll *find* her."

Reagan nodded weakly. She wanted desperately to believe. She *needed* to believe. "Okay. Thank you."

"It's no problem. I assume Max is already out looking."

Reagan hesitated for a split second before answering. She'd been trying not to think about Max all evening without much success. She'd been struggling to stop wanting him with her, to keep from needing him at her side in this crisis. But it wasn't working. Whether she wanted to admit it or not, she wasn't strong enough to go through this alone.

"He's out in the field," she told Stacy. "Working."

"He didn't come back to help?" Stacy looked shocked. "That doesn't seem like him at all."

"He doesn't know about Jamie," Reagan admitted. "I don't even know how to reach him."

Stacy frowned and her brows drew together. "He doesn't have a cell phone?"

"If he does, he didn't give me the number."

"He's *so* secretive."

Reagan's natural instinct rose like a wall in her heart, but protecting Travis's reputation didn't seem so important anymore. Neither did her own. "He's only being secretive to help me," she said quietly. "He's here to arrest my brother."

Stacy fell back against her chair and did her best not to look stunned. "I didn't…I…" She shook her head and laughed weakly. "Listen to me jabbering like an idiot. It's just that he never let on, not even once."

"No. He wouldn't have. He didn't want to embarrass me by letting people know why he was really here."

"Now, *that* sounds like him." Stacy patted Reagan's arm. "He's a good man, Reagan. The kind a smart woman would hang on to for a long time."

Reagan lifted her cup again and, heartened by the fact that she didn't spill any, took a sip. "It's not that simple."

"Why not? You like him. He likes you. Sounds pretty simple to me."

"I can't think about that now. Not until Jamie's home again."

Stacy's fingers traced a pattern on the table. "Sorry. I thought maybe talking about Max would help to take your mind off it."

"I don't think anything could do that."

"Then let's find that daughter of yours." Stacy stood again. "I'll go make those phone calls. We'll have a whole crew of people here before you can finish that coffee."

CHAPTER SIXTEEN

IT WAS NEARLY TEN O'CLOCK when Max pulled into the parking lot in front of Serenity's city offices and shut off the engine. His eyes burned from fatigue and his arms and legs ached from his trek up and down the mountain. He'd kept the heater blasting most of the way back to town, but his pants and boots were still wet from the snow and he hadn't been able to get warm. Donovan didn't look much more comfortable, and Travis sat in the back seat, shivering.

Once Max turned Travis over to the police and stopped by Reagan's to let her know they were back in one piece, he'd head back to the Wagon Wheel for a long, hot shower.

Travis leaned forward in his seat, his face a mask. "You're leaving me here?"

"Yep." Max opened his door and put one foot out on the pavement. "I can't let you go back to Reagan's and pretend like nothing's happened."

"She won't like it, you know. She'll be mad that you left me here."

Max took a deep breath and swung his gaze back to the kid. "I doubt that, but if she is, I'll deal with it. Personally, I think you need to face the facts. You stole from her and you lied. You destroyed what little trust she had left in you. She might very well want your butt in jail for a good, long time."

Donovan muttered something and stepped out into the night.

Travis shook his head and looked away. "Whatever."

"Exactly." Max climbed out of the car, holding back a groan when the stiffness of cold, overworked muscles hit him. He shut his door and rounded the car to let Travis out. Lights gleamed from the tiny building, making it look warm and welcoming. Max was grateful that Donovan had insisted on calling to let the chief know they were on their way in.

Max took Travis by the elbow and nudged him toward the low-slung building just as two cars drove past and pulled into the parking lot of the diner on the next block. To Max's surprise, the diner was still brightly lit and he could see people inside a full hour after it usually closed.

There could have been a game tonight, but even so the diner didn't stay open this late. Something was going on, though. And he felt a pang of melancholy that he wasn't part of it.

He ignored it. Even if he stayed, he wouldn't expect the people to feel the same way about him now that they knew the truth. He just hoped he hadn't burned all his bridges here in Serenity. "Come on," he growled at Travis. "Let's get this over with."

The chief of police was waiting for them inside, his tie loosened, the top button of his shirt undone, a fine stubble of dark beard shadowing his cheeks. One hand rested on the telephone, but he pulled it away when Max and Donovan came inside with Travis. "Glad to see you made it," he said, pushing to his feet. "I've been waiting."

"It's a long drive from Thayne," Max reminded him. "Especially in the dark."

"True enough." The chief tried ineffectually to stuff his shirttail into the waistband of his uniform trousers. "So this is our boy, huh? You want to put him in that first cell in the back?"

Donovan didn't wait for Max to answer. He took Travis's arm and led him toward the cell.

"If you don't mind," Chief Henley said, "we can do the paperwork in the morning. I want to get on over to the diner. Imagine you will, too."

"I noticed all the cars," Max said with a glance out the window. "What's going on?"

"You haven't heard?"

"I haven't been here. What is it?"

Chief Henley looked from Max to Travis and Donovan, and shifted his weight uncomfortably. "Jamie McKenna's gone missing."

Max was so bone-tired, he thought for a minute he'd heard wrong. "Jamie? Are you sure?"

Donovan took a step back into the office. "Someone you know?"

"Reagan's daughter. She's thirteen." Max stole a glance at Travis's shuttered face and turned back toward the chief. "How long has she been gone?"

"Since about noon, best we can figure. We can't do anything official yet, of course. It's too soon. But folks are getting together to help search. I figured Reagan would've called you."

"She didn't have any way to reach me." He should have given her his cell phone number, but he and Donovan usually kept their phones turned off when they were on a case. "Nobody has any idea where Jamie is?"

"None of her friends seem to know anything," the chief said. "And her sister claims she doesn't know. I told Reagan I didn't think there was anything to worry about. Teenagers, you know. But Stacy's roused the whole town, and it's getting so late now, I'm not quite as confident as I was."

Max's heart slammed against his chest, and his head began to buzz. He couldn't even imagine how frightened Reagan must be. Forgetting Travis, he crossed to the door and jerked it open. "Is Reagan at the diner?"

"Far as I know."

Max started to pull the door shut, but Travis called after him. "Max? Wait. I might know something."

The whole town was searching for her and Travis knew something? Max barely resisted the urge to throttle him. "What is it?"

"I don't know anything for sure, but she's been talking a lot about taking those rock climbing lessons. Maybe that's where she went."

"Are you saying she might have taken off for Jackson? *Alone?*"

"Not alone. She told me she'd found some people who were taking private classes from some guy who used to teach at the school. Maybe she went with them."

"What responsible adult would take her that far without her mother's permission?"

"I don't know what she told them. All I know is that I was supposed to tell Reagan she was sleeping over at a friend's house tonight."

Max resisted the urge to pummel Travis. "You knew she was planning to run off, and you didn't tell Reagan?"

"I didn't think it would hurt anything. I used to go

where I wanted, and I was always okay." Travis set his jaw stubbornly. "Jamie knows what she wants, but Reagan doesn't listen to her. I know what that feels like, and I felt sorry for the kid."

"Jamie is *thirteen,*" Max shouted. "She's not mature enough to make decisions like that for herself, and she sure as hell isn't old enough to be out there on her own. *Dammit,* that's why kids *have* parents." He forced himself to put a little more distance between them, afraid of what he might do.

"Yeah, but she's a smart kid," Travis countered. "She knows how to take care of herself."

"Considering the source," Donovan grumbled, "I'm not sure that's much of a recommendation." He nudged Travis toward the cell again, and Max turned his attention to Chief Henley.

"She won't get very far with the lessons," Max said to reassure himself. "She doesn't have her mother's permission to take them."

"Yes, she did," Travis said as he dug in his heels and stopped again. "Kind of, anyway."

Chief Henley glowered at him. "Kind of? You want to explain that part?"

"Well...I kind of signed a permission slip for her."

"You forged Reagan's signature?" Max demanded.

Travis held up both hands to ward off the attack he felt coming. "It was a mistake, okay? I just didn't think it was that big a deal when I did it."

Max clenched his fists at his side and made himself take another step backward. He had to stay focused. Everything else could wait. "You said she was taking private lessons? Where will I find her?"

"Right now? I don't know. But they're meeting the

instructor in Albertson's supermarket parking lot in Jackson tomorrow morning.''

"You'd better start praying that she's all right,'' Max said through clenched teeth, ''or you can really start feeling sorry for yourself. You'll have good reason to.''

Max let himself out the door and raced toward the diner, narrowly missing being hit by a car as he darted into the road.

REAGAN WAS QUICKLY LOSING every bit of calm she'd been able to dredge up. She'd called home so often to see if Danielle and Andie had heard from Jamie, she'd drained the battery in her cell phone. Since then, she'd moved a table to just inside the front door so she could be near the pay phone.

She ached to be out searching, but Stacy had finally convinced her to stay behind. Stacy was probably right. Reagan was too tired to think straight and too worried to be any help. She took a sip from the diet cola she'd been nursing since the coffee began to taste bitter, and rested her head on her arms.

Rapidly approaching footsteps outside the window brought her head up sharply and she peered through the glass into the darkness, hoping someone had news of Jamie. She couldn't breathe as she waited, and it seemed to take forever for the person to come around the corner.

When she saw Max, whatever had been holding her together seemed to evaporate. She jumped to her feet and ran to him. Sobbing so hard she couldn't speak, she threw herself into his arms. All the worry over Jamie, over Travis and over Max—all the questions she'd been asking herself, and the answers she'd found—became one overwhelming mass, and Reagan couldn't seem to get control over herself.

Max pulled her close and held her without speaking. His body was tight with worry, his arms strong and sure, his eyes nearly black with concern. He smoothed her hair and cradled her while she cried. He demanded nothing of her, asked no questions. He just held her until she could finally speak again.

"You heard about Jamie?"

"Chief Henley told us."

"Does that mean you found Travis?"

"We did." Max tightened his embrace, as if he needed to feel her as much as she needed him. "Sweetheart, I think I know where Jamie is."

Relief and almost overpowering hope nearly dropped her to her knees. "You do? How? Where? Did she tell you something?"

"She didn't, but Travis did. He thinks she's gone to Jackson."

The hope evaporated, and Reagan pulled away from him. "I've already thought of that. She's not signed up for the classes."

"Apparently, she found someone who's willing to give private lessons and Travis encouraged her. He even forged your signature on a permission slip. She arranged to ride up there with someone else, and Travis was supposed to cover for her."

Reagan felt the blood drain from her face, then surge back an instant later. The parking lot began to swirl, and for a moment she thought she might actually pass out. She gripped Max's hand, partly to hold herself up, partly to make him listen to her. "We have to go find her. Please."

"Of course we will. What about Danielle? Where is she?"

"At home with Andie." Reagan forced her head up again. "I have to call her."

Max led her inside and pressed her gently into the seat she'd left only a moment before. "You sit down and try to get your legs back. I'll call the house."

More grateful for his help than she could say, Reagan listened while he talked briefly to Andie, then to Danielle. The gentleness in his voice as he reassured her daughter touched her deeply.

Stacy was right. Love didn't come along every day. Good men didn't just drop from the sky. And Reagan would be a fool to let a few little differences, a few inconveniences and a little fear keep her from grabbing hold of this one and hanging on.

"We'll be home in a few minutes," she heard Max say. "Just as soon as your mom's ready to leave here." He glanced at her, his eyes clearing slightly when he saw that she looked stronger. "Maybe I'll ask the cook to whip up some sandwiches for us to bring with us. I'll bet your mom hasn't eaten since Travis left." He listened to Danielle and scowled at Reagan. "A *whole pear?* Well, no wonder she's dizzy."

Before she could tell Max she was okay, a caravan of cars rounded the corner and pulled into the parking lot. Almost immediately people began pouring out of the cars and rushing toward Max and Reagan.

Bart reached them first and nodded to Max. "Good to see you're back. Any word?"

"We think she's gone to Jackson," Reagan told him. "It's a long story, and I promise I'll explain it all later. Right now, I'd like to go find her."

Bart pushed his baseball cap back on his head and looked at Max. "You're going tonight?"

"I have to," Reagan answered. "I can't sit here until morning. We *think* that's where she is, but we don't know for certain."

"I doubt either of us will rest until we know," Max added.

"You want me to come along?"

Reagan stood on tiptoe and hugged Bart quickly. "You have no idea how much I appreciate everything you've done. If you could just stay here and let the others know, that would help more than another set of eyes in the car."

"You got it." Bart stepped away and drew the crowd with him, leaving Reagan and Max alone.

Feeling stronger still, Reagan glanced toward the city offices and took a deep breath. "What's going to happen to Travis?"

"Donovan and I were going to transport him to California tomorrow. I won't leave until I know Jamie's safe, but I know Donovan won't mind taking him alone. Travis will stand trial, of course. There's no way out of that. And he does have some prior convictions, so he probably won't get off with a suspended sentence. But I'm hoping that if he has good character witnesses, he'll only spend a year in jail before he gets parole. After that, it'll be up to him."

"I have no idea who could testify for him—besides Dad and me, of course. How much weight would our testimonies carry?"

"I don't know," Max said, leading her back inside. "But Donovan and I will help if we can." He rubbed her arm and kissed her cheek. "Don't worry about Travis. He'll be fine. Let's focus on finding Jamie."

Reagen nodded quickly. "I'm going to call my dad and tell him to meet us there," Reagan said. "Then we'd better go get Danielle. She's probably anxious."

"And I'll get those sandwiches." Max pulled her close and kissed her quickly. "Don't look at me like that. Humor me, okay? I'm not used to caring about someone else, and I may not always get it right."

Reagan leaned her head against his chest and took a long, deep breath. The scent of fresh air and pine drifted up from his shirt and mixed with his own unique scent. She felt warm and safe for the first time in years. It would be so easy to get used to this. So easy to grow dependent upon it. "Don't worry," she whispered, "you're doing fine, so far."

REAGAN AWOKE SUDDENLY, chilled and confused. In the next heartbeat, she remembered where she was and sank back against Max's chest, where she'd slept for the last few hours while they waited for sunrise. Danielle's soft breathing came from the back seat and Max slept soundly, his head tipped back and his mouth slightly open.

He was exhausted, obviously, and all because of her and her family. He should be angry and frustrated with her. Instead, he'd held her for hours, pulling the blanket back onto her shoulders when it slipped and rousing himself occasionally to run the engine and warm the car.

Hoping to let them both sleep awhile longer, Reagan eased away from Max's embrace and let herself out of the car. She closed it soundlessly and waited to make sure she hadn't woken either of them, then walked away from the car across the parking lot of Albertson's supermarket.

The lights had come on inside the grocery store and traffic had begun moving on the four-lane highway. She jogged across the pavement and found the public rest room in the back of the store. She washed her hands and face, smoothing her hair back from her face and grimacing at the dark circles beneath her eyes.

Jamie had better be here, she told her reflection silently. She didn't know what she'd do if they didn't find her daughter. She also didn't know what she'd do if they *did*. What punishment was appropriate for an act like this? Right now, she felt like grounding Jamie for the rest of her life, but she knew she'd have to handle the situation wisely.

Yes, Jamie had done a foolish, irresponsible thing, but Reagan didn't believe that she'd have run off without Travis's encouragement. He deserved at least part of the blame.

A hefty share belonged on her own shoulders, as well. If she hadn't been so distracted by Max and Travis, she would have gone with Jamie to check out the class. Then, even a definite "no" might have been acceptable. Her actions had led Jamie to believe that her needs came way down on her mother's list of priorities.

She gave herself another quick check in the mirror, dug a lipstick from the bottom of her purse and slashed a little color onto her face. Not good, but better. She tucked her T-shirt into her jeans, slung her purse over her shoulder and hurried back into the store. On impulse, she picked up fruit, milk and doughnuts on her way out.

Max was awake by the time she got back. He stood outside the car and shielded his eyes from the sun with

one hand as he scanned the parking lot, probably looking for her. She waved to catch his attention.

He came to meet her, his eyes shadowed. "I
thought I'd lost you."

"Sorry. I didn't want to wake you."

He nodded toward a beat-up Chevy truck behind
them. "The climbing instructor got here a few minutes
ago. He's expecting Jamie for the class he's teaching.
They should be here in about half an hour."

Reagan's knees buckled. "Then she *will* be here?"

"As far as he knows. He has her signed permission
slip, so I'd say the chances are pretty good." He
pulled her into his arms and kissed her. "There. *Now*
I feel better."

Reagan looked up into his eyes. "Do you?"

"Mmm-hmm." He followed up with another kiss,
this one longer and more demanding. "I could get
used to this," he said when they came up for air.

"To staying awake for days at a time while you
chase my family all over creation?"

"Maybe. And to waking up next to you—or at least
in the same general vicinity." He kissed the tip of her
nose and moved to her chin. "To sleeping with you
in my arms."

Waves of fire moved through her. "I could get used
to it, too," she whispered against his lips.

"The question is, what are we going to do about
it?"

"Give me some options," she teased. "Let me see
if anything sounds appealing."

"This isn't the best place to ask me for 'appealing,'" he said, his voice low and intimate. "But I'll
give it a shot, anyway. I did a lot of thinking while I
was climbing that mountain after Travis. I came home

cold and wet and hungry and tired, and I'm not sure that's what I want to do with my life anymore.''

Reagan gaped at him. ''You'd give up your career for me?''

''For us. That is, if you're interested in having me around.''

''Oh, I'm interested.'' She threw her arms around his neck and kissed him, putting all the emotions she'd been fighting for the past few days behind it. ''But what will you do if you don't hunt fugitives?''

''I'll find something. I thought maybe I'd talk to Bart and see if he could use a hand while I'm figuring it all out.'' He glanced over his shoulder to where Danielle's head was visible above her pillow in the window. ''The past couple of weeks have taught me a thing or two about priorities, about people, and about myself. I don't want to lose you, Reagan. And if that means I have to make a few changes, that's what I'll do.''

She nestled against him, battling an uncomfortable twinge in her stomach. ''The past couple of weeks have taught me a few things, too,'' she whispered. She tried to relax, to savor the moment, but the edginess persisted.

This was exactly what she'd asked for, so why did she feel so uneasy? Maybe it was just because she still didn't know for certain that Jamie was safe. Yes, that was it. When she had Jamie back safe and sound, she'd be able to relax. When the present was settled, she'd be able to look to the future and make plans. That's all it was.

She didn't have time to worry anymore about it because a white Chevy pulled into the parking lot at that moment. When she recognized her dad driving, she let out a cry and ran toward it. He slid out from behind the wheel just as she reached him and gathered her into a warm embrace. He wore his usual striped denim overalls and plaid shirt and he looked so good she vowed never to let so much time pass between visits again.

He held her tightly for a minute and kissed her cheek. "How are you, sweetheart? Have you had any word about Jamie yet?"

"We're pretty sure she'll be here in a few minutes." She held on to his arm and motioned for Max to join them. "I want you to meet Max."

Charlie squinted to see him better and held out his hand. "You're the man who talked my son into turning himself in?"

"One of them." Max shook Charlie's hand and Reagan knew instinctively that they'd like each other. "Reagan told you he's at the police station in Serenity? My partner's waiting until you get there."

Charlie tucked his hands into his pockets and rocked back on his heels. "She did. After we find Jamie, I'll follow you back there in my rental car. I'd like to know how you got through to him. I've been trying for years to reach him."

"Don't give up," Max said as he slipped an arm around Reagan. "I know it may not seem like it, but he really wants to know that you care."

"Well, that's good to know." Charlie smiled gratefully and glanced with interest at Max's hand on Reagan's waist. "Is there something else I should know?"

Reagan grinned, but Max spoke before she could answer. "As a matter of fact, sir, when this is all over, I'd like to ask you for permission to marry your daughter."

Charlie regarded him for a moment. His face was utterly serious, but Reagan could see a sparkle in his eyes. "What does my daughter want me to say to that?"

She laughed softly, again ignoring the twist of uneasiness. "I want you to say yes."

"I'll give it some thought," he said with a teasing grin and nodded toward a van that was pulling into a spot not far from the climbing teacher's truck. "Right now, sweetheart, it looks like you have some work to do."

THE VAN PARKED and three young girls Jamie's age climbed out, chattering, laughing and tossing equipment to one another. Reagan started toward them, but the look on her daughter's face made her grind to a halt. How long had it been since she saw Jamie smile like that? How long since she'd heard that laugh? In the years since Paul's death, she'd almost forgotten that Jamie could look so carefree, so...*happy*.

Just then, Jamie wheeled around and saw her standing there. The joy on her face evaporated and her eyes shadowed, and Reagan's heart constricted painfully. She'd never meant to take the joy from her daughter's life.

Max stepped up and put an arm around her. "Do you want me to come with you, or would you rather talk with her alone?"

It would be so easy to lean on him, but she shook her head. "Thanks, but I need to do this on my own." She drew away, but he caught her hand and squeezed it. Somehow she knew this is how he would always be. He'd never push, but he'd be there if she needed him.

Suddenly nervous at the prospect of facing her daughter, she pulled the edges of her sweater together and crossed the lot. She had no idea what to say. Apologies were needed all the way around, and Reagan didn't know where to begin.

Jamie shuffled her feet and dropped her gaze to the ground as Reagan approached. "You're going to kill me, aren't you?"

"Not exactly. I'm feeling many different things right now. I'm so relieved to know that you're all right, it's going to take me a few minutes to know just how angry I am." She took Jamie's arm gently. "You and I need to talk, sweetheart. Leave your things here and come with me."

Reagan didn't speak again until they'd put some distance between themselves and the others. "I could ask if you had any idea how frightened I've been, but you couldn't possibly know. You must know how angry I am that you lied to me. And I'm furious with you *and* with Travis for forging my signature. What on earth made you think you could get away with this?"

Jamie ducked her head. "I know it was wrong, but—"

"Wait. I'm not finished yet. I'm also sorry, Jamie. I'm sorry that I didn't pay enough attention to what you were asking me, sorry that I didn't realize how important this was to you. It must be very important to make you go to such lengths to get it."

Jamie's stunned gaze flickered to Reagan's face. "Mom, it's the only thing I've found since we came here that I really want to do."

"I realize that now." Reagan took a deep breath. "Unfortunately, this was the *wrong* way to get it. We had half the town out looking for you last night, Jamie. There were a lot of frantic people searching the fields and the forest. Your teachers are worried, Danielle's been half sick, and Max has only had about an hour's sleep in the car because he had to turn around and come back out to find you the instant he got back with Travis."

Jamie's gaze faltered again and a slow flush stained her cheeks. "I'm sorry, Mom."

"I'm sure you are." Reagan put her hands into her pockets. "I know you want these lessons more than anything, but I don't know how I can let you take them after everything you've done."

Jamie paled and her mouth quivered. She tried to act tough, but Reagan could see the heartbreak in her eyes. "I knew it. I *knew* you wouldn't let me do it."

"Not this session." Reagan lifted Jamie's chin until their eyes met again. "But if we don't have any repeats of this kind of performance, I will let you take them from the climbing school when the next session begins."

It took a minute for her meaning to sink in. "Are you serious? You'll let me take classes this summer?"

"If you follow the rules between now and then. And if you'll help me make all this up to the people who've helped us."

"Sure."

"Absolutely no more lies. No more sneaking around. If you do *anything* like this again, you won't take the lessons. Are we square on that?"

Jamie nodded and glanced over her shoulder to her waiting friends. "I guess I'd better get my things, huh?"

"Yes, you'd better. I'll talk to the instructor and explain what's happened. And I'll talk to the people at the school before we drive back home and put our names on the mailing list for summer session.''

Jamie started away, then darted back and threw her arms around Reagan's neck. "Thanks, Mom. And I really am sorry. I knew I shouldn't have done it. I knew how mad you'd be. But—"

"For the record, Uncle Travis might not be the best person in the world to take advice from.''

"Yeah, well, I know that now.''

Reagan spoke with the instructor who was horrified at what he'd almost allowed to happen, then turned back toward Max, who leaned against the car, talking to Danielle. Charlie was helping Jamie. Reagan took only three steps before she realized why she'd felt so uneasy earlier. She'd done the same thing to Max that she'd done to Jamie. Apparently, she'd been letting fear run her life for a long time.

Was she so afraid of losing Max that she'd change him just to keep him beside her? What kind of life would that be? What kind of love? Didn't she love him exactly as he was right now? If she insisted that he change, wouldn't that make him a different man than the one she'd fallen in love with?

She leaned against the car beside him and wrapped her sweater around her.

Max studied her expression carefully. "Did everything go okay?''

"Fine.'' She brushed a stray lock of hair away from her mouth. "She's getting her things together. I'm going to let her take lessons in the summer.''

"That's pretty generous.''

"There are a few conditions, but I'm also aware that I'm partly to blame for this. And Travis, of course.'' She turned to face him, taking in his clear gray eyes, his kind face, his full, generous mouth. "I'm afraid I'm not going to be able to take you up on that offer you made earlier."

"Which offer was that?"

"The one to stay here and find work with Bart."

Max's face froze and his smile slipped from his mouth. "Why not?"

"Because it's wrong, Max. I can't let you change who you are just to make me feel better."

"I can't let you push me away just because of that one part of who I am. I don't want to lose you, or the girls." He watched Jamie and Danielle, who were working together now to get Jamie's things into the car. "I'm growing kind of fond of them, too."

"I don't have any intention of losing you," Reagan assured him. "And that's exactly why I'm changing my mind. I want you exactly as you are, and that means you have to be able to do what you love. I'll just have to learn to live with it."

Max took her gently by the shoulders. "Can you do that?"

"Yes. That's part of what I've learned since I met you. What I *can't* live with is the possibility that you'll turn into a shell of the man I love because I'm so afraid. Look what I've done to Jamie by clinging too tightly. I'm not going to do that to her any longer, and I'm not going to start doing it with you. If the girls and I have to move to San Diego, then that's what we'll do."

Max ran his hands along her arms, as if he wanted to hold her but wouldn't let himself do it yet. "Well, see…I've been meaning to talk to you about that, too. I've gotten kind of attached to Serenity and the people in it. And the way they all pulled together last night to look for Jamie— It was amazing."

Reagan gaped at him. "You'd move to the country?"

"I'd move to the moon if you were there."

"You're serious?"

"That's a pretty weak word for how strongly I feel about it. What do you say we try things this way for a while—I'll stay in Serenity and we'll see how things work. Donovan wants me to go into business with him, and since it's all I really know, I'd like to try it for a while. If my job bothers you too much, we'll adjust. If I'm miserable in Serenity, we'll figure *something* out. I love you, Reagan McKenna."

Reagan slid her arms around his waist and held on for dear life. "And I love you, Max Gardner."

"How do you want to break the news to the girls?"

She pulled away and took him by the hand. "There's only one way I want to do anything from here on out. Together."

Max grinned and slipped his fingers through hers. Two short weeks ago, the word would have sent cold chills up and down his spine. Now he didn't think he'd ever heard anything sound more beautiful.

"Together." He pulled her close for one more kiss. "It doesn't get any better than this."

"Oh, sweetheart," she whispered with a sly smile. "This is just the beginning."

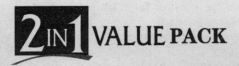

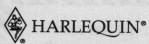

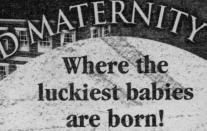